Life Goes On

Amy Iketani

Published by Amy Iketani, 2024.

This is a work of fiction. Similarities to real people, places, or events are entirely coincidental.

LIFE GOES ON

First edition. November 30, 2024.

Copyright © 2024 Amy Iketani.

ISBN: 979-8230385448

Written by Amy Iketani.

Also by Amy Iketani

Coming Home
The Last Wish
I Never Knew
Second Chances
Life Goes On

Watch for more at instagram.com/amyiketaniwrites.

To my sister, Leigh Ann

Siblings, the longest relationship we will ever have.

Chapter 1

There are those moments in life when you feel the hair on the back of your neck stand up, when that pit in your stomach tells you to keep pushing forward. You just knew you were about to uncover one of the biggest stories of your career. Well, for Emma, today was the day!

Emma Reese was an investigative journalist who had been working on a story about corruption in the city government for a couple of months. At first, she thought it only went as far as bribing and politicians looking the other way, but Emma had just gotten a break in the case that confirmed her suspicions that it ran much higher than she had even imagined.

As Emma drove to the Channel 2 news studio, she was feeling the excitement that only a new and promising story could bring. She couldn't wait to tell her boss what she had just learned. Emma was returning to her office to show all of her proof of bribery, mishandling of funds and corruption that she was beginning to uncover. Her meeting with her whistleblower went extremely well.

Emma parked in her assigned parking spot and nearly sprinted into the offices of the St. Petersburg News. With her black coffee in one hand and her computer bag slung over her shoulder, she rode the elevator up to the third floor and merely smiled at her co-workers as she laid her things hastily at her desk.

She glanced over at her boss's office and smiled. The wall of glass made it easy to see that she was in, but she was even more excited to notice that she was alone. So Emma gathered her paperwork and knocked on her door. A simple nod let Emma know she could enter.

Liane Lincoln was a woman with power and a heart. As news director, she oversaw everything and everyone at St. Petersburg Channel 2 News. Liane had been Emma's boss for four years and thankfully, had a wonderful working relationship. Liane had a reputation of being firm but fair.

Emma had been working on this bribery case for a couple of months now and had gone on air with parts of the story a few times. She had gotten some attention from other media outlets who found her story intriguing and covered it, too. However, Liane wasn't convinced that it ran any deeper than local officials and didn't want Emma to be spending any more time on it. In the end, she had offered to give her only a few more days to dig something up and today was her cut off day, Emma was to move on.

"But, I met with an unnamed source today," Emma started, eager to convince her boss that there was so much more to this story. "She gave me some documents that prove they are lying. These show where the money came from and more importantly, where it went."

Emma handed her boss the papers and bit her lower lip as she anxiously waited for Liane to review all the numbers. Her boss flipped through the papers and read the descriptions. All Emma could do was watch and wait. It was agonizing. Finally, slowly, Liane placed the papers on top of her desk and looked up at Emma.

"I'll admit that there may be something here," Liane Lincoln began. "There are names here that a reasonable person would definitely question…but…"

"But?" Emma interrupted.

"I might need you to cover another story," Liane replied.

"What? You're telling me to stop investigating this one?"

"Not stop exactly, just hold off."

Emma couldn't believe her ears, she had been working this case day and night and finally found something she could sink her teeth into and she was being told to walk away? Emma looked out the floor to ceiling windows that surrounded her boss's office and exhaled sharply.

"Is your source willing to go public?" Liane asked.

"Well, no, not right now," Emma answered.

"Has anyone else come forward to confirm her information?" Liane continued evenly.

"No..." Emma felt defeated.

Liane went on to explain that Emma could continue with this story for a few more days. If she couldn't get any more evidence or sources, then it was time to let it rest. Reluctantly, Emma agreed even though she knew there was something more to find. It was Liane's newsroom and her rules.

She collected her papers and with shoulders slumped, walked back to her desk. Everyone in the newsroom knew Liane could be harsh and unyielding, but she was also fair. She had given Emma plenty of extensions and it was time to give in, there was no argument. Emma passed anxious faces as she sat down with a thump on her chair.

Donald first exchanged glances with Miriam before approaching Emma. He sat on one of the chairs opposite Emma and folded his hands in his lap as if waiting for her to begin a speech. Emma just smiled. It wasn't long before Miriam sat down on the other empty seat beside Don.

Emma took a deep breath before starting. "She's taking me off the story."

Again, Don and Miriam exchanged concerned looks before speaking.

"Did she say why?" Don asked.

"But I thought you had your meeting with the informant today?" Miriam asked.

Emma took another deep breath and explained everything to her co-workers. As she spoke, their facial expressions changed from anger to understanding and then concern. They were worried that Emma would take this news from Liane as a rejection of her story or worse yet, her ability. They knew Emma well enough to know that she didn't like giving in easily, she could be very stubborn.

The three of them met when they all started working at Channel 2 and became fast friends. Donald Day and his wife, Cindy, were married last year. It was a beautiful wedding on the Clearwater Beach at sunset. They knew each other from college and they just couldn't stop looking at each other the entire ceremony. It was the kind of love everyone could just dream about.

Miriam Post, on the other hand, was single. She was always going on dates in the hopes of meeting the right guy, but so far he was still evasive. Miriam was in her thirties, a few years older than Emma and Don and the life of the party. It was always fun to come in on Monday mornings and hear all about Miriam's dates and what the guy did to annoy her this time.

Emma considered all of them her friends. With her long work hours, it was hard to make friends outside of work. She had her brother, James and his wife, Joanne, but those were really the only other people she hung out with. Her mother, Nora Reese, died a few years back from a heart attack. Shortly after that her father, Joseph, had a stroke. Emma's circle of family and friends was small.

Her father was still recovering but in a wheelchair. Emma and her brother had agreed that neither one of their lifestyles were conducive to taking care of their father while he recovered from his stroke. His need for care and physical therapy was more than they could provide at this time. It was an agonizing decision, but they finally had to find a care facility for him.

Emma and James had both agreed that the facility they put their father into two years ago would be temporary. It was the only place they could find at the time that could provide a room, provide care and also allow a physical therapist access when he needed it. It was also very expensive. They visited as often as they all could, but it wasn't daily. This guilt weighed on Emma but there wasn't a lot she could do about it right now.

James was even less help because he and Joanne had just bought a restaurant that was monopolizing all of their time and money. The Salty Waves Restaurant was on Madeira Beach and was in desperate need of renovation. It had been in foreclosure when they found it and after driving past it for months, James and Joanne finally decided to take the plunge and make an offer to buy it.

It took months to get it back up to code and even longer to get people to come. Emma loved what they did to it and tried to go and help out as much as she could. This included painting walls and scrubbing floors to get it open but now her duties evolved into waiting tables on weekends when they needed her and when she could spare her own time.

Getting pulled in three different directions was wearing Emma thin. Her normal bouncy and positive disposition had turned irritated and quiet. With so many responsibilities competing for her attention, it was easier for her to get distracted, like now.

"We need to go out!" Miriam announced. "What are you doing tonight?"

Emma blinked a few times, trying to focus on the two people still sitting in front of her desk. She shook her head as if that would clear the fog from her brain. Emma's long dark hair fell into her face and she carefully pushed it back over her shoulders.

"I can't," Emma replied.

Miriam rolled her eyes. "You mean you won't."

"Maybe. Either way, I'm not," Emma said. "I just have too much going on to think about trying to meet a man."

Miriam's laugh startled Emma. "Oh honey, that's not the only reason to go out. Sometimes you just need to let your hair down and have a couple of drinks."

This time it was Emma who let out a laugh. "I appreciate the thought Miriam but I can't, not tonight, maybe another night." Emma didn't really know when she would feel like it.

In the past, she would not need persuading to go hang out with her friends. Emma would accept Miriam's invitation and, if Don and Cindy were free they would come, too. There was a bar down the road, Ferg's Sports Bar and Grill that would have live music and that was their favorite hang out. Those nights were some of her best memories. But tonight, she knew she had a schedule to keep.

Liane had unwillingly given her a few more days and she knew that was all she would get. She would be busy making more phone calls and coaxing more anxious people to turn over evidence. Emma had to stay focused.

She thanked Miriam and Donald again, but Emma needed to get back to work. They quietly went back to their desks and sent concerned texts back and forth. Emma didn't care, they could be concerned about her later, right now she needed to stay busy and focused because she knew this story could be big.

Staying busy was exactly what Emma did. After leaving work around four o'clock, she went to visit her father. It was not on her way home but that never stopped her, there wasn't anyone waiting for her at home anyway.

Pulling up to Rainbow House was anything but cheery. It looked old and run down from the outside with the inside was not that much better. She walked in and greeted the older woman at the front desk. The staff had such a high turnover rate that Emma didn't even bother learning their names anymore.

The magazines on the lobby table were months out of date, the vending machine was consistently out of order and there was always that smell. It was a mixture of rubbing alcohol, bleach and sickness. Emma's father never complained. It didn't matter if his dinner didn't arrived hot, the cable went out for a week or the mail was always a day behind.

Emma walked the familiar hallway with the usual sights and smells until she turned the corner and walked into Joe's room. He was sitting in his wheelchair and was reading a book when he heard Emma enter.

"Hi Sweetheart!"

"Hello, dad."

Emma walked over and gave him a hug and kiss. He immediately put his book down and looked at her. He smiled and gestured for her to sit down on the only other chair in the room. Emma was exhausted and knew she couldn't stay long, but she also didn't like to go longer than two days without visiting. James took longer between his visits, but Emma made sure she came.

They talked about their days, Joe informed Emma that they now had lasagna on the menu and they played bingo in the main room every Friday. Emma smiled and told her father all about her day, too. Joe was a big baseball fan and told her that the St. Petersburg Sharks were doing really well. Joe thought they might even make it to the World Series. Somehow her father always brought the conversation back to baseball.

Emma was not a sports fan, she had to look up the scores each time she visited because she never kept track of that kind of thing. She didn't even know when the World Series was, but her father informed her it was in a couple of weeks. The Sharks were in the playoffs. She tried to sound excited but she really just wanted to go home and crawl into bed.

A knock on the door brought their attention to Kevin, Joe's nurse. Kevin came in to help Joe clean up and then get him into bed. Emma watched Kevin do his job with such care and empathy. She had many things to say about how this place was run, but she never had a bad thing to say about their nursing staff.

When Kevin left, Emma said her goodbyes to her father, too. She could see that the day had been draining for him as well. She was always kept in the loop with his doctors and therapist and she could tell that progress was being made. His left side was getting a little stronger.

"Goodnight, dad," Emma said. "I love you."

"I love you more, Sweetheart," said Joe as Emma left the room.

Chapter 2

Despite all of Emma's best efforts, the extra time that Liane had given her was up. As Emma entered the Channel 2 offices, she felt a little bit of dread at having to face her boss today. Emma had been doing this job long enough to know that sometimes a story just ran its course, that there wasn't anything more, there wasn't anything else to find. Only this wasn't one of those stories, she just knew it. She just didn't have any more time to prove it.

She also knew better than to keep pushing her luck with Liane. She had given her three more days and Emma had tried her best to find more evidence and she didn't. Time to move on. That didn't mean she would, she just couldn't let on that she was still going to dig deeper.

Emma didn't look around when she entered the offices on the third floor. She just looked straight ahead and sat down at her desk. She knew eyes were on her, especially Don and Miriam, but she was afraid she would crack if she glanced in their direction. She did, however, allow herself to glance in Liane's direction just in time to see her gesture for Emma to enter her office.

Emma tried to read Liane for any signs of what mood she might be in. There was a palpable tension in the air and she couldn't yet find out the reason for it. As she approached the glass office, their eyes met briefly but Liane quickly looked away. Emma opened the door, slowly sat in the chair opposite Liane's and waited.

Liane calmly took a long sip of her coffee, smoothed out her skirt and then placed her hands in her lap before looking at Emma directly.

"Since no further evidence has come forward, we are placing this story in the 'finished' file for now, correct?" Liane asked.

"Correct," Emma replied, reluctantly.

"Great," Liane started. As she spoke she gave a sideways glance out into the newsroom. Those who were watching, quickly diverted their gaze and tried to look busy. "Gary is out sick."

Emma waited. Surely there was more to the story that involved her. Gary was their sports reporter. He lived, breathed and ate sports. It didn't matter the team or the season, he could spout scores and stats that coincided with every coach and player.

"The St. Petersburg Sharks are in the playoffs. With Gary out, I need someone to cover the game and get quotes, sound bites, anything from the coach and players. I need someone who is, shall we say, 'in between' stories at the moment. I need you," Liane said.

Emma didn't know whether to burst out into tears or laughter. Surely this was a joke. Emma looked out into the newsroom and expected to see everyone doubled over in laughter as if she was the punchline of a cruel prank. She allowed herself a small smile as she stared back at her boss.

Liane was not smiling, she was completely serious.

"You can't be serious!" Emma exclaimed. "This has to be some kind of joke."

"This is not a joke," Liane confirmed. "You can call Gary for any insights as to who to approach and what questions to ask. I don't care, I just want the Coach, the pitcher and who ever else might be around them."

Still in shock, Emma stood up and turned towards the door.

"I don't even know who they are or what they look like," Emma said.

"Well, you have until tomorrow night to do your homework, that's their next home game," Liane replied.

Emma mumbled some obscenities under her breath as she made her way back to her desk. As usual, Don and Miriam were right behind her. They didn't even need to ask a single question, Emma blurted out everything Liane said to her and then she threw her head on her desk.

Trying to sound supportive, Donald pulled out his phone and tried to get Emma to look.

"Well, this is the coach, Mike Walters. He's short and stalky but everyone says he as sweet as a grandpa," Emma raised her head in interest and he continued. "This is the pitcher, Andy Anderson. Good looking, a bit of a player if you know what I mean, but he's definitely a team favorite. You're going to want to get an interview from him for sure. Gary always does."

At the mention of Gary, Emma threw her head onto her desk, again. Don and Miriam just looked from her mop of hair spilling all over her desk to each other. After shrugging their shoulders they decided it was better for them to leave her alone right now.

Emma was sure she was in her own personal hell. Sports?! Her boss expected her to fill in as a sports reporter? Why not Don? Why not any other person in this entire building? She was sure that she was being punished, exactly by whom and why she just didn't know.

After taking time to get herself some coffee and clear her head, she knew she had no other choice than to do the story she was given. First, she called Gary. In between the coughing, sneezing and everything else he was doing, she was able to get some information and some questions to ask the coach and players when she went to the game tomorrow night.

Emma had no idea the Sharks had gotten into the World Series last year and didn't win. Everyone was calling this their redemption year. She wrote that down. Gary had a good rapport with the team, so he wasn't sure how they would react to Emma walking onto the field in his place. He warned her that she might get some ribbing, but to just get the interview and then she could leave.

She wasn't sure what Gary meant by ribbing. She had heard about female sports reporters getting harassed but had never personally had to deal with it. Gary also gave her more logistical tips such as where to park and how to get in. His cameraman would meet her at the stadium and he knew where to go from there.

After hanging up the phone, she called her brother. Emma wasn't exactly sure why she did and when James picked up the phone, he sounded surprised by her call.

"I can't call my big brother?" Emma teased.

"Of course," James replied. "What do you need?"

This made Emma a little mad. It was usually the other way around, James was always asking her for favors, except when the topic was their father. Emma was always telling him to visit more.

"It's dad," Emma said.

"I know, I know," James replied. "I was going to go tomorrow."

"Good, but that's not why I'm calling. We need to find a different place, a better place for him." Emma explained.

James let out a heavy sigh. "I told you I would try. I just don't have a lot of free time right now. Business is starting to finally pick up a little, but Joanne and I are still barely getting home by midnight."

Emma knew it was pointless to ask James for anything. He was doing the best he could, but it wasn't enough in Emma's eyes. This task of finding a better facility was going to fall on her shoulders, too. She ended the conversation with letting him know she would be the sport reporter tomorrow night.

After waiting for him to finish laughing, he said he would have every television in the restaurant tuned in to see her. After he suggested that she might meet someone there, she hung up. Emma would not be finding love at the baseball game, that was for sure!

There was nothing left for Emma to do in the newsroom. She packed up her briefcase, grabbed her jacket and went out towards the studio. She liked checking in on the live broadcast and saying, 'hi' to friends that worked over there.

Emma loved being a reporter on the ground, but her dream was to be a news anchor. She liked watching them at the news desk sending it over to weather, sports or traffic. How exciting that would be! The only problem was that those jobs didn't become available very often and to wait around for one was unrealistic.

Before visiting her father, Emma decided to get some food from his favorite restaurant, Bob Evans, and take it to him. She ordered two turkey dinners and when she couldn't decided between the cornbread muffins and banana bread, she told them to add some of each.

The aroma from the food made her car smell delicious. When her stomach growled, she realized she hadn't eaten lunch today. What a day it had been! When she let herself replay all of the events from today, she still couldn't understand how she was now the interim sports reporter. She was sure that her boss had a good laugh when she decided to give Emma the job.

Everyone knew that Emma and sports did not mix. She was still thinking about it when she pulled up to Rainbow House and entered the lobby. The woman at the desk looked familiar and they smiled and waved to each other. Emma made her way down the long dark hallway and turned the corner.

Joe was sitting up in bed watching Wheel of Fortune when Emma walked in with the smell of the delicious food. She wheeled his table up to the bed and laid it all out.

"Thank you, Sweetheart," Joe said.

"I got your favorites," Emma replied.

"With banana bread?" He asked.

"Of course with banana bread!" She said.

They both eagerly ate their meals in comfortable silence. Emma never pushed her father about the progress he was making. It was slow, but steady. She knew he was lonely, there just wasn't anything she could do about that right now. Her mother was gone, James and Joanne were building up their business right now and it could be years before they had free time to do anything outside of the restaurant.

That left Emma. It wasn't that she didn't want to help her father, sometimes she wanted help, too. She watched as her father ate. He had always been a good cook, it was where James got his love of cooking. Emma, not so much. She thought about how he would cook the family meals on the weekends and how her mother would have a cake or pie fresh from the oven. Those where the moments when there was no fear of the future or worries about death.

Emma was thankful for their serene childhood, where the worse thing they worried about was the occasional hurricane in the summer. Her father, once the pillar of strength for their family was now so weak and immobile. It made her sad to think about how young he really was and how drastically his life had changed over the last few years.

Life could be cruel. It could hand you lemons all day long without any sugar to make the proverbial lemonade. It could even turn a bright and charismatic investigative journalist into the dreaded sports reporter. Emma would just have to find a way to make her own lemonade.

Chapter 3

Emma was never one to feel nervous before showing up to do a story. Her job was to get facts and then go on air and tell her audience what she found out. It was simple and concise. She knew what to do and how to do it. Tonight, however, was completely different. She was out of her element being a sports reporter and she hoped it wouldn't come across on television.

She has driven this route a thousand times from her home in Pinellas Park to work in St. Petersburg. Tonight, though, she was going to Tropicana Field for a baseball game and she was actually nervous about it. Gary had given her detailed instructions on where to park and meet up with his cameraman and Emma followed his every word. She just prayed it didn't end in disaster tonight.

As she entered the parking lot and showed her credentials, she easily found the area and met up with Fred. He had all his gear out and ready, he was just waiting on her. Emma shook hands and introduced herself and Fred gruffly told her to follow him.

Emma had changed outfits at least a dozen times before coming because she had never even been to a baseball game, but she wanted to look professional. She opted for a white blouse and blue trousers and threw on a black cardigan she had in the backseat.

She followed Fred through a side entrance as they showed their press credentials. Fred led them down long concrete hallways and through doors that were marked 'do not enter'. Emma knew they were getting closer to the field when the noise level increased. There was music blaring and just a constant hum of enthusiasm from the crowd that echoed down the never ending hallways.

As they entered the last door, Emma was shocked to see that they were now directly on the field. She had never envisioned an indoor stadium looking like this. It was bright with a constant pleasant temperature and alive with energy. There was no other word for the feeling of the crowd and the teams together except electric.

Fred pushed his way through the crowd and pointed out the coach. Coach Mike Walters was exactly as Gary described him. His hair was turning white, he had a belly hanging over his belt but a smile that could warm up any non-sports fan. Emma walked right up to Coach Walters with her microphone.

After a nod to Fred to start recording, she reached out and shook the Coach's hand.

"Hello, Coach Walters, I'm Emma Reese from Channel 2 News."

"Well, hello there Ms. Reese, nice to meet you," Coach Walters replied with a smile.

"How are you and the team feeling heading into game three of the Championship playoffs? What do you think your odds are for winning tonight?" Emma asked, feeling completely out of her element but trying desperately to fake it.

"Oh, we're confident we are going to win tonight. We're coming into this one and one, so a win tonight will put us that much closer to getting into the World Series. Andy is feeling good, he's been warming up this afternoon and of course with Greg and Bobby on bases, how can we lose?" Coach Walters smiled and waved to another reporter and Emma felt an elbow in her back. She took that as a cue to move on.

"How was that?" She asked Fred.

"It'll do," he replied with a slight eye roll. Fred pointed at another man on the field and then pushed his way through the other reporters. "This is Andy Anderson, the pitcher."

Emma looked quickly at her small notebook for what to ask the pitcher and then followed Fred. Emma found herself standing in front of a man who was six feet four inches tall and had the most beautiful blue eyes she had ever seen. It took a moment for Emma to compose herself and remember why she was here. She glanced back at Fred who nodded he was ready.

Emma had heard that Andy Anderson had an ego the size of the stadium, so she was determined to ask some intelligent questions so that she could be done with this interview quickly. Andy worked his way down the line of reporters and was using words like 'honey,' 'doll' and 'sweetie' to all the female reporters. Emma rolled her eyes.

Beautiful blue eyes or not, she would not be sweet talked by this full-of-himself baseball player. She also wasn't going to play by his timetable either. Eager to get this night over with, Emma leaned over another reporter and tried getting Andy's attention.

"Excuse me! Excuse me, Andy Anderson! May we have a few minutes?" Emma shouted.

Andy looked over in Emma's direction and wondered who it was calling for him. Andy saw the Channel 2 microphone and immediately looked confused.

"Hey, you're not Gary!" Andy remarked then smiled. "But it's okay, you can call me anytime." Then he winked.

Emma immediately turned on her heals and walked past Fred, brushing his shoulder on her way out towards the exit. Not even bothering to turn around and look to see if Fred followed her, she made her way through the crowd of journalists. Fuming, Emma wanted out of that stadium as fast as possible.

"What did I say?" Andy yelled out to her.

Fred stood there in shock for a minute before realizing Emma wasn't coming back. He shrugged his shoulders at Andy and he followed Emma out the door. Andy let his gaze follow the two figures until he got called into the next interview.

Emma returned the way she and Fred came into the stadium the whole time mumbling under her breath about what a jerk he was, who did he think he was, she was a professional, he can't talk to her like that...

Back outside in the night air, she sat against her car bumper. She knew what she did was stupid and childish and worse yet, unprofessional. She let her feelings get in the way of her job. Liane was not going to like this. Fred made his way to Emma and he looked furious.

"You're jeopardizing my job, too, you know!" Fred yelled. "What kind of stupid stunt was that? Channel 2 does not walk out of interviews with local teams that are on their way to the World Series!" Fred was angry and he had every right to be.

Emma could just watch as he loaded his gear back into his truck and left. She had no response, Fred was right. She was ashamed of how she reacted to Andy's smart remarks. There was no excuse. She also didn't want to go home.

She walked over to Ferg's Sports Bar and Grill and ordered some tacos and a beer. Of course they had the game playing on every single television. This was probably the first time she really watched and paid attention to it. Sure over the years her father and brother watched sports, James even played some kind of sport in school, but she never paid attention. Tonight she did.

She watched Andy on the mound look over his shoulder at Greg Reynolds on first base to see if he could tag the runner out. Then Andy looked over at Bobby Bishop on third base to see if his runner could get tagged out. Just when you thought he would throw the next pitch, Andy lifted his foot off the pitching rubber and turned his body to throw to Bobby at third base.

The move was so quick and fluid that when the runner was called out, Andy smiled and went on to strike out the next batter. Andy Anderson was good. It was like watching the conductor of an orchestra. Every other player on the field looked to the pitcher, it was his symphony.

Emma was starting to think Andy's reputation was well earned, he was good and he knew it. He was allowed to indulge in a big ego because his fans told him he earned it. How could you not let that go to your head? Emma would not be another adoring fan, she had approach him as a professional and had expected to be treated as one.

She was enjoying her taco and beer when she heard someone call her name.

"Emma!" Emma turned around to see Miriam approaching with a man. "I didn't know you were coming tonight."

"Well, I wasn't planning on it. I had to go to the game for my interview, remember?" Emma asked.

Recognition showed on Miriam's face. "That's right, Mr. Pitcher! How did it go?"

"I don't want to talk about it," Emma said, taking another sip of her beer. "You go have fun, I'm leaving soon."

Miriam hugged her and said they will talk about it Monday morning at work. She said everything will be fine, there will be more games to make up for it, not to worry. Another game was what Emma worried about. How many will she have to go to and what if she reacts the same way? She decided to order another beer and watch the game a little while longer. It was research.

Emma almost didn't hear her phone ringing, only catching the last ring and then it was too late. She took it out of her pocket and saw that the caller left a voice mail. It was from Pat. She stared at the name for what seemed like minutes, debating what to do next. She hadn't heard from her ex-boyfriend in months and couldn't imagine why he would be calling her now.

She decided to listen to the voicemail but had to plug her other ear to hear over all of the noise. She strained enough to make out that he would be in town soon and would love to get together. He wanted her to call him back.

Emma didn't want to see him. Patrick McNeil moved to Atlanta a few months ago for a new job. They had broken up before that and it was nice to know they wouldn't have to awkwardly run into each other anymore. Pat was part of her past. He was controlling and possessive and she needed to get out of that kind of relationship. She deleted the message.

Hearing that Pat would be back in town made her wonder why. She hoped he wasn't coming just to see her. She was starting to feel uneasy about it already and he wasn't even here. She took another sip of her beer and tried to get back into the game. Andy had just struck out another batter and now the Sharks were up. The Sharks were beating the Nashville Eagles four to nothing at the bottom of the fourth inning.

Emma didn't want to sit here all night, so she paid her tab and left. The cool air was comforting and inviting. She walked back across the street and found her car. At least she would beat the traffic since the game was only half over. Emma saw a text from her boss that had come through earlier. She had almost forgotten about her fiasco at the interview, almost.

She wasn't going to deal with that right now, that could wait until Monday. Tonight she was going home and taking a long bath to wash this night away. Then maybe she would watch the end of the game, maybe. She tried to psych herself up to meeting the pitcher on the field again. Maybe if she didn't let him talk first, it would go better.

Emma drove back to Pinellas Park with the windows down. Fall was here and she was welcoming it. It was her favorite time of the year with Halloween decorations everywhere she looked. Florida didn't have a lot of leaves changing colors or drastic temperature drops like the North did, but they still had seasons.

Changes were coming, Emma could feel it. What those changes would mean for her and her family, she didn't know but she welcomed them. Change was inevitable and wasn't always a bad thing, so she was ready for whatever life threw at her. Good or bad, life would go on.

Emma pulled into her little rental home and walked in the door. Her sanctuary, it was warm and welcoming and after a night like tonight, it was the medicine she needed to forget about all her problems if only for a little while. She would take it, she didn't know how many peaceful nights she would have to just relax and enjoy the quiet.

Emma watched the end of the game, the Sharks won. Another missed call. Emma turned off the light and went to sleep.

Chapter 4

Nerves were getting the better of Emma during the whole drive into work the next day. She kept thinking about how she could explain why she did what she did at the baseball game. But no matter how she imagined it going, she knew Fred would tell the whole story differently than she would.

Even Emma didn't fully understand why she bolted out of the stadium. As she walked in the front doors to the Channel 2 news studio and rode the elevator to the third floor, she always came back to the same thing, she just wanted to be treated like a reporter, male or female, it shouldn't matter.

Liane was standing at her glass door and watched as Emma briskly walked to her desk, laid down her things and then, without even looking up, walked into Liane's office. They both sat down opposite each other and waited.

It was Liane who started. "Well, imagine my surprise when I watched as my star investigative reporter ran out of Tropicana Field without even getting an interview, which I requested I might add, of the team's pitcher!"

"I know, I'm sorry." Emma offered.

"Sorry? Is that really all you have to say?" Liane was angry but in control of her emotions, only her swinging foot gave her true inner fury away. "I had to watch what footage you did manage to get and I could have easily fired you after that."

Emma's hands were folded in her lap but her knuckles were turning white. She deserved the wrath of Liane, but she also needed to make it up to her. "I don't know what happened. I just felt so...so...unprepared for what it was like being a sports reporter. I won't let it happen again."

"No, you won't!" Liane glared at her and then a smirk rose at the corner of her mouth. "Gary still isn't back and there's another home game tonight. You're going to redeem yourself with full interviews of the coach and team members, including the pitcher, tonight."

Emma's head snapped up to look at Liane who was now wearing a full smile. Emma deserved it, expected it even. She really shouldn't be surprised.

"Okay," was all Emma could say as she stood up to leave.

"One more thing," Liane began. "Smile. This is not investigative journalism. It's sports...baseball, America's pastime. Everyone is usually smiling and happy at a baseball game."

Emma looked confused. "I was."

Liane let out a laugh that made Emma flinch. After such a serious and uncomfortable conversation, the sudden howls of laughter were startling. "No, Emma, you definitely were not smiling."

Still stinging from that remark, Emma went back to her desk and sulked. She pulled up her own footage from a few days ago and rewatched her interview from the game. Fred's camera had been focused on her until she had gotten close enough to Coach Walters for the interview.

Not only was Emma not smiling, she looked downright confrontational when throwing the microphone in their faces. She had studied and practiced the questions and faces, but not how other sports reporters feel the room and go with the flow. Her boss was right, she was not smiling at all.

What Emma really couldn't believe was that she had to do it all over again. She promised herself she would be better. She would smile, joke around and be spontaneous. A smile crept up on her face because even she knew that those things were not her normal personality. She would also have to become an Oscar worthy actor in the next eight hours.

Emma was now becoming more aware that people were looking at her and whispering. She stood up, looked around the newsroom and everyone looked away and went back to work. It wasn't until she spotted Miriam and Don that she smiled and nodded that they could come and talk to her.

As if sprinting down a race track, Miriam and Donald were sitting opposite Emma in seconds. Eager for the scoop on what was said in the boss's office, they waited until Emma started.

"Well, it didn't go well," Emma said.

"She looked upset, but not too upset," Miriam replied as Don nodded.

"She was upset but she said I can make up for it tonight," Emma lowered her gaze.

Don and Miriam gave each other confused looks until Don inhaled sharply and brought his hand to his mouth. "Oh my goodness! You have to interview them again at the game tonight?"

Now Miriam understood her dilemma. She, too, inhaled loudly and looked over at Don.

"Oh Emma, you can do it. Well, you have to," Miriam said, trying to be supportive but was met with Don's elbow. "Ouch!" Miriam said while rubbing the arm he had hit.

"It'll be okay," Don said. "Just go there with the intention of having fun rather than your next big scoop."

They both realized they didn't know what else to say to Emma. She was in a precarious situation and it all came down to whether she could perform tonight because that's exactly what she needed to do, perform. Don and Miriam stayed a little while longer, trying to cheer Emma up, but they soon realized it was no use. They excused themselves and went back to their own desks.

Emma was alone, again. She got herself into this mess, she would get herself out. She looked up some of Gary's old pre-game interviews on the field and watched how at ease he was with the players. They would nudge Gary on the shoulder and they would both laugh about some inside joke. Gary was a natural. Emma was quickly losing confidence.

She ended up watching videos at her desk for over an hour. There was nothing more she could do there. She had tried her best, gotten reprimanded, and then was given her next assignment. Now she had to get back on the road and do it all again. Emma packed up her things and walked out into the sunny Florida afternoon.

Emma decided to grab some lunch and head over to visit her father. It had been a couple of days since her last visit, so it was time. This time she picked up some sandwiches at his favorite fast food chicken restaurant, PDQ, and headed in his direction. Emma rolled down her windows and turned up the radio.

If she couldn't pull off this interview tonight, today could be her last day as an employed woman. She laughed at the absurd reality she was living in right now and was determined to not think about it for the next few hours. Beside her, the food smelled delicious. Emma just knew her father would be pleasantly surprised by her mid-afternoon visit.

She pulled into the same depressing parking lot and walked into the same sad lobby. There was a new man at the front desk whom Emma had never seen before. She signed in and got a badge before walking down the familiar, drab hallway.

Joe was already sitting in his wheelchair reading a book. His lunch on the tray beside his bed, untouched. Joe was in a bathrobe but looked clean with his hair combed.

"Hi dad," Emma said.

Startled, Joe jerked his head up and smiled. "Hello, Sweetheart," he replied.

"We're going on a date, are you all dressed?" Emma joked as she walked behind her father's wheelchair and released the hand breaks.

"Oh sure! Where are we going?" Joe asked with a smile.

"Well, I was thinking Paris or Rome, how does that sound?" Emma laughed easily steering Joe back through the old hallway and out the backdoor that led to a pretty decent garden.

"Oh, well, you know I'm more partial to Edinburgh, to see the land of my grandparents," Joe replied.

Emma steered them to a bench and table under a large oak tree. When shaded from the sun, it almost felt cool in the late October afternoon. She unpacked their sandwiches, fries and drinks and helped her father hold them up to eat.

"Okay, dad, Scotland it is. Isn't it a nice day in Edinburgh today? You can almost see the castle from here." Emma took a bite of her own sandwich as they admired the imagined scenery.

"Well, to be honest, I wouldn't know what it looks like. I've never been there myself, but it is a dream," Joe replied as he struggled to hold the sandwich with just his right hand.

Emma reached over to help. "Maybe one day, dad, maybe one day."

There were so many things to do on her plate already, she was not about to be planning any trips at the moment. Sitting in this beautiful outdoor garden almost made her forget how bad the inside looked and felt…almost. She had made a few calls around town, even going up as far as Largo, but nothing was available.

Emma would keep looking, though. Her father was too important to her. Even though she was desperately trying to stay in the moment with him, her mind kept drifting to the baseball game tonight and the importance of her performance.

She talked to her father about how the Sharks were doing and his excitement was not easily contained. He went on and on about the different players and how the coach was so good at holding back certain ones so they didn't get too tired for later in the game.

Emma was mostly half-listening until he mentioned Andy Anderson. "Do you like Andy?" She asked.

"Oh yes! He's the best player in the league," Joe declared. As far as Joe was concerned, there was nothing else to say about him.

Emma chewed slowly and envisioned how a potential interview would go with Andy Anderson. She wanted to wipe that smirk right off his face and slap him when he winked at her, but why? Why did he infuriate her so much? Maybe it was the fact that she didn't feel like she was controlling the interview. Andy had a way of taking the spotlight and the focus from anyone within a four mile radius.

"Are you happy here, dad?" Emma asked. She wasn't sure where that came from. She had never had cause to question it before.

"I guess so," he replied. "I don't have any complaints. I get my meals, my medicine, physical therapy and it's peaceful." Joe continued to eat his lunch and looked out at the garden.

Emma wondered if 'peaceful' was another word for bored and lonely. It made her sad that James didn't visit more often. If she were a betting woman she would put a million dollars on the fact that he probably hadn't been there in a week.

Joe needed a place with more interaction and activities. Emma needed to make this more of a priority. She could hear notifications on her phone letting her know she had some missed calls. She glanced at the screen and saw one was from Pat, again. Well, Pat could wait.

The other numbers were unknown. She would deal with them later. Now was her time with her father and she didn't want it interrupted. Emma took a deep breath and wondered how her life had gotten so complicated. She was twenty-eight, on the verge of breaking a big story, single with a brother who didn't have time for their father who was in a home recuperating from a stroke. Their mother passed away leaving everything to fall on Emma's shoulders while trying to maintain a healthy work and life balance. It was starting to sound impossible. Maybe she did need a break or a change.

They had finished their lunch and were cleaning up when Emma glanced at her phone again. It was nearly four o'clock and she still needed to go home and get ready for tonight. She pushed her father back inside and settled him in bed to rest. Joe always enjoyed the fresh air, but it tired him out.

Emma kissed him goodbye and drove home. Now there wasn't anything else to distract her from what was coming next. The whole ride home she tried to picture what she would wear, what she would say and how she would say it. She tried to visualize herself smiling and enjoying the evening, all up until she visualized herself running out the exit door, again.

Chapter 5

Emma drove into the Tropicana Field parking lot with a confidence she didn't feel. She would fake it, she told herself. She spotted Fred's familiar truck and parked right next to him. They were early. It was Fred's idea to come early so that all the nervous energy would burn itself out and she could, maybe, relax a little bit before the game.

The St. Petersburg Sharks were winning the playoffs against the Nashville Eagles three to two. If the Sharks won tonight they would be going to the World Series. Fans were already arriving and there was a palpable excitement in the air. Maybe Emma could bring some of that with her inside. Fred asked her if she was ready and she nodded her head that she was even though she wasn't being completely honest.

This was it. She followed Fred through doors and down hallways, showing their credentials when asked. The door that led onto the actual field always took her breath away. She could imagine the feeling for someone who was a true fan, how this would invoke such awe and elation.

Fred led them further onto the field and they waited with the other reporters. Emma tried to give Fred an encouraging smile, but she didn't think he was convinced. His word of advice was to not leave without talking to the pitcher. Emma took a deep breath and tried to muster as much cheer as she could before she had to go live on the air.

They watched as the team crossed the field to talk to the reporters who were hanging on their every word. Emma rolled her eyes as she spotted Andy Anderson getting closer to their position. She smiled at the thought of Andy needing to fit that huge ego under his cap.

Luckily Coach Walters approached them first and Emma found herself genuinely smiling when asking Coach how he felt about their chances for tonight's win. She was engaged and interested. It was the first time she thought she actually could do a real sports interview without having to pretend. That was until Andy came up behind her.

"Hey, you're still not Gary," Andy said with a smile and a wink.

Still on a high from a great interview with Coach Walters, Emma turned her microphone to Andy. "Hello, I'm Emma Reese with Channel 2. How do you feel coming into the game tonight?" Emma stood, smiling, proud that she moved past the ego and charm.

"Well, much better now that you're here," Andy said with another wink.

Emma's cheer was fading but one glance at Fred made her gather up enough courage to keep going. She would not let Andy Anderson's charm ruffle her.

"So you feel like you have an edge over the Eagles to clench the Championship?" Emma asked.

Andy didn't miss a beat. He went on to give a great interview about how his arm felt good, his teammates Bobby and Greg were looking sharp as well as the whole team. They were ready and they would bring the World Series to St. Petersburg. Then he added that he hoped she would be watching.

That was Emma's cue to cut this short and not press her luck any longer. She politely thanked him and wished him and his team luck tonight and then quickly turned and left. Andy watched her go and then moved on to his next reporter. Fred followed her to the parking lot and congratulated her on getting a complete interview.

She was being congratulated for doing the bare minimum, that was okay with her tonight. Fred had no idea how difficult it was for her to even do *that*. Emma was sure Liane would be happy and that's all that mattered right now. She was tired and ready to call it a day.

THE NEXT MORNING EMMA walked into the office tall and proud and went straight to her desk. Liane smiled and waved which was a good indication that she was pleased. The Sharks won, they were going to the World Series! Better yet, Gary was back.

Emma remembered the missed calls she had from yesterday and pulled out her phone to investigate. The ones from Pat she would ignore, for now. The other ones she decided to call back. They could be important and even pertain to her investigation. They were local numbers and that was promising.

With her note pad and pen poised, she dialed the first one. It was answered by a man who immediately asked how she had gotten this number. Emma explained that she was returning a call and then went on to introduce herself. It was a man who wanted to meet, he had information that she should see.

Emma tried to contain her excitement as she wrote down an address. It was something that could tie this investigation to the higher ups in the city government. She tried to question him on how he got this information but he didn't want to talk on the phone. Fine, she would meet a stranger in a strange place.

First, Emma went to Liane's door and knocked. She gestured for her to enter and Emma went on to explain that she was contacted by someone who was willing to talk. If this turned out to be what the man said it was, it could be the missing piece to tie up her entire investigation.

To Emma's surprise, her boss was willing to let her continue her story, for now. The fact that she actually did a fairly decent sports interview was in her favor. Emma let Liane know where she was to meet the informant, just in case. She promised to stay in touch and keep her informed on her progress.

Walking back to her desk, Emma thought about what evidence she needed. She still needed something to show where the money went and who benefited from the transaction. This could go beyond city officials, it could even include county or even state officials! Emma review her notes and wrote down some questions in the margins. This was going to be the break she needed, she could feel it.

JAMES REESE WAS GETTING ready to open for the day. His restaurant, Salty Waves, was a dream come true for him and his wife, Joanne. James had been a chef for most of his life and loved it more than anything. When they had gone for a quick vacation to Madeira Beach a year ago they had come across this run down restaurant and James immediately got excited.

It wasn't very far from home, it was just the right size and after calling the realtor, found out it was also affordable. Joanne needed a little more convincing. It would mean leaving her retail job and devoting day and night to getting the restaurant up and running. Even before they could do that, it needed to be cleaned and fixed up.

James didn't know exactly how long it had been vacant, but it was long enough to need new everything. The salt air only added to the neglect which meant it needed painted and scrubbed. They were happy to put their heart and soul into Salty Waves and after four months of around the clock cleaning and repairs, it was now open for business.

Customers came back slowly. It was clear that locals were unsure how a new restaurant would compete with some that had been around for decades but it was getting a solid base of customers. James kept the name and embraced the surfer vibe of the place and of the area. He, himself, did not surf but there were surfboards on the walls and some used as benches.

After being open for business only six months, business was steady but not what they had hoped. James knew they needed to advertise more. How could they expect to draw in crowds if no one knew they existed? James mainly took care of inventory and cooking. Joanne was front of the house hostess and waitress. She also did the books at the end of the night.

The bar was the biggest draw for folks right now. James made sure he had plenty of televisions playing as many games as he could find. It was a fun atmosphere and they just prayed they could keep their dream going. At thirty-two years old, there just wasn't much time for errors in judgement. If this restaurant couldn't stay in business, they would lose everything.

Joanne had hoped to have started a family already. She could hear and feel her biological clock ticking and as much as she tried to ignore it, it was like Poe's Tell Tale Heart, getting louder everyday. For now, the restaurant and James would have to be enough as their priorities were focused on the business. Hopefully a family would come next.

As James unlocked the front door and turned on the lights and televisions, he took a moment to sit and reflect. Maybe he was feeling down because he knew winter meant less people coming to the beach and he had expected a better summer turn out than he had. One thing he didn't tell Joanne was that in his head he gave himself six more months to make Salty Waves a success. If things didn't get better by then, he would have to sell it.

James walked into the kitchen to start preparations for dinner. They were trying to help their bottom line by cutting out lunch service and it helped a little. He was thankful for his sister's help, too. Emma came on weekends and helped wherever she was needed.

Some days it was washing dishes and other days it was waiting tables. He could always count on Emma.

Joanne was wiping down tables and cutting up lemons for the bar. She was also reflecting on how the restaurant could survive the winter. They didn't have a backup plan. This was it, this was their livelihood, their future and their retirement. Maybe she could talk to Emma to see if there was something she could do to help get word out for them.

EMMA LEFT HER SECRET meeting with her new informant absolutely frantic! It was everything she had hoped for and more. She immediately drove back to the studio and ran right into Liane's office. Out of breath from excitement, she showed, explained and laid out everything that led her to believe that county officials were definitely involved.

Liane gave her permission to run with it, she could get a camera crew and go right to the men and women who were caught red handed. Emma was eager to get back out there with her microphone in the faces of those responsible. She was hoping that after her investigation and reporting on air about what has been going on for years, arrests would be made.

Emma returned to her desk to start typing up her report and tried to get out there before everyone left for the day. This was it! She could feel it! Months of work went into this story and it was finally getting told. Miriam and Don were excited for her, everyone loved a great ending to a story that meant corruption was not only stopped but uncovered for everyone to see.

Emma was out the door as soon as she closed her laptop. After meeting up with her cameraman, they headed out in the Channel 2 van and hopefully they would be all set for the five o'clock news. This was the kind of reporting that got Emma's blood pumping, not the fluff and smiles of sports, Gary could have it. This was the adrenaline rush that Emma lived for.

As soon as they parked, everything else was like clockwork. Her cameraman carried this equipment into the building and Emma had her microphone in hand. At the front door, they showed their credentials and were allowed inside. Emma knew exactly where to go. With her camera in tow, all you could hear were her high heals clicking on the marble floor.

Emma stopped in front of the large wooden door at the end of the hallway. The men behind that door had no way of knowing what was about to happen. The crimes and corruption they have been a part of for years was about to be breaking news in minutes. Emma nodded to her cameraman who knew that meant to start recording.

After a deep breath Emma knocked on the door. "Hello? This is Emma Reese from Channel 2 News. I was wondering if I could ask you a few questions?"

Chapter 6

It wasn't until later when Emma watched a recording of the breaking news that she reported live on the air that she let it all sink in. Liane had popped champagne and poured everyone a glass as their own reporters where saying how city and county officials were being arrested after confessing to bribery, money laundering and even wire fraud. Police were raiding their offices and homes as they spoke.

So far, six county and ten local officials were being booked on multiple counts of fraud all because of Emma Reese and her persistence. Everyone in the room toasted to Emma. She was proud of herself for not giving up on the story. They continued to watch the news as handcuffed men were being put into police cars and driven away.

Emma was already prepared to do follow up reports as more crimes became uncovered. There was a steady murmur of voices throughout the news room as Emma returned to her desk and leaned back in her chair. She loved her job, especially on days like this, when the criminals were arrested and hopefully brought to justice. It was just her job to follow the clues and decipher what they meant and she enjoyed every minute of it.

Calls and texts were coming to her phone faster than she could respond. Well-wishers and congratulations would expect a reply. Some were fellow reporters, but most were family and friends...and Pat. She decided to bite the bullet and call him back.

"Hello," Pat said, surprised.

"Hi, I saw you had been calling and thought I would find out why," Emma replied. Not exactly friendly but not as rude as she wanted to be, either.

"Well, I'm going to be coming back to St. Pete next week and wondered if we could get together?" He asked.

"Umm, why exactly?" Emma was getting impatient.

"Just to catch up," Pat said, then added, "I miss you."

There it was. "I don't think that's a good idea," Emma responded.

"Why, are you seeing someone?" He asked.

Emma hesitated. Saying 'yes' would probably be the easiest way to get him to stop calling, but if he did show up unannounced next week, it would also be hard to hide the fact that she wasn't seeing anyone. "Maybe," was the response she decided to give.

"Okay, well, I understand. It still would be nice to see you. Maybe we could just have lunch?" Pat insisted.

"I don't think so. Goodbye, Pat." Emma hung up before he had a chance to say anything else. She didn't know how to make him understand that she didn't want to see him. She had to admit that she did miss him, too, but it was not a healthy relationship. Better to cut ties completely.

Her next call was to James. Since there wasn't any baseball on the television tonight, he had the local news on and caught her breaking news story all by accident. It was meant to be a jibe at her but he was too proud to make her feel bad for not letting him know she was working on something so dangerous but important.

Emma tried to explain that she really didn't know until the last minute if it was actually going to amount to anything big. But once she received all the evidence to go public, she did. James let her know that she could come get dinner on the house. She reminded him that her dinners were always on the house because he never paid her a salary.

They laughed together just like old times. Emma was glad to hear from him, it had been too long. She would have to go help out at the restaurant soon, she was sure it would be busy now with the World Series coming to town. Emma promised to come out and watch the game with them one of these nights. He laughed but agreed.

LIANE LINCOLN DIDN'T often pop champagne at the office, but she always had a bottle ready when the circumstances called for it. Today was one of those days! Liane was a shrewd business woman who worked her way up to the top as Director. It wasn't easy but it sure was worth it.

Through the years, many choices presented themselves to Liane and some decisions were much harder than others. Her love life was a mess. She turned down a marriage proposal in order to stay in St. Petersburg and never regretted it. The only thing she occasionally reflected on was not having children. At forty-four years old, she always lingered on the thought of adoption. Then she remembered her job.

Being Director of the newsroom wasn't exactly a nine to five job and it certainly wasn't conducive to being a single mother. Marriage, on the other hand, was a possibility. She wouldn't mind being a step-mother. These thoughts were fleeting but persistently regular. This was probably why Liane threw herself into her work.

Sitting at her desk and sipping champagne made Liane a little melancholy. She remembered *her* first big break in a story and was so excited when it finally became public. That was years ago, decades even. It was the thrill that all journalist live for and are always on the hunt for the next big story.

Liane remembered when Emma first walked into her office for an interview. She was fresh out of college and had worked at her college newspaper. Emma had told Liane that she like the newspaper, but it was a job in front of the camera that she wanted. That was when Emma knew her true calling was investigative journalism. Liane even thought she would be a natural on the anchor desk. She had no doubt now that every news outlet in the Southeast just became aware of who Emma Reese was.

Losing Emma to a competitor was Liane's worst fear. She would just have to make sure Emma was happy here and not wanting to look elsewhere. Liane turned her chair so that she was looking out her glass wall and into the newsroom. Everyone was gathered around Emma's desk. Her instinct was to go and join them but she decided not to, let them have their celebration.

It was Miriam who first suggested they all go to Ferg's Sports Bar to get something to eat and continue the party. Emma was already feeling tipsy but it was within walking distance so she was all for it. Altogether seven co-workers walked to Ferg's and got a table near the bar. Miriam took control of ordering the food and another round of drinks.

Emma was starting to get emotional when she looked around the table. All of these people came to celebrate her and her achievement today. She had never felt such support ever in her life and it felt good. She felt tears well up in her eyes but blamed the jalapeños in the nachos when someone asked her if she was okay. These were her friends.

Right now life was good. Emma couldn't imagine how it could get any better than it was right now. Well, maybe an anchor job, but this was pretty good for now. She just wished her family was with her. Emma suddenly felt guilty about not calling her father. She was sure he saw or heard about her news story, but he did not hear it from her.

That guilt only compounded the guilt she already felt about him in that terrible facility. She had called a few more but they were either full or way too expensive. She even looked into home care if she brought him to her house, but twenty-four hour care was not feasible. She was running out of options. What she needed was a miracle or a guardian angel, either one would do.

Emma yawned and realized she was exhausted. After an hour of celebrating, she said her goodbyes to everyone at the table and gave Miriam a hug. Miriam was always her biggest supporter. Emma walked the short distance back to her car and enjoyed the cool evening air. Soon this area would be swarmed with fans coming to see the World Series.

She was starting to feel some hometown pride in her St. Pete Sharks and thought she should get a t-shirt or something. It was funny, Emma had lived in this area her entire life and had never been to a hometown sports game of any kind. Maybe she will go to one of the home games next week.

Thinking about the Sharks brought Andy's face to mind. She hated the way he winked at her or made snide comments about how he was glad she was there. What an ego! But what beautiful blue eyes, as blue as the sky on a cold winter day. There was nothing wrong with admiring the tall, handsome ball player while being disgusted by his huge ego, right? Well, luckily she would never have to be put in the position of interviewing him ever again.

At home, Emma kicked off her shoes at the door and went to take a shower. She loved her cute little rental home and the quiet neighborhood in Pinellas Park was the perfect getaway from the city. Emma wasn't quite ready for bed so she made herself a bowl of chocolate ice cream and turned on the television.

She found an old Katharine Hepburn movie and let the familiar voice lull her into a cozy sense of comfort. Realizing she had dozed off at the end of the movie, Emma decided it was time for bed. She turned off lights as her best day had finally come to an end.

OVER THE COURSE OF the following week, things became busier for Emma. More stories of suspected criminal activity were coming to her desk as well as more whistleblowers coming forward about the story she had just reported. It was an endless stream of calls, texts and emails.

On top of all that, the World Series was in full swing. The St. Petersburg Sharks were playing against the Savannah Storm and the games were tied at three each. Tomorrow's big game would decided who got the World Series trophy. Emma had gone to the Salty Waves to watch a game and tried to use her social media to create a buzz, but it only attracted her friends.

James and Joanne were happy to have Emma stop by and it was a great time to catch up. They seemed busy but Emma knew it should be busier. James confirmed that business was bad and he was giving it until next summer. If things didn't turn around by then, they just couldn't afford to keep it going. Emma hated to hear that. She knew how much he loved his restaurant and how much time and money he and Joanne had put into it.

She wished there was something more she could do. Emma just didn't have the pull to bring people down, even with her new found local celebrity status. It wasn't enough and they all knew it. It was a sad way to end a pretty nice day.

Well, it was a nice day until she got a call from Liane. She wasn't sure why her boss would be calling her at this hour, but she answered it anyway. There was a pit in her stomach that seemed to grow very quickly with every word Liane said. No, this wasn't happening, not again! Liane was not prone to practical jokes and this was no exception, only there was no other way of comprehending what she was saying.

"Hello, Emma?"

"Yes," she replied.

"Emma, I have some bad news," Liane started. "Gary is sick again. I need you to cover sports reporting for the last game of the World Series tomorrow night, only I need you to stay for the whole game because we want to report on the winning team, of course. Be there for the pre-game interviews and then the post-game interviews. Fred will be your cameraman, again."

Silence.

"Hello, Emma, are you there?" Liane asked, concerned.

Yes, Emma heard her but she couldn't respond. Emma had already ordered and drank another shot of whiskey.

Chapter 7

The traffic problems around Tropicana Field stretched for miles in every direction. The whole county, if not the state, were here to support the Sharks on the last night of the World Series. Cars were arriving early to get a good parking spot and join in on the festivities that were popping up all around the stadium.

Everyone wanted a glimpse of the team, especially Andy Anderson, who was rumored to be named the MVP of the series. Andy had been playing superbly all season and had really been a key player these past few weeks. Everyone loved Andy, everyone except Emma.

As Emma inched her way towards the stadium she began to feel the butterflies. She thought this was all past her. Damn it, Gary! Why are you sick, again? Emma felt bad for cursing Gary, she knew that he hated missing this last game of the series. He was one of those sports fans who would have been here all day just for the excitement of it if he could.

Not Emma, she was pulling up later than she would have wanted to, but still early enough to get inside and situated before the team interviews. She showed her credentials to the parking attendants and they showed her the area were she was to park. Fred was already waiting for her. Emma called out a casual greeting, but Fred was not in the mood.

Fred knew what having Emma with him today meant. The interviews would be short, spirits would be low and the time in between the pre-game and post-game interview would be excruciatingly painful.

"Come on, let's get this over with," Fred mumbled as he led the way into the stadium.

Even when they came to the games during the earlier playoffs Emma thought the stadium was alive with its own hum. Today it was downright vibrating! Music was already playing, the crowd was cheering and the teams were out on the field warming up. Emma smoothed her long hair and held the microphone out for her first interview. She nodded to Fred as Coach Walters approached.

"Hello, Coach Walters," Emma started. "Congratulations on your team getting to the seventh game. What are your thoughts on tonight's game?"

Coach Walters, with his ever-present smile looked from Emma to the stands. "Everyone is so excited, as you can see! I feel good about it, the team feels great. I think we will come home with the trophy tonight."

Emma went on to ask Coach Walters about his thoughts on the season and how certain player injuries were a factor this year. The coach was quick to say that having other players step up and play more may have been their key to success. Emma was able to get a few more questions in before Coach Walters was called away.

The next player Emma called over was Greg Reynolds, the first baseman. Emma asked how he felt going into tonight playing against the Savannah Storm. The Storm had been a strong team this year and she asked if there was anything they needed to adjust in their game tonight. Greg replied that they would do what they've been doing all year and that was 'win'.

While waiting for their next player to approach, Emma asked Fred if they should move locations. When Fred's eyes darted to the right, she knew there was a player approaching, she could feel a presence behind her. As Emma turned around with her microphone, there was Andy Anderson standing just inches away.

Before the game the players always looked so clean and fresh. Their white uniforms where freshly laundered and they were smiling in anticipation of the start of the game. It was the best time to interview a player in Emma's opinion. Being this close to the six foot four pitcher was always a little intimidating, but today it annoyed her a bit. She didn't like it when people snuck up behind her, even a potential MVP of the World Series.

"Hello, Emma," Andy said.

Now Emma was speechless. She was expecting to be called Gary, a wink or a sexist comment, but not this. How did he remember her name? They had only met twice and that was for a minute and it was weeks ago. Emma stared at Andy, trying to compose herself and remember the questions she was here to ask.

"Are you okay?" Andy asked, only half joking.

"Yes, yes, of course," Emma began, partly stuttering. "So how are you feeling coming into this last game tonight?"

Emma was only half listening. She tried to maintain direct eye contact but it was making her lose concentration. She decided to look down at her notes, up in the stands and then at the camera in order to finish the interview. Luckily, her questions seemed to come from auto pilot and when Fred nodded that they had enough and it was time to get off the field, she could breath again.

She could see how easy it would be for a female fan to get caught up in the centrifugal force that is Andy Anderson. It was a good thing Emma was strong enough to withstand the pull of such a charismatic man, no matter how handsome he may be. Emma and Fred walked to the press box that was set up for all the media personnel to watch the game.

She had never been in a press box before. There were more than one, but she was in the television news box. Here they would wait out the game and hopefully be interviewing the Sharks as the winning team later. Emma had never watched an entire baseball game from start to finish and expected to pass the time on her computer but ever since the first pitch, she was hooked.

The game started slow, Emma thought, but having met a few players gave her a new connection to the team that she never felt before. She watched Andy as he looked over his shoulder and faked a throw to first base. How he rubbed his shoulder in between innings, possibly indicating an injury that he was fighting through. Emma watched Coach Walters as his facial expressions changed from one batter to another depending on how they were doing.

Fred had brought Emma a hot dog, chips and a soda. She didn't realize how hungry she was and thanked him for the food. It wasn't what she was craving, but it was typical stadium food and she enjoyed it. Being there was awakening a new love for the game she had never expected. She was seeing the men on the field as more than just players with big egos, although that was still true in her opinion, she now saw the athletes that put in years of hard work to get to this stage in their careers.

Emma was appreciating their job and their sport. She asked one of the staff if they would bring her a Sharks t-shirt or jersey that she could purchase. She wanted to wear it at the post-game interview. She didn't know how her boss would react, but she was actually enjoying the moment. Maybe she could share the sports reporting with Gary next season. Emma laughed out loud at the thought of her suggesting that to either Gary or Liane.

At the seventh inning stretch the game was close. The Savannah Storm were beating the St. Petersburg Sharks with a score of six to four. With only two innings to go, it wasn't impossible, but the energy in the stadium had changed. They would have to rally back in order to win the trophy.

Emma had gotten calls throughout the game, mostly from Gary. He was watching the game and told her she did pretty good with the pre-game interviews. That was actually high praise from Gary. But he also warned her that the post-game interview was the most critical. Emma didn't want any more pressure on her than she already felt. She would do her best, it was just another interview, right?

Neither team got any more runs during the eighth inning. It was starting to look like the Storm might win this game and the series. Other journalists where agonizing over having to do their post-game interviews with the Sharks if they lost, if they could even get them to talk. Fred remembered being in this situation many times before. He was confident that they could still pull out a win.

All anyone could do was watch and wait. At the top of the ninth, the Savannah Storm were hitting pretty good. Andy was on the mound and was pitching strikes, until he wasn't anymore. After striking out the first two batters Andy walked the next two. Coach Walters was visibly distressed and called for a time out. He walked to the mound and was joined by the infield players.

Whatever they were saying to Andy, he was shaking his head furiously. He didn't want to be taken out of the game, not in the last inning. With two men on base and two outs, anything could happen. If the next player got a home run or even a hit, it could be too much to come back from for the Sharks.

Andy was feeling the pressure but stayed on the mound. Coach Walters and the other players returned to their places and the game went on. As the next player stepped into the batting box the whole stadium was silent. The crowd collectively held their breath as the count went to two balls and two strikes. Andy looked over his shoulder at the base runners, now at second and third base.

With a quick fake throw to third, he regained his composure and leaned in to watch the catcher. The catcher flashed what he thought Andy should throw and then the wind up. Andy threw the most perfect pitch and the umpire yelled 'Strike!'. The Sharks managed to hold the Storm's lead at two runs and now they were up to bat.

Emma was torn between not wanting to watch and needing to see every detail. It was so quiet in the press box that she could literally hear the slow exhaling of the breathing around her. The Sharks needed two runs to tie and three to win. It was a lot to ask for in the bottom of the ninth inning. Everyone watched as the Storm took their positions on the field.

The first player at bat struck out, a collective sigh filled the room. The next player was able to hit a line drive to center field and stood safely at first base. Emma breathed a little easier knowing he could help score a run. The third player got walked and the Storm called for a time out and they approached their own pitcher.

The Savannah Storm were in the same position that the Sharks were in only minutes before. The pressure was on and the stakes were high. Everyone wondered how they would play this out. Would they change their pitcher now or let him finish the game? Just like Andy, the pitcher refused to leave. He would finish what he started, for better or worse.

The next player up was Greg Reynolds, the first baseman. The crowd's cheers were deafening. Fred came over and nudged Emma's arm, he said if anyone could pull this off, it was him. Emma felt like she and Fred were bonding tonight. They were the ones in the trenches of this emotional journey together.

Emma smiled at Fred and they both focused on Greg at home plate. The pitcher was looking over his shoulder to check the runners, now at second and third base. It was like déjà vu, only this was it, this was the Shark's last chance to win. The pitcher focused on his catcher and nodded, then the wind up.

Emma didn't even see the ball but she heard the crack of the bat when Greg Reynolds connected with it! Everyone in Tropicana Field was on their feet as they watched the ball land somewhere in the section of seats behind the right field fence. Pandemonium broke out as all three players rounded the bases and stomped their feet on home plate.

The game was over. The Sharks won the game seven to six and won the World Series four games to three. It was probably the most exciting night that Emma ever experienced and it was at a baseball game of all places! Fred was pulling at Emma's elbow to get her to follow him, they had to get down on the field as soon as possible. They probably should have already been down there but they didn't want to miss a second of such a dramatic finish.

Wearing her new St. Petersburg Sharks jersey, Emma and Fred pushed their way onto the field. It didn't take long to get caught up in the celebrations as streamers and confetti were being dropped from above. They were bringing a makeshift stage along with the trophy to the field and that was where Emma headed.

It was a joyful time for players and fans alike. There were hugs and cheers coming from all directions. Players were making their way towards the stage and giving high fives, slaps on the backs and hugs as Coach Walter was handing out shirts and hats that said, 'World Series Champions' on them.

Even Emma was getting emotional when she felt a hand on her shoulder. It was Andy Anderson, he was giving her his first interview after winning the World Series! Fred nodded that he was ready and Emma conducted the best sports interview of her career. It was heartfelt and cheerful, Gary would be proud. Afterwards, Andy hugged Emma.

It was so quick and fleeting, but in that moment, it felt right. All past grievances were forgiven. The Sharks had just won the World Series and everything was right with the world. That is until she got back to her car.

As much as she tried, it wouldn't start. The crowds had cleared out by then. Her and Fred had stayed for more celebrations and the fans had thinned and eventually went home. Fred offered to drop her off at home, but she had gotten ahold of James and he said he would swing by on his way home. Now that the game was over, his restaurant had emptied, too. She would just have to wait for him.

Emma was sitting in her car and watching James's location which never moved. She let out a long, deep sigh knowing that it could be another hour before he came to help her. A knock on Emma's window startled her so badly, she had her pepper spray in one hand and her other on the door handle.

It took a moment for Emma to focus on who this smiling man was waving at her from the darkened parking lot. It was Andy Anderson.

Chapter 8

Surprised, Emma stepped out of her locked vehicle and stood in front of Andy, the new MVP of the World Series. Emma was shocked to be standing face to face with him in the dark parking lot. First of all, she didn't know anyone else was still here, let alone the star player.

"What are you doing hanging out in the parking lot? If you wanted my autograph, you could have just asked," Andy said with a smile.

Emma noted that he didn't wink this time, this was possibly the real Andy Anderson, the one that the fans didn't see all that often. Andy started to look concerned when Emma didn't answer right away.

"Is everything okay?" He asked.

Emma managed to clear her head and answer. "My car won't start," Emma said, gesturing to the dead vehicle beside them for emphasis.

"Well, I'm not really good with cars, not my specialty if you know what I mean. Plus, I don't like getting my hands dirty," Andy replied as he brought his dirty hands up for both to see.

Andy and Emma both laughed. She was starting to relax and realized that Andy was pretty funny, a real comedian.

"It's okay, I called my brother and he's on his way," Emma said even though it was only a half truth. She glanced down at her phone and knew it was still going to be a long wait.

"Listen, let me take you home," Andy started. When he saw her physically take a step backwards he put his hands up, again. "Wait, no, that's not at all what I meant."

"Really, you can go," Emma replied. "I'm sure you have some celebrating to do. You just won the World Series for crying out loud!" She let out a nervous laugh because this whole interaction was unbelievable. All she could think about was telling Miriam and her family.

Andy laid his bags on the ground and said he wasn't leaving her alone in the dark and empty parking lot. So she would either let him drop her off at home or he would wait with her. Embarrassed that she had exaggerated that her brother was on his way, Emma decided to trust Andy. She made a quick call to James to explain about needing to pick up her car tomorrow then she grabbed her bags and followed Andy to his truck.

No one was ever going to believe this was happening so she snapped a quick photo for evidence then proceeded to send it to James, just in case. Emma laughed as she imagined his expression when James opened her text. She put her phone away and caught up with Andy.

Andy Anderson was just thankful she agreed to let him take her home. He really didn't want to spend any more time just sitting around the parking lot. He already felt like he had been at the stadium for days and was ready to go home, put his feet up and relax. He didn't mind the detour, at least he was still on his way home.

Heading north on Highway 275, Andy asked where exactly Emma lived. She found herself talking easily to Andy and probably giving away too much personal information. She said she had moved to Pinellas Park after her mother's death and her father's stroke. Once he went into a care facility that she didn't even like, her brother took the house and she moved out.

Andy was fascinated and was genuinely interested in this investigative journalist turned sports reporter. He admitted he saw her breaking news story, that's why her name stayed with him, but even back when she first interviewed him, he was interested in her. Emma was one of the few people who weren't susceptible to his charm.

Andy asked about her father and why she didn't like the facility he was at. She went on to describe the conditions and how impossible it was to find anything better. Emma talked about her father and how he deserved so much better and wanting to take him to Scotland to visit but that there just wasn't time right now. Then she explained why her brother couldn't come and get her. That he and his wife just opened a restaurant on the beach and were putting all their blood, sweat and tears into it and that may not even be enough.

"What's the name of it, maybe I know it?" Andy asked.

"I doubt it, it had been vacant for so long," Emma replied. When she saw that Andy was still waiting for the name, she added, "The Salty Waves."

Andy shook his head, he never heard of it but then again, he didn't have much time to go to the beach. His days were either playing, practicing or training. It left little time for anything else. Andy was thirty-three and baseball was all he knew. He also knew that the constant pain in his right shoulder was a warning that his time was running out. He would be lucky if he had three or four more good years of playing professional baseball.

"What about your family?" Emma asked. She felt like she had been babbling on about her family long enough and wanted him to talk about himself a little.

Andy laughed. "Oh, that's a story for another time. It's much too complicated to get into this late at night." He glanced over at Emma and saw that she was still waiting for more. "Suffice it to say that I have a brother, a mother and a father but none of us spend any time together."

Emma let that sink in as she turned her gaze to the road ahead of them. They were nearing her house and she was now giving him turn by turn directions. She thought about asking follow up questions about Andy's family, but she got the impression he didn't want to talk about it, especially with a stranger who was also a reporter.

Andy turned onto Park Lake Drive and made a right onto 98th Avenue. Emma pointed out the house and he pulled into the driveway. She gathered her things and expressed her gratitude for the ride and the company.

"Anytime, Emma, the pleasure was all mine." Andy replied.

As soon as Emma left his truck his mood changed. He waited until she waved and then closed the front door before backing up and driving home. Emma had lightened his mood tonight. Next came the realization that he was going home to an empty house. Andy had meant what he said about his family, they were all living their own separate lives.

Andy's father was an alcoholic who just couldn't get it together. His mother couldn't take it any longer and left when he turned eighteen. He supposed she thought that was old enough to not need a mother anymore. Well, she was wrong, wrong about a lot of things. Being left alone with an alcoholic father and an eight year old brother was extremely hard on him.

When his father remembered to come home and remembered he had kids, he was decent. He would actually buy groceries, give him money and clean the house. When he didn't, well, it fell on Andy's shoulders to take care of the house and his little brother. He wished he did have a supportive father who came to his games or practiced with him in the backyard but that never happened. Instead, he was left with a family he never saw.

It wasn't much of a detour to drive through Pinellas Park on the way to his home in Clearwater. Andy had a beautiful house on the beach because he figured that was the only way he could enjoy the ocean was to bring it to his backyard. Andy always liked the feeling of coming home. This was his sanctuary.

Andy pulled into his private driveway but noticed an older model car on the street. It wasn't until he was entering his front door that a man approached him from the bushes.

"Hello, son," the man said.

"Dad?" Andy was so startled by his father's appearance out of nowhere that he wasn't sure how he even knew where he lived.

"I heard that you guys won the game tonight and I wanted to congratulate my son," he replied. "Can I come in?"

Andy was reluctant to let his father inside. In the past, his father was known for stealing anything he could fit into his pockets to pawn for more booze but Andy was still feeling generous tonight. He opened the door for his father and tried to not let the man out of his sight.

Ronald Anderson was not quite sixty but looked seventy. Life had not been kind to him. Andy never tried to figure out why his father was the way he was, he never cared. All Andy knew was that Ron Anderson was not a good father. Wendy Anderson would never win any mother-of-the-year awards, either. She just left and never came back.

It took every ounce of self preservation to keep himself out of trouble and focus on baseball. It was the teachers and coaches in his life who provided the encouragement his parents couldn't. It was why Andy loved Coach Walters like a father, because he basically was one.

"You got any food in here? I'm starving," Ron asked his son.

Andy locked away as many valuables in his bedroom as he could before returning to the kitchen. He didn't know why he really showed up tonight but he was damn sure it wasn't to congratulate his son on winning a game.

"Yes, I think I have a couple steaks in here," Andy replied while looking in the refrigerator. Maybe if he fed his father he would leave.

Tonight did not turn out the way he thought it would. Helping a stranded reporter and feeding his father were not on his radar at all. Having a girl over might have been more his plan but not tonight. Now his plan was to get his father out of his house as soon as possible. Ron always brought bad luck wherever he went.

Bad luck and pain followed Ron Anderson everywhere.

Chapter 9

The city was still celebrating. Shark merchandise was everywhere. You couldn't walk into a store without seeing something with the St. Petersburg Sharks on it, everything from cereal to potato chips. Having a Championship team brought the city and county together like nothing else ever did.

Every news outlet in the country had stories about the players and coaches. They were seen having dinner out and boarding planes. Even buying a coffee or getting gas was reported on social media. The Sharks were the local celebrities being reported worldwide.

Emma walked into the newsroom and had to admit that she was getting caught up in the excited chatter about their amazing win. It couldn't have played out any more dramatically, either. Everyone was congratulating her on her interviews and even Gary gave her a raving review.

As soon as Liane saw her, she called Emma to her office. Liane informed her that there was talk in other markets and Emma's name was being mentioned. Big cities were calling and asking whether she might be willing to relocate or what her future plans were. Liane had done her best fielding questions, but was not wanting to play Emma's secretary.

Emma couldn't believe she was being talked about and maybe even sought after by other cities. This was what she dreamed of, only she didn't really want to leave St. Pete. She would if the right position opened up, though. Her head was spinning and Liane told her to consider all her options before making any rash decisions.

"Remember, today's news is tomorrow's trash," Liane called out to her as Emma left.

Liane loved that phrase and used it in every conversation. Emma was never quite sure what she was trying to say, but she was smart enough to know not to wait too long if she was going to accept any job. There was always a new, young journalist just waiting for their next big break and to steal the spotlight.

Emma spent the remainder of her day working on other stories and daydreaming. She wouldn't mind moving to Atlanta, that was a huge market and only a six hour drive home. The thought of moving made Emma feel guilty about leaving her father behind. She was the only one who visited him regularly and that would be a huge change for him.

Unable to concentrate any longer, Emma said goodbye to her co-workers and left for the day. November brought cooler air and she put on a sweater before walking to her car. She decided to visit her father before going home. Emma was frustrated with the progress she was making in trying to find another facility and James was no help at all.

Joseph Reese was sitting in the chair by the window and Emma was quick to note that it wasn't his wheelchair.

"Dad, how did you get over there?" She asked.

" I walked," he answered proudly. "With help."

It was only a few steps, but it was more than he had done before. Emma was so happy that it was progress. It was slow progress, but who cared. Well, she did care because this should have been happening months ago. This place was simply old and understaffed.

"Well, I brought you a present," Emma said, handing her father a gift bag.

"It's not my birthday," he replied.

Joe was so tickled to unwrap a baseball cap and t-shirt that said, 'World Series Champions' on them. He hugged her and put the cap on his head. She didn't think there was a bigger fan in the world than Emma's father. She had debated on getting one or the other but in the end she decided on both.

She spent a little more time with her father before she had to leave. She had originally planned to drive straight home, but she was hungry and knew a great restaurant on the beach she could go to. She thought about calling James and letting him know she was on her way but decided to just show up instead.

Salty Waves was on Madeira Beach and had the potential to be very profitable. It had everything going for it...on the beach, near shopping and lots of parking. The only problem they could figure out was that no one knew they were open. It had been closed for so long, people drove right past it even though there were cars in the parking lot and lights on.

When Emma walked in Joanne came over and gave her a big hug. They hadn't needed her help in a while, so Emma didn't get out there very often. Joanne led her to the bar and got her an iced tea and a menu. Emma ordered chicken tenders and waited for James to come out from the kitchen to join them.

Reluctantly, James came out with his sister's food and waited for her to reprimand him. He knew the real reason she was there was to yell at him for not visiting their father more often. Instead, Emma complimented him on the food and how much she liked the place. A little taken off guard, he thanked her.

To his surprise, Emma didn't mention their father once. Maybe it was reverse psychology. By Emma not talking about him, made James think about him more. If that was her plan, it was working. James already felt guilt, but he had more than his father on his mind right now. More immediate was how to pay the bills. Joanne said she had gotten a job in the mornings to help until things picked up...if they picked up.

Emma had wanted to bring up the possibility of her moving, but decided that this wasn't the time. She didn't even know if it would happen, so there wasn't any reason to mention it now. Instead, she just enjoyed the company of her brother and sister-in-law.

They asked her about the final game of the World Series and what it was like being there. They had seen the game and her interviews and were very impressed. She tried to explain the excitement of being there when all the drama of the ninth inning took place but she couldn't do it justice. There was just something in the air at Tropicana Field.

James asked about the night she needed a ride and who, exactly, did she get to take her home? He had seen the picture she sent, but didn't believe it. When Emma said Andy's name, James and Joanne started laughing. When they realized she was serious, their eyes were on Emma. They made her explain every detail without leaving anything out.

Emma insisted it was nothing. He drove her home out of guilt or obligation but that was it. He had already been spotted out recently with models and actors, so she was only a footnote on an otherwise chaotic night. She tried to convince them that he was nice to her but she wasn't interested in a baseball player with a big ego.

James and Joanne merely exchanged looks. They knew Emma well enough that when she protested that much, there were feelings behind it but they let her change the subject. Emma brought up Pat's name and James became defensive. James didn't like Pat and was glad when Emma had finally left him.

"Wait, why is he calling you?" James asked.

"He wants to meet me," replied Emma.

Again, James looked over at his wife. Neither one of them wanted Pat to come back in the picture. "What did you tell him?"

"I said, no."

Relief showed on his face as he refilled his sister's iced tea. He felt protective of her but knew she could take care of herself. Emma had proven that time and time again. Maybe it was time for James to trust her more since she probably knew what she was doing when it came to Pat.

Emma enjoyed her evening with her family but she was tired. She walked out onto the sand before leaving. This really was a beautiful location. She took a few pictures and posted them. If she could use her social media to help them even a little bit, it would be worth it.

She took her time walking back to her car. There were so many things she wanted to tell her brother, but she was tired of saying the same things over and over. James was older, he should be the one worried about their father but it fell to her. It would be a very hard conversation if she did decide to move.

Back at home, Emma was more determined than ever to make sure her father was settled into a better home. Maybe she was looking at this all wrong. She decided to search care facilities that weren't specifically for stroke or injuries but rather disabilities. Her search brought up a whole new avenue of possibilities and Emma reached out to some in her area.

Emma felt more encouraged by this new breakthrough and thought some of these places were very promising. There was one in particular called Sunnyside Home that was absolutely beautiful. She filled out their online form for consideration and would follow up in a couple of days. Even the name made her smile. Feeling more accomplished than she had in months, she poured herself a glass of wine and sat down to watch television.

Emma found it hard to stay focused on the movie. Her mind was wandering and was drifting from one worry to another. She ended up wondering what moving would really mean to her. She would be giving up her little slice of peace in this quiet neighborhood for what? A small apartment in a big city where she didn't know anyone?

Well, if she chose Atlanta, she did know one person...Pat. She changed her mind and decided to call him back. What was the harm in meeting him for lunch? They had been separated long enough that maybe they could, at the very least, be friends. She would call him tomorrow and set it up.

Emma heard the faint sound of rain outside and decided to sit out on her front porch. She put on a robe and carried her wine to one of the chairs by the front door. It was calming to hear the drops hit the roof and the leaves of the trees. Seeing the wet surface of the pavement reflect the street lights had a way of bringing everything into perspective.

She had a nice and comfortable life here in Florida and maybe that was worth more than chasing a dream in the big city. After all, she would be leaving so many things, and people, behind. Emma stretched her legs out and closed her eyes. She could almost mistake the sound of the rain for the ocean waves. Every storm uncovered new treasures. Maybe this rain would also bring her answers and closure, whichever she needed most.

Emma thought of her mother, Nora. What would she make of all that was happening to her daughter now? What advice would she give? Emma could only imagine what she would think but she was probably looking down and smiling. She trusted her daughter to make the right decision, perhaps even more trust than she allowed herself.

Chapter 10

One day after work Miriam announced they all needed to go out for dinner and drinks. She had met a new man and was eager to tell Emma all about him. Don decided to tag along as well, since Cindy was at her mother's out of town. It seemed like weeks since they had all gone out together and it felt good to just laugh with friends and catch up.

Miriam's new boyfriend was someone she met while taking her car in for repairs. He was divorced and very nice but she was concerned that he didn't want to get married again. Miriam definitely did, but not this very minute. However, it was a red flag when the guy she was dating says it was out of the question.

She liked him but wondered if she should cut ties now before they got too serious or should she see what happened. Miriam didn't want to get her heart broken, again. Emma and Don each gave their perspective and advice but in the end it was up to Miriam. It was hard to tell someone what to do when you had so much going on yourself.

Donald asked Emma if she ever heard back from Andy Anderson. Emma quickly replied, no. Why would she? They had all seen the magazine and social media posts of him at a holiday party in Paris with a beautiful blonde on his arm or the photo of him on a yacht with the young actress. He was spotted getting coffee in London with a few women walking with him down the street.

There was no way she could compete with those famous and beautiful women and she didn't want to. She was surprised his ego fit in the picture with the rest of his body. She was right about him from the very beginning, he liked to chase women. It was all a game to him. The only reason he acted interested in anything Emma had to say the night he drove her home was probably because he thought he'd get lucky.

Well, Emma was not one of his groupies that were waiting on his every word. He could keep his pretty actresses and she wished them well. She was sure he was driving them home at night, too, maybe that was his plan, to wait until they needed a ride somewhere and then pounce. Miriam and Don weren't buying all of Emma's explanations. When someone gets under the skin that much, they meant something to them.

It may have only been a brief moment, but Miriam was sure that something happened on that ride home between her and Andy. Maybe nothing physical, but there was a connection and now it was gone. Miriam decided to change the subject. Thanksgiving was right around the corner and Miriam wanted to host another Friendsgiving.

"Hey, maybe we could have it at my brother's restaurant," Emma offered.

"Sure, we could all pitch in," Miriam replied. "It would be less work for me."

Don liked the idea, too. He would confirm it with Cindy and get back to everyone. Maybe they could meet Miriam's mystery man, if he was still around. They all joked about taking bets but in the end they just wanted Miriam to be happy.

It was Don who had to leave first. He had gotten a text from Cindy that she was home and had dinner ready. Emma and Miriam could only hope for such a relationship as theirs. The bar was getting busier and noisier so the women followed him out, too.

They said their goodbyes and each went their separate ways home. Instead of going home, Emma went to see her father first. It was a clear night and she drove with the windows down. She made a mental note to call James and let him know they wanted to have a Friendsgiving party there. He would be happy about that.

Joe wasn't in his room when Emma arrived so she went to the dinning room to look for him. There he was sitting with a couple of friends eating meatloaf and mashed potatoes. She kissed her father and pulled up a chair to join them. Everyone greeted her and then went back to eating their dinner. Her father asked about her day and she said everything was great.

Emma was working on anther story but it wasn't anything as big as a corruption scandal. Her father said he couldn't wait to see her on the television, again. Every time she was on, he made everyone come around the television and watch her. Joe was Emma's biggest fan. She patted her father on the back and smiled.

After dessert was served, Emma helped him back to his room. He could walk part of the way but needed his wheelchair to make the whole journey. It was still progress. Just as Emma was getting her father settled into his bed, she got a call from one of the care homes she contacted.

Emma walked out into the back garden to take the call. It was Sunnyside Home and they were wondering if she could stop by and pick up some additional paperwork about her father. It looked like they had an opening for him and would like to start the process as soon as possible. Emma had to sit down before she collapsed.

She said she could be there in twenty minutes. Feeling elated, Emma said goodbye to her father and hopefully Rainbow House as she put the address in her phone. She was afraid to get her hopes up but this was the one place she really hoped would call her back. It was such a blessing that it was actually happening. Someone was looking out for her today.

As Emma pulled up to Sunnyside Home she felt an immediate calmness. It was beautiful. The lobby felt like a hotel. There was a concierge desk up front and Emma gave her name. A nice older woman led her through the lobby that opened up to a grand living area. There was a fireplace on one wall, a large television on another wall and in the corner was a pool table and then bookshelves full of books.

It was so inviting, Emma didn't know where to look first.

"Hi, I'm Sam," said a young man from behind her. Sam had been reading a book but quickly got to his feet when Emma entered the room. "I live here. Are you going to live here, too?"

"No, Sam, I'm just visiting," Emma replied.

Sam watched as Emma was led into the manager's office then went back to his reading. Emma sat down and reviewed the paperwork that she needed to fill out. The manager, Mr. Marc Brown, was happy to answer any and all of Emma's questions.

"Why is this facility so cheap?" Emma asked.

Mr. Brown laughed. "Well, we are a state of the art facility that caters to the needs of many different types of patients whether they are short term residents or long term. You do not need to worry about the needs of our residents being met. The reason our cost to the residents are so low is that our expenses are mostly covered by a foundation that was set up to cover all costs. It is a non-profit foundation that has various activities and events to help raise money, too."

Emma just couldn't believe her luck. She filled out everything they needed and said they would arrange transport for her father in the next day or two. They were customizing his room right now. He would be able to bring any personal belongings, within reason, to make it feel more like home if he wished, but Sunnyside Home should be able to accommodate whatever he may need.

LIFE GOES ON

Her head was spinning, she hoped this wasn't a dream. Mr. Brown said he would contact her as soon as transport was arranged so that she could be here when he arrived. He also invited her to walk around and become familiar with the Home so that she knew were everything was. Mr. Brown handed her a map of the facility and she thanked him before leaving his office.

Back in the living room, Sam greeted her again. Only this time there was a woman sitting with him. They were quietly reading in the corner library, undistracted by the game of pool being played in the other corner of the room. The living room led into a large dining hall with tables covered with tablecloths. There was no pass through serving window like in a school, this felt more like a restaurant. There were windows looking out onto the garden, lights and flowers at every table and soft music coming through the speakers.

Emma didn't have time to see everything, but according to the map, there was a swimming pool, a gym, a sauna, a movie room, extra rooms for out of town guests and the garden wrapped around the whole building. Before she left, she stopped at the concierge desk and picked up a November calendar of events. She really couldn't believe a place like this existed. It really spoke volumes about the type of person who started this foundation.

At home, Emma reviewed all the materials she was given and cried. She didn't even know where the tears came from. It was like a physical relief of all the pressure that had been heavy on her shoulders. That pressure was released as soon as she walked in the doors of Sunnyside Home. She had held it together long enough to get home. Now Emma could relax, her father would be well taken care of and would no longer be a factor in her decision making.

She called James and sent him a link to Sunnyside Home's website. She explained everything Mr. Brown had told her and would let him know when their father arrived. It was even in St.

Petersburg so it was more convenient for both of them. James said he would be there, just let him know what time.

It was nice being on the same page with him again. Perhaps this meant she didn't have to keep reminding him to visit their father more often. There was always that hint of tension when they met or talked on the phone. She knew it even if he wouldn't admit it. Those days would soon be over.

Emma rewarded herself with a bowl of chocolate ice cream. She deserved it as well as a pat on the back. What a year it had been! The year was winding down and with it meant the promise of new beginnings. Emma had accomplished so much this year, more than any other year. Hopefully that also meant that her father would finally get the therapy he needed to become independent again.

Just the thought of her father moving back home, driving again or even taking care of himself used to be a faraway dream, now it was so close she could almost see it in the shiny new brochures. It was as vivid as the paintings on the lobby walls. And Sam was there to greet them every time they walked in the door.

Emma knew she would sleep like a baby tonight. Her mother had a hand in this, she just knew it. Her mother was always looking out for them. There was another angel out there somewhere, too. Emma couldn't stop smiling. She washed up her dishes and walked outside in her robe. Sitting in her chair out front was where she could think best. Tonight she just wanted to feel the cool air on her face and be thankful for everything that was happening to her family.

Everything else could fade away right now. She didn't need to carry everyone's problems on her shoulders. Sometimes she needed a shoulder to lean on, too. Emma missed having a companion and promised herself that next year would be different. She would allow herself to love and be loved. It sounded easy, but she knew that it wasn't.

She was worthy of unconditional love and wouldn't compromise this for anyone. Maybe this time next year her whole life would look very different, if she was lucky.

Chapter 11

Now that her father was all moved into his new home, Emma could start focusing, really focusing, on her own life. James and Joanne were amazed when they walked into Sunnyside Home for the first time. Sam was always there to greet them each time they went back, too. It was so convenient to drop by that James found himself visiting with his father on his way to the restaurant each morning.

It was such a relief to have a fresh outlook on life. Emma felt encouraged by her father's new, cheerful demeanor as well. Joe was always optimistic but at Sunnyside Home, it was contagious. Even Emma smiled when she was greeted by Sam each day. She found out later that the woman who sat quietly in the corner and read with him was his mother. She was very unassuming and never offered up a smile or a friendly wave the way Sam did.

Emma never pushed, if Sam's mother wanted to engage with her, she would. Sam was a tall young man in his early twenties, she would guess, and autistic. Sunnyside was his home since it had opened. Emma didn't know why his parents couldn't take care of him, but she would never ask, everyone had their story.

In the newsroom, Emma was called into her boss's office. At first Emma thought it was about the story she reported on last night. She had wanted to do a follow-up piece about it but was waiting for some documents through an open records request. Armed with reasons and rebuttals Emma entered Liane's glass office.

"Sit, please," Liane said. Her voice was firm but her smile gave her away. She was not angry or upset. After waiting for Emma to do what she asked, she continued. "As you may know, the city's big gala for the Hometown Heroes Awards is coming up."

Emma nodded her head. She had covered the gala each year and reported on the newest award recipients each time.

"Well, this year I will not be sending you to cover it," Liane said with a straight face. Emma frowned, confused. "Because you will be receiving an award this year!"

Liane's face lit up with excitement. She had done her best to hide it but couldn't wait to give Emma the news any longer. Emma brought her hands to her face in shock. She was getting an award?

"For what?" Emma asked.

"What do you mean, for what?" Liane asked with a laugh. "For your incredible journalism uncovering corruption and money laundering that put a dozen officials in jail, that's why! The city is most grateful and are giving you a Hometown Hero Award on Friday."

Liane watched her as Emma let the information sink in. She didn't do this job for the accolades or awards, she just loved what she did. But an award...

"What do I wear?" Emma asked.

Liane laughed again. "Something long and sparkly I would think."

Emma thanked her before walking slowly back to her own desk. Miriam and Don were anxiously awaiting the news and Emma was quick to oblige. Shrieks of excitement came from the newsroom as word spread that Emma was receiving an award at the annual gala.

"I wonder who else is getting one?" Don asked.

There were plenty of people who could be awarded one, but the city liked to make it special and only chose a few each year. How special would it really feel if you were only one out of a hundred, but one of only four or five felt fantastic!

"Well, I don't know," Emma began. "But what I do know is that I need a dress."

Miriam clapped her hands excitedly, "I can go shopping with you!"

It was set, Miriam and Emma would go fancy dress shopping for her gala dress tomorrow evening after work. They planned to drive to Tampa and visit the International Plaza. If they didn't find a long, sparkly dress there, she didn't know where else to look.

EMMA DROVE UP TO THE entrance of the Vinoy Resort right on time. She had never been there before and was amazed how grand it was from the outside and could only imagine what the inside would look like. She carefully stepped out of her car as the valet attendant took her hand. Emma maneuvered her dress so that she didn't step on it as the valet took her car away.

Other guests were arriving as well so Emma followed everyone inside. Feeling a little self conscious about being here as a guest of honor, she smoothed out her dress and touched up her hair before walking inside. Emma walked through the lobby and was escorted into the ballroom. Trays of champagne were being passed around and Emma gladly took one. She took a moment to get her bearings and scanned the room. There was a string quartet in one corner, a table of food and refreshments along the wall and a bar near the door.

The stage was set up directly in front of her and she could see the table covered in blue velvet with four awards sitting proudly on top. The spotlight was aimed at the podium and Emma was glad she had practiced a short speech. She made her way around the back of the room looking for her table and noticed that there were place cards at each setting.

Winding her way around each table, she finally found her name but was struck with a sudden wave of anxiety when she realized it was right up front. Of course it was, the award recipients wouldn't be expected to walk all the way from the back of the room. It was logical but unnerving. Emma had never been the center of attention like this before and was starting to question her decision to come at all.

Just as she was planning her escape, Liane Lincoln tapped her on the shoulder and gave her a brief hug. Liane told Emma she looked stunning! Emma felt stunning. If nothing else came from tonight, she knew she picked the perfect dress with the help of Miriam. Emma chose a long red strapless dress. This dress had small, clear beading all over and as soon as she put it on, she knew this was the one.

Emma wore her hair up and had a simple necklace and dangling earrings to complete her look. She couldn't remember the last time, if ever, she had gotten this glamorous for anything. There was still time before the event so Emma walked over to get a plate of food. She turned around when she heard a loud commotion coming from the entrance to the ballroom. Emma took her plate and walked closer to get a better look.

Amidst camera flashes and news reporters was Andy Anderson. Andy was wearing a custom fitted navy blue suit and was charming all of the photographers and reporters. Emma's mouth opened in surprise when she recognized one of them as Don. Don had a microphone in Andy's face asking one question after another.

Emma wanted to call him a traitor but knew he was only doing his job. As Andy Anderson made his way around the room, Don came over to Emma.

"Hey, you look fantastic!" Don said, impressed.

"Why are you only interviewing Andy?" Emma blurted out.

"I'm here for you, too," Don quickly replied. "I just ran into him in front of the hotel and followed him in. I'm here to interview you, too."

"Fine," Emma said and answered all of Don's questions on camera. It was the normal round of questions such as how she felt about winning, did she know she was getting this award and what did she have to say to those that chose her. But it was Don's last question that stumped her.

"Emma Reese, has winning this award changed your life in any way?" Don asked.

Emma paused and thought for a moment. "Yes, Don, it has. I have learned that it doesn't have to be the big earth-shattering stories of government corruption that change you, sometimes it's the small stories that make a big impact."

Just then Emma felt a hand on her shoulder.

"Hello again, Emma."

Emma turned around to find herself face to face with Andy Anderson. He held out his hand and she shook it, all very formal. His smile, however, reminded her of that night a month ago when he offered her a ride home. Emma couldn't decided if she was still upset about how he acted when his ego took over or if she was warming to his softer side.

"You look amazing!" Andy proclaimed with a huge grin.

Emma was definitely feeling his warmth. "Thank you, so do you," Emma replied.

Neither one of them even noticed that Don was still standing there with his camera until he cleared his throat.

"Can I get a few pictures of the two of you together?" Don asked.

"Um, no..." Emma started.

"Sure!" Andy said, cutting her off.

They stood for a few photos before the emcee asked for everyone to now take their seats. That was Emma's cue to remove herself from

Andy's arm around her and find the table for Channel 2 News. Relieved to be able to sit and be out of the spot light for a moment, she let her eyes wonder the crowd. There was a great turnout for this year's gala and as she brought her attention back to the podium, her eyes caught Andy's, watching her.

Just as she was beginning to warm up to him, he winked.

The emcee began by thanking everyone for coming tonight. It was a wonderful turnout for such a prestigious event that St. Petersburg holds every year to honor those who represent the best of the city. This year they would be honoring a news reporter, an educator, a doctor and the MVP from the St. Petersburg Sharks.

Everyone cheered and clapped as each were called to the stage. Emma Reese was first and delivered her speech perfectly. She wasn't nervous talking in front of a crowd, she did it everyday on camera, it was only one pair of eyes that bothered her. She avoided eye contact with Andy and his whole table until the end. His smile was big and genuine.

Emma managed to walk down the steps and to her seat without embarrassing herself, so that was an accomplishment. The other two award recipients were just as worthy and their stories equally inspiring. She clapped when they each finished their speeches and returned to their seats. That only left one more person.

Even before Andy Anderson stood up, the room started cheering. The city was still celebrating their boys for bringing home the World Series trophy. Andy stood up at his chair, took a bow and then waved. At the podium, he gave a heartfelt account of how it wasn't only him who won, or even the team, it was the city. This was answered by more applause.

Andy made it clear that his job is only possible if they have the support of their fans. Baseball wasn't just a game they played for each other, they played if for their fans. He was proud to be named the MVP, but that was because they could only chose one player, in reality it belonged to the whole team.

It wasn't until people at his table stood up to cheer that she noticed some more familiar faces. Coach Walters, Greg Reynolds as well as Bobby Bishop were all in attendance to support their teammate. Emma looked around her table at her own team. Liane Lincoln, Miriam Post and Donald and Cindy Day were at her table supporting her. Maybe they weren't all that different after all.

After the speeches there was music, dancing and more food and drinks. Emma began to relax and have fun, after all, this was a once-in-a-lifetime party in her honor and why not enjoy it. Greg asked her to dance and she agreed, then Bobby asked. She was having fun.

As the evening wore on she sought out a quiet corner for a moment of peace. She found herself walking down a long hallway and was about to turn around when she heard the faint sounds of a piano being played. Before walking any further, she bend down and removed her high heels. She had been wanting to do that for hours and it felt good to be walking down this unknown hallway barefoot on the plush carpeting.

Emma stopped in front of each closed door and listened. It wasn't until she got to the end of the hall that she knew that was the one that contained the lovely melody of Beethoven. She was tipsy enough to go in, curious enough not to knock and disturb the pianist. All she could make out in the dimly lit room was that the man playing the grand piano wore a custom tailored navy blue suit.

Chapter 12

Andy didn't hear anyone enter the room. He had quietly escaped the crowd in search of some solitude in this huge hotel and didn't think anyone had followed him. He had found peace and quiet in one of the smaller rooms down the main hallway and snuck inside. He didn't think anyone would mind, he wouldn't make a mess, just play the piano.

Music was Andy's refuge in life. He knew that it would always be there when he felt down, sad or scared. No matter what he played he could change his mood and feel better instantly. Even as a child, he enjoyed music class the most. His teacher had taught him to read music and Andy gravitated to the piano. He was a quick learner and could even play by ear.

Most of his friends chose the guitar or saxophone to play, anything sexier than the piano. It wasn't an instrument he could take home or carry around, which made his time with it even that much more precious. Andy would find time to practice before school and after school. He would even make time to practice around his baseball schedule. Now that he could afford to have one in his home, he preferred to play it to watching television or playing video games. Music let him escape his memories.

Emma thought she was being quiet in the back of the room until she dropped one of her shoes. Startled by the sound, Andy suddenly turned around and stood up. Surprised to see Emma standing barefoot behind him, he hesitated a second before offering her a seat on the bench. Emma looked around for another chair, but the room was empty except for the piano and bench.

Reluctantly, she slowly approached Andy and the piano. Still surprised at what she found behind the door, she considered turning around and leaving but something in his eyes persuaded her to stay. Her bare feet lead the way to his side.

"Please don't stop," Emma said, sliding in next to him. "It was very soothing."

Andy turned around to face the piano leaving Emma facing the opposite direction. He placed his hands on the keys and did what she asked. Andy chose another Beethoven piece, this time, Fleur De Lis, one of his favorites. Emma listened and closed her eyes, agreeing that it was hers, too. They were both deep in their own thoughts until the song came to an end.

Andy didn't want to return to the main ballroom and neither did Emma. He wanted to talk to Emma and learn more about her. This woman intrigued him so much. It actually surprised him how much he had thought about her since that night in his truck.

Andy thought about that night many times. Was it luck that brought the two of them together that night in the parking lot? Maybe. Or maybe it was fate. He was glad that he was able to offer her a ride home but he also wanted to be invited in, however improbable that may have been. It was better this way, he needed to know his feelings were real. He also desperately needed to know this woman.

"I noticed you didn't come here with anyone," Andy said softly in the quiet room.

"I noticed you didn't, either," Emma replied. "Weren't any of your model or actress girlfriends free tonight?" She couldn't believe she had just said that out loud. She definitely had too much champagne.

Andy laughed. It was so organic and deep that she felt it through his arm that was touching hers. They were still facing opposite directions but Emma knew he was smiling. She could sense it. She was learning that he had a great sense of humor and she liked that.

"You don't believe everything you see about me, do you?" Andy asked. There was a tinge of hurt in his words.

"Well, why shouldn't I, you looked so happy and together..." Emma didn't know what else to say.

"Those were publicity photos. My manager thinks that if I'm seen with those women it's good for my image," Andy replied. "Besides, my life is crazy enough. I can't keep up a long-distance relationship with someone in France. I can barely keep a plant alive here at home." They both laughed. "That's also why I don't even have a pet."

For some reason, Andy was desperate for Emma to understand that none of those women were important to him. He knew that sounded bad, but all of those women were just arranged for photos or events. They weren't women he met or misled, they were in it for the publicity, too. His life might be glamorous on the outside but it was really just a series of hotels and events, like tonight.

Emma hadn't considered that before. Tonight, although it was a highlight in her life and career, was just another thing to do on a Friday night for Andy. This was his normal. She started to get a sense that maybe she was being too hard on him. Emma let out a huge yawn and Andy turned to her and laughed.

"I'm sorry if I'm boring you," he said with a smirk.

"No, it's not you, you are actually very delightful," Emma said and immediately turned beet red. Luckily the room was dark enough for Andy not to notice. He noticed. "Actually, I'd better get going soon. I have to get up early and help at my brother's restaurant tomorrow."

"That's right, I remember you saying something about a restaurant on the beach. What was the name of it, again, the Salty Dog?" Andy asked.

Emma was surprised he remembered any of their conversation from last month. "The Salty Waves. It's barely hanging on and I help out when I can. If they don't survive this winter, he will close it down for good. It was his dream but not every dream works out, right? At this point he needs to make decisions like should he pay the electric bill this month or use that money for more advertising. The utilities usually win out each month."

Emma felt like she was doing all of the talking and maybe saying too much personal information, again. She wasn't sure James would appreciate strangers knowing all of his financial troubles but Andy wasn't exactly your average stranger was he? It seemed like they had very personal conversations when they were alone together in dark places.

Andy remembered everything about that night in his truck. He had divulged some personal information of his own. Not a lot, to be honest, but more than he ever did to a stranger. He didn't usually bring up his father, mother and brother to anyone other than very close friends. Some teammates and coaches knew, but that was it.

Andy didn't want anything leaking out to the press about his dysfunctional family and here he was telling the press. Emma was different, though. She wouldn't be putting it on the five o'clock news even though he never explicitly said not to. He felt he could trust her.

Emma complimented him on his music and encouraged him to continue playing whenever he could, just in case this baseball thing didn't work out. Emma laughed, not realizing how close she was to the truth. Andy had been nursing his shoulder for months, maybe even years if he was really being honest with himself. He could still perform with a sore shoulder and that was all that mattered to his coaches.

Andy always turned to music when life got to be too much. He also liked talking to Emma. It was surprising to him that he had never met anyone like her before. From that first moment when she came to interview him and he realized his charm didn't work on her, he was hooked. He followed her social media just like he knew she followed his, but that had been the extent of his involvement with her, until tonight.

Emma stood up and collected her shoes not even realizing she was still carrying her glass trophy from earlier in the night. As she turned around she noticed Andy's trophy was sitting on top of the piano, the only witness to tonight's conversation.

"It was nice talking to you, Andy," Emma said as she walked backwards towards the door with her shoes in one hand and trophy in the other.

Andy turned around. "The pleasure was all mine, Emma."

"And we even got bookends out of it," Emma said, holding up her trophy.

Andy let out a soft, gentle laugh and returned to the piano. He started playing so softly she wasn't even sure his fingers were touching the keys. It was hauntingly beautiful. When Andy heard the door close behind him, he stopped playing and brought his hands to his face. He wasn't really sure why he was so sad all of a sudden, he just needed a minute.

Perhaps it was that he was given a glimpse of what a real relationship could be, a tease of what genuine care and compassion felt like. It had always been a dream to feel the warmth and touch of someone who didn't want anything from him or to be seen with him. Andy longed to be with someone who simply enjoyed being in the same room with him to talk.

It felt possible tonight. Without even realizing she had done it, Emma showed him that he could have it all. He could have a real relationship and a career, he just needed to find the right girl. Maybe he already had. He didn't think it was too late for him, he just needed to be willing to open himself up and be vulnerable to someone.

Andy went back to playing Fleur De Lis. He let the music carry his thoughts to another time and place until he knew it was time to leave. He had wasted enough time here and it was time to go home. Andy stood up, carefully closed the piano and started walking away. He thought about leaving the glass trophy behind but knew that it would be found and returned to him anyway so why not save them the trouble. He picked it up and carried it out the door.

Back in the main ballroom, Andy noticed that most of the guests had already left. How long had he been hiding out? He saw that Greg had waited for him, knowing he was around here somewhere. Greg put his arm around his friend and asked him if he was okay. Andy assured him that he was now.

Outside, the cool evening air sobered him up even though he hadn't touched any alcohol this evening. He was coming out of his melancholy and feeling a little lighter. His spirit was lifting and he only had Emma to thank.

It was funny, Andy walked into tonight dreading another event where he had to smile and give a speech. He had been doing this kind of thing non-stop for as long as he could remember but it was part of the job and he loved his job. Little did he know that by the end of the night he would be so grateful for coming.

Life sure had a way of kicking you when you were down and then next thing you know it was offering you a hand to get up.

Chapter 13

Andy's new cheerful mood changed as soon as he drove into his driveway. The same old familiar car was back. Andy got out of his truck and looked around, he knew his father was lurking around here somewhere. The last time his father visited, he was able to send him on his way after he fed him. He hoped tonight would be that simple as well.

Ron got out of his car when he saw his son approaching and his greeting to his son was not reciprocated. Andy just wanted to know what he wanted this time, was it money?

"Hello, son," Ron said.

Andy unlocked his front door and went inside. Ron followed.

"I was wondering if you had any more of that steak from last time." Ron said.

Andy was not in the mood to entertain his father. He also wasn't about to leave him alone while he went to change out of his suit and tie.

"Wow, where were you all dressed up?" Ron asked, trying to lighten the mood.

"Listen dad, I'm tired. What do you want? If you just want food I will make you a sandwich, otherwise I need you to leave." Andy had had enough.

Ron pretended that he was hurt by his son's suggestion that he only came around for a free meal and a few bucks. It was true but he wasn't proud of it. Ron really had nowhere else to turn. He never had a father figure growing up, either. As he struggled through life, he found alcohol numbed the pain and made it all go away, for a little while.

Andy had tried everything. He had taken him in at first, but when things started disappearing in his home he threw his father out. Then he took him to rehab. It lasted just enough for Andy to trust him again until things went missing. The last time he offered to help he said that if he left rehab early, he was done helping. Well, Andy was done.

There was only so many chances a son can give a father before he felt like he was hitting his head on a brick wall. Andy was focusing on self-preservation now, no longer willing to let his father hurt him like he had in the past. Andy felt he had tried to help him enough.

"Sure, I'll have a sandwich," Ron finally answered.

Andy sighed heavily and took off his jacket and tie. As he rolled up his sleeves he let his mind travel to earlier in the evening. He wanted to be anywhere by here right now. As he made his father a sandwich, he imagined how Emma's relationship was with her father. A widower with a stroke but who had a daughter and son who loved him and would do anything for him.

What a contrast to the father and son in this room! All the fame and money couldn't buy a loving family that supported him. Even his mother ran away and never looked back. Where was she now and who was she with? Andy would probably never know. At least he knew where his brother was, he just couldn't be with him right now. The Andersons weren't going to be the stars of any Hallmark movie, that was for sure.

Andy finished making the sandwich and slid it over to his father. He thanked him and ate hungrily. In between bites his father tried to carry on a conversation with his son but to no avail. Andy wasn't giving in until his father said something that stunned him.

"That ninth inning of the last game was a real nail-biter," Ron said.

Andy looked at his father. "You watched it?"

"I was there!" Ron said with a smile.

"You...what...?" Andy stammered.

"I was there, in the stands. It was high up but I saw every throw," he said. "It was the best game of the whole series."

Andy watched his father finish his sandwich and then he reached into the fridge and handed him a soda. Ron nodded in thanks and drank it. Andy's head was spinning with this new information. A man who couldn't remember to come home from the bar to feed his children went to watch his son play in a major league baseball game. Maybe all those times Ron had said he had changed weren't just words after all.

Well, it would take more than watching a baseball game to earn back Andy's trust. His father had thirty-three years to make up for, just sitting in the stands wouldn't cut it. Andy shook it off and led him to the door. He was beyond exhausted and wanted to be alone.

Ron didn't protest. He thanked his son for his hospitality and went out to his car and drove away. Andy tried to imagine what it would have been like to look up into the stands and see his father watching him. It was something he had dreamed of for years, he just couldn't believe it had happened and that he didn't even know it.

EMMA LOVED VISITING her father now. Sunnyside Home was an answered prayer. Walking in the front doors was like a breath of fresh air. The desk clerks knew her and greeted her each time. Even James and Joanne were regulars. Emma felt like a weight had been lifted off her shoulders.

Sam was always walking around doing something and today he was painting. Even Sam's mother saw Emma often enough to offer a nod as she passed by. Joe's room faced the back garden and today he had the windows cracked open a little. He had gotten much of his mobility back and was even using his left side more than he had the last several years.

The physical therapist took him to the gym every other day and in the pool twice a week. Emma was so happy she could cry. Donald had sent Emma all of the photos he took from the gala and Emma was showing them to her father when he saw the one of her and Andy.

"Hey, I didn't know you two were hanging out," Joe said.

"Dad, we aren't. We just happened to be standing next to each other and a picture was taken. These were all from the gala, nothing else." Emma replied.

Joe just smiled. He liked teasing her but he also wanted her to find a nice man. A rich one would be nice, but he wasn't picky. Emma wanted to change the subject and offered to take him for a walk. It was odd not needing the wheelchair anymore, but Joe insisted he could do it.

They walked down the hall, through the living room and out the back doors to the large backyard. There was a vegetable garden, fruit trees and a pond with a dock. Emma noticed a family fishing on the dock and wondered if her father might want to try. Maybe James could bring some fishing poles next time.

Emma smiled at the possibilities available to her father now. It was like a resort rather than a care facility. Before coming outside, Emma had grabbed a game of checkers and was now setting it up on the table. This game in particular was suggested because it made Joe concentrate on using his left side. Emma played a dozen games before she said she had to leave.

Joe helped her pack up the game and they walked back inside. Sam eagerly walked over to Joe and offered to play a few more games with him and that was where Emma left him.

Emma was running late for her dinner date with friends, but she didn't want to rush her time with her father. She would rather be late than miss one more game of checkers. On the way to Ferg's Sports Bar she got a call. Without looking at who was calling, she hit the green answer button.

"Hello, Emma?"

It was Pat. She hadn't heard back from him and hoped he would just go away.

"Yes," she replied.

"Hi, I'm here in St. Pete for a little while and hoped we could get together," Pat said.

"Gosh, Pat, I'm on the way to meet my friends right now, so today isn't good for me," Emma answered.

"Okay, well, maybe I'll see you later?" He asked hopefully.

"Um, maybe," Emma answered, trying to sound as noncommittal as possible.

At Ferg's, everyone was already eating appetizers and having a cocktail. They waved Emma over as soon as she walked in. Miriam got up to give her a hug and pulled over a chair next to hers. All eyes were on Emma and she didn't know why.

"So... what happened?" Miriam asked. Even Don and Cindy were waiting for her to answer.

"When?" Emma asked after ordering herself an iced tea.

"At the gala, we all noticed that you and Andy Anderson were no where to be found for hours and then all of a sudden you pop out of some random room with your shoes off," Miriam explained.

Emma laughed and ate some nachos that were in the middle of the table. "Nothing, that's what happened."

Sideways glances were exchanged by the others at the table and Emma kept trying to defend herself. She tried to explain that she just wanted to find a quiet place and happened to find the same room that Andy was hiding in. It did sound far fetched, but it was the truth. Emma didn't know how else to say that nothing happened but she thought they eventually believed her.

"Besides, if there was something, you all would be the first ones to know," Emma promised.

"Well, I should hope so!" Miriam replied.

It was nice kicking back and having fun after such a stiff and formal night at the gala. This was the kind of night she preferred... laughing, talking over each other, reaching across the table and making jokes.

Emma was having the best time until she heard her name being called from behind her.

"Hey Emma!"

Emma turned around to see Pat coming towards their table. Her face felt flushed and she hadn't even had anything stronger than iced tea. Everyone was staring at Pat.

"Pat, how did you know where I was?" Emma asked nervously.

"Well, don't forget this is the same place we all hung out when we were dating, too," Pat replied then looked at the others around the table. "Hi Miriam, Don and Cindy."

"Hi Pat," they all answered in unison.

Pat pulled up a chair and ordered a soda from the waitress. It was Pat who broke the silence first.

"Emma, I was wondering if we could maybe talk in private," he asked.

Emma knew he would never leave her alone until she talked to him so she figured that here with witnesses was probably the best option. They walked to one of the tables right outside, within sight of her friends. Emma sat and waited for Pat to say what was on his mind.

"Emma, I miss you," Pat started. "I've been seeing a therapist and I know that the reason we broke up was all my fault."

Emma was listening. This was the first time Pat had acknowledged his part in the break up. Being apart didn't help either because when he first planned his move to Atlanta, he would always question where she was and who she was with. It had finally gotten too much and Emma called it off.

"Thank you for that, Pat," Emma replied.

"I'm sorry for everything. I know I was smothering you and that's not how I wanted our relationship to end. I'm not asking to get back together, I just want to be friends again."

Emma considered his request and wondered if there was a catch. "What does 'just being friends' mean to you?"

"It just means that we can talk and text without any expectations and if we visit each other's city, we can have lunch or dinner without it being so uncomfortable," Pat replied.

Again, Emma considered his answer. She always did like Pat. When they first met, he was sweet and respectful to her. Emma was a sucker for his blond hair and dimples. It really only changed once he took the job in Atlanta, maybe if he had stayed they would still be together. She decided to give him the benefit of the doubt and agreed to be friends.

Pat was visibly relieved and asked if he could hug her, she agreed. At first he said he should go, but Emma felt bad. He had already driven all the way down here, the least she could do was let him join them tonight.

The others at the table tried to be discrete but they were spying the entire time Emma was with Pat, so when they saw them return to the table together, they were even more curious.

"So, what was that all about?" Miriam asked both of them.

"Emma agreed to be friends again," Pat answered.

More looks were exchanged, but they all remained quiet. Emma smiled and nodded, trying to give the impression that everything was okay. She really wasn't sure what she thought, but she didn't want any more drama.

Miriam wasn't convinced and texted Emma under the table. "You okay?"

Emma texted back, "Yes".

Miriam gave her a sideways glance and Emma smiled. One thing she could always count on was that Miriam had her back.

Chapter 14

Emma was nervous. Today was their Friendsgiving and she was busy loading things in her car that she needed for decorations. She invited everyone she could think of which included Liane and Pat. That was why Emma was nervous. This could either go horribly wrong or kind of great. The only reason she invited them was to help save the restaurant.

According to the invitation, everyone knew that they didn't need to bring anything, just pay for their own meals. It would be a win for everyone involved. Emma didn't know why she was stressing herself out more than was necessary since it still only meant ten people might show up. She just hoped everyone had a good time.

Emma had cute little turkey favors to place at everyone's seat as well as mini pumpkins and orange table cloths to make it look more festive next to the surf boards. Emma closed her trunk and gave a heavy sigh, it was happening whether anyone showed up or not.

The whole way to Salty Waves she considered what she would tell James when it was just her and Miriam ordering the turkey dinner. He would understand but Emma would be devastated. She could make it up to him by organizing a Christmas party, she was sure that would draw a crowd better than Friendsgiving would.

Emma's nerves were getting worse the closer she got to Madeira Beach. As she turned into the parking lot, she couldn't believe her eyes. It was full of cars. Not just full, it was overflowing. There were people everywhere, in the parking lot, in the restaurant and on the beach. Decorations forgotten, Emma ran to find her brother.

She pushed her way through the people and tried to call out his name over the music but there was no way he could hear anything over the crowd. Emma just kept her head down and used her shoulder to make a path to the kitchen.

Before she could find James, Miriam grabbed her elbow.

"Hey great idea by the way!" Miriam exclaimed. "But I wish you would have let me in on your little secret."

"What are you talking about? It was only supposed to be just us," Emma replied.

"So you didn't know they were coming?" Miriam pointed out towards the beach where a large group were dancing and partying.

Emma's mouth dropped when she took a closer look at the tall figure in the middle of the crowd. How did this happen? Now Emma pushed her way towards the beach. When she was standing in front of Andy Anderson, he beamed.

"Emma!" Andy yelled. "You finally made it!"

Emma looked around and realized the entire team of the St. Petersburg Sharks were here and more. They were eating, drinking and dancing, it was a real party. Emma still didn't know how this happened. She grabbed Andy's hand and led him to quieter place and they sat right on the sand.

"What is going on here? Why is the whole team here?" Emma couldn't get the questions out fast enough.

Andy laughed. "I guess it is a bit of a shock to you, it was to your brother, too," he started. "When we talked at the gala, you mentioned how Salty Waves was suffering, and even dying a slow painful death. Well, I looked it up, made a few calls and some social media posts about the place and my two million followers are coming through, at least the ones who are local."

Emma was trying to process this information and let it sink in.

"Emma, I just wanted to help. I wanted to pay you back for helping me, that's what friends do, right? Miriam said this was supposed to be your Friendsgiving, so this is my gift from one friend to another," Andy said.

"Wait, what do you mean you were paying me back for helping you?" Emma asked. She didn't recall helping him with anything. He was actually the one always helping her.

"You probably don't even realize how much you have helped me just by treating me like a normal person. In fact, you make me want to be better," Andy answered.

"I don't know what to say," Emma replied. She was at a loss for words which was new to her. She could just look at the hundred or so people at her brother's restaurant and smile.

"You don't have to say anything," Andy said. "But I would like to ask you something."

"Sure," Emma said.

"Would you like to go out sometime?" Andy asked.

Emma didn't know what she expected him to ask, but it certainly was not that. She blinked a few times and then looked down at her feet.

"Listen, I don't want to scare you, but I like hanging out with you and I thought maybe you did, too," he said.

"I did like our talks," Emma admitted. "But I just got out of a bad relationship and I don't know if I'm ready for another one, especially one as high profile as yours. I'm not a model or an actress so I don't understand why..."

"Emma, stop it," Andy said. "That's exactly why I like hanging out with you, you don't let me get away with anything and you keep me on my toes. If I wanted to date a model or an actress I would be asking them, but I'm asking you."

Emma's hesitation made Andy back off and take another approach. "Can we at least exchange phone numbers? That way we can still talk without any pressure of a date. A simple call or a text would be enough."

"Okay," Emma conceded that it was a good first step to see how things went. They put their numbers in each other's phones and sat awkwardly not knowing what to do next. "Thank you, by the way, for this."

Emma gestured to the large crowd that was gathering at the Salty Waves. All she could do was smile at his selfless gesture. There were so many people here, they were spilling out onto the beach.

"You're welcome," Andy said. "It was the least I could do. I like to use my power for good sometimes rather than just evil."

This time it was Emma who laughed. Andy loved making her laugh and stood up and then offered her his hand. They returned to the restaurant and got lost in the crowd. Emma was still searching for her brother and made her way into the kitchen.

James looked busy but happy. He was cutting, slicing and frying with a huge grin on his face. When he saw Emma he waved.

"Is this all your doing?" James yelled. "I thought it was supposed to be a small group of ten."

Emma laughed. "I decided to invite a few hundred more."

She spotted Joanne waiting tables and clearing plates. Emma put on an apron and started helping wherever she could. It was so much fun. Andy was helping take orders and serving drinks, always making sure everyone paid first. They would catch each other's eye from across the room and smile. That exchange did not go unnoticed by their friends, either.

Liane Lincoln did show up and could not believe Emma had gotten the Sharks to come to this little party. She was very impressed and mingled in the crowd. Andy and Emma were sitting on bar stools laughing about something when Pat walked in. When Emma's mood changed, Andy became concerned.

"That's Pat," she said to Andy.

"The ex?" He asked.

Emma nodded as Pat walked directly to her. He did a double take when he saw Andy and asked if he was really the pitcher for the Sharks. Andy said he was and moved to Emma's side. Pat looked from him to Emma and then walked in the other direction. She felt bad for making him think that she and Andy were a couple, especially since she had just agreed to be friends with Pat again, but this was her party and she would deal with the ramifications later. Today was Friendsgiving.

It was getting late and the crowds were thinning. James said he ran out of almost everything but promised that if they came back it would be ten times better. Everyone said they would be back. It was a miracle. Ever since Andy came into Emma's life wonderful things have been happening.

What was amazing to Emma was that Andy saw these as small things, making a social media post, playing the piano and giving her a ride home. They were minor things to him but major things to her. If she wasn't so skittish about jumping into another relationship and getting hurt, she would date him in a heartbeat, but she was very skittish about it.

When everyone else had gone home and the doors were locked, it was James, Joanne, Emma and Andy washing dishes. The simple mundane task of washing and drying seemed so normal, yet when she really thought about who Andy was, it made her smile. She supposed this was what he meant by her treating him like a normal person because deep down he was.

When everything was clean and put away, James locked up and shook Andy's hand.

"Thanks, man," James said. "I know Emma probably thanked you already, but you don't know what this means to me and my family." James put his arm around his wife and gave her a squeeze.

"Yes, sir, I think I do," Andy replied and looked over at Emma. "Good luck."

As everyone walked to their cars, Andy headed to the sidewalk.

"Hey, where's your truck?" Emma asked.

"I came with Greg, but they left long ago," Andy replied. "I just live up the beach. I'll walk."

"No, you won't, get in," she said. "It's my turn to give you a ride home."

Andy smiled, nodded and got in her passenger seat. He meant it when he said he was just up the beach. It was only a ten mile drive but it would have taken a long time to walk it. Andy probably knew she would offer to drive him and didn't want to ask.

Andy asked how Emma's father was doing. She said he was much better now that he was in a better facility. She went on to explain how they all loved it and how much he was improving. Andy was glad to hear it. She asked about his family and he reminded her that they don't see each other.

"I know that's what you said, but things can change," Emma replied. "People can change, too."

There was no way for Emma to know how accurately that statement stabbed him in the heart. It was a bullseye, for sure. Andy said that he actually had seen his father since then and he wasn't sure if he changed yet or not.

"What do you mean you don't know?" Emma asked.

"He's an alcoholic," Andy stated. "He's made promises before and never kept them. I don't know how many times I have to fall for them before I give up."

"Seven times seventy," Emma said. "That's how many times the Bible says we should forgive someone."

"Oh Emma, you're too good for me," Andy said in a whisper.

Chapter 15

For the next week, Emma was receiving daily updates from James on the restaurant. Business had picked up so much he had to hire more staff. It was truly a blessing how one person could inspire so many people to help out a stranger, but Andy Anderson could. James was so thankful that he wanted Emma to personally thank him the next time she saw him.

Emma didn't know when that would be. After the night they exchanged numbers, he started texting her. They were sweet and loving messages, but Emma didn't know how to respond to that. At first she replied with short answers until she eventually stopped responding altogether. Every once in a while Andy would still reach out wanting to get together, but Emma ignored them.

She wasn't sure why she wasn't eager to date one of the most eligible bachelors in St. Pete, but maybe that was why. In the back of Emma's mind, she still pictured him out with prettier, more famous women and never felt adequate enough to be seen by his side. In the end, she figured he would move on if she waited long enough.

At work, it was easy to forget all about Andy. Even with the constant looks and questions from everyone who was at Friendsgiving, Emma wanted to put it all behind her. When Liane called Emma into her office, she wasn't sure if this was business or personal.

"Emma, sit down," Liane said. It was business.

Emma sat and waited while her boss looked for a paper in the folder on her desk. Liane took her time finding it, looking at it and then handing it across the desk for Emma to take. Emma searched Liane's face for any clues about the letter's contents but she gave none away.

Emma read the letter and read it again. Was this a joke? She glanced up to her boss and she was not laughing. Liane was smiling, arms crossed and leaning back in her chair. Emma laid the paper back on Liane's desk and took a deep breath before slowly exhaling.

"Atlanta wants you," Liane finally said, confirming that the contents of the letter was true. "I'm so proud of you. I hate to lose you, but I figured this was coming."

"How? I..." Emma didn't know what to say.

"You don't have to answer now," Liane replied. "Take some time and talk it over with you family. It would be a huge change and you have to be sure this is what you want."

Emma simply nodded and took the letter with her when she left the office. Wow, Atlanta wanted her! She had dreamt about this moment but now that it was really happening, she was questioning her ability to follow through with her plan.

If she moved, she would be leaving James and Joanne as well as her father. It would be so difficult, maybe too difficult, especially now that the restaurant was doing so well. And that made her think of Andy. She would be walking away from any potential relationship for good, but wasn't she pushing him away already.

Realistically she knew that none of that should be a determining factor in her decision. Ultimately she had to do what was right for her and her alone. Emma knew everyone would be fine without her. They would miss her, of course, but they would be okay. Would she? Maybe that was the reason she was hesitating more than she thought she would when she actually received a job offer from Atlanta. Maybe she wasn't ready to leave.

Miriam and Don were already sitting at Emma's desk and had read the letter. They congratulated her but had mixed feelings as well. They had all worked together for four years and worked on some really big stories, but they were also good friends. It would be a loss for them, too.

Emma admitted that she wasn't sure anymore. A month or two ago she would have packed her bags already and booked her fight, but now things were different. She was different. Miriam persuaded her to at least go for the interview and listen to what they had to say. Emma agreed that she would go and hear what they offered her. It may turn out to be too good to refuse.

Her nerves felt better, too. Agreeing to go and just talk to them made her feel better about telling her family. Emma knew they would be supportive and encourage her to take the job but maybe she still needed to hear it. She called her brother and they agreed to meet at Sunnyside Home tomorrow for lunch so that she could tell everyone together.

Now that it was all settled, Emma could get back to work. Well, at least she tried to work. Her phone kept notifying her of all the text messages coming in. At first it was just her brother and friends, then she received one from Andy.

"I miss you," Andy texted. Emma stared at those words a long time before closing it.

The next text she received was from Pat, "It was good to see you last week. Friendsgiving was fun." Again, Emma stared at that message then decided to respond.

"Yes, it was quite the party!" Emma texted. "Hey, I'm coming up to Atlanta in a few days, maybe we can have lunch sometime." She hesitated before adding that last sentence but if she was going to be living in the same city as her ex, then she had better start off on the right foot and be friends.

Pat immediately replied, "Great! I'll pick you up from the airport."

Emma put her phone down before she typed anything she might regret. It was only lunch, and a ride from the airport, how much trouble could that cause? She started thinking about what life would be like in Atlanta with only Pat as her friend. It would be awkward at first, of course, but she was confident she could make friends easily.

At five o'clock Miriam went to Emma's desk and declared that they were going out to celebrate. Don agreed and said Cindy would even be meeting them at Ferg's. Even as they were pulling her out the door and helping her put her coat on, she was thankful to have friends that always celebrated her wins. It would be impossible to find these types of friends no matter where she moved.

Cindy motioned to them from the table she secured in the back. She even gave Emma a hug when they made their way through the crowd. They ordered food and drinks and spent the next hour or so just reminiscing about their favorite stories of Emma. Some were funny and others were embarrassing, either way Emma enjoyed the camaraderie with her friends.

Miriam told the group that her latest boyfriend might be 'the one'. Everyone was happy for her yet skeptical. Emma knew that anything was possible at this point. She has had so many surprises this year, she was willing to let someone else take over. Miriam deserved happiness and if finding 'the one' did that, then she hoped it would all work out.

It was Cindy who asked Emma if she had heard from Andy. Emma caught a glimpse of Don nudging her with his elbow, but Emma insisted it was okay to talk about him. She didn't want to but she would. Emma went on to explain that he had been reaching out to her ever since Friendsgiving. He started with texts and calls and then eventually only the occasional texts.

With confusion on their faces, they wondered why he wasn't reaching out more.

"Because I'm not responding," Emma replied.

Everyone around the table looked perplexed. Why was she not responding to Andy Anderson's calls and texts? Even if it didn't work out, at least she would have given it a chance. Emma wasn't even doing that much. No one could understand her reasoning for ignoring the man's calls.

"I don't want to be another one of his girls," Emma replied.

"You follow his social media, right?" Miriam asked and Emma nodded. "Then you know he doesn't hang out with one girl more than one time. That's just for the public image. He doesn't date. But, he has been gravitating towards you for weeks and it looked like you felt the same way last week."

"Yes, but that didn't mean anything," Emma defended.

Don couldn't remain silent any longer. "I think it did. What he did at the Salty Waves wasn't for the Sharks, the city or for your brother...it was for you."

Emma shook her head and took another sip of her drink. She hadn't really thought of it that way but it was too late anyway. She had let the calls fade away and she was moving to Atlanta. In her mind it didn't matter what they all said, it was in the past.

LUNCH WITH HER FAMILY went almost the same as dinner with her friends the night before. They were happy for her and encouraged her to go and see what it was all about. They insisted they would be fine if she decided to accept the position. Her father was particularly supportive because she had always been there for him and if being more independent was any indication of how well he could do if she moved, then she had nothing to worry about.

Sam even stopped in to say hello and ask if anyone wanted to play a game. Joe promised he would later and he wouldn't let him win, either. Sam returned to the main room and continued to solicit for an opponent. Everyone loved Sam, they just wondered why only his mother ever visited and no one ever came to take him out.

Attention was focused back on Emma and inevitably the conversation steered towards Andy. James was still serving to a full house every day and he still couldn't believe it. He was so thankful. He wanted to thank Andy in person and kept asking Emma to invite him back.

"I don't talk to him," Emma announced.

Her statement was met with silence. Finally James asked, "Why?"

"It's a long story, plus I might be moving," Emma replied.

"Emma, sometimes you are too stubborn for your own good. He was clearly into you," James said and Joanne confirmed with a fervent nod of her head.

"Well, nothing is going to happen. I've made my decision and I'm moving forward. Life goes on," Emma said.

It was clear to her family that there wasn't anything they could say to change her mind, she was too strong willed to be influenced by words. Unless Andy could perform another miracle, she would probably be deleting his number very soon.

It was a shame, really. James actually liked the guy for doing something so selfless that not only helped her but helped her family. James thought Emma had seen another side of him that night, his true self. Not many celebrities would bother or open themselves up to criticism like that, but Andy did and he did it to impress a woman.

James just hoped that his sister wasn't going to regret it. Andy would not wait around forever, that was for sure. For Emma, it might already be too late.

Chapter 16

Emma enjoyed her time in Atlanta. She had never been there before and was impressed with how large and exciting the city was. When she visited the Channel 4 studios on Peachtree Street, she couldn't stop looking up. There certainly weren't buildings that tall in St. Pete.

She had met with the news director and they were interested in her as a news anchor. They had a beloved anchor who was retiring at the end of the year and hoped to permanently fill her seat soon. Emma expressed her interest and gratitude for the opportunity to meet with them about it and would get back to them soon. This was a great opportunity for her, not to mention, her dream job.

She spent the rest of the week touring the city. Emma had never used vacation days before because she never trusted to leave her father alone that long, but now she could. She even met up with Pat a few times and they fell into a familiar friendship touring The World of Coke and the Georgia Aquarium. Emma even said she could see herself living there.

Having fabulous restaurants and places to visit within walking distance was a dream come true for her. She loved walking through Centennial Olympic Park and enjoying the sights and sounds of the big city. It was dressed festively for Christmas, which was only a week away. The huge Christmas tree was lit up at night and there was a large white tent set up for outdoor ice skating. Emma was very impressed with what she saw of Atlanta and hoped that she could work here.

Pat worked for Channel 11, a competitor, so they wouldn't see each other at work if she took the job. Emma thought that might be for the best anyway. She wasn't looking to get back into a relationship with him, just maintain a friendship. How hard could that be, they were both adults. When Emma finally left Atlanta, she promised Pat that she would let him know her decision. Her visit to the city made her excited for this next adventure and admitted to him that she was leaning towards accepting the job.

WITH ONLY A FEW DAYS remaining until Christmas, Emma's days were full of events that she reluctantly attended. One of the parties she was actually looking forward to was the one at Sunnyside Home. Her father, Sam and the whole staff kept telling her that it was a big deal around there. Even before she left for Atlanta, they had started decorating. Now she was seeing it all finished and it looked beautiful and festive.

There were thousands of lights outside that led the way to the front entrance. Trees and bushes also were adorned with lights as well as a few reindeer on the front yard. Since winters in Florida didn't usually produce any snow, Floridians were used to making this time of the year festive by letting the decorations do all of the work.

Inside the front lobby was a Christmas tree filled with red ribbons and silver and gold balls. In the main living room there was green garland and lights on the mantle but the main attraction was the ten foot Christmas tree in the middle of the large room. It had colorful lights and it looked like handmade ornaments from top to bottom. But it was hard to miss the stacks of wrapped presents under the tree. The smell of dinner was coming from the kitchen and Emma was told that Santa would be there shortly to hand out gifts to all of the residents.

In the meantime, Emma went to her father's room. He was standing in front of his mirror, straightening his tie when she entered.

"Looking good, dad," Emma said.

Joe turned around and gave his daughter a hug. Emma had worn black pants and a red sweater and looked festive as well. She handed him a present and they sat down while he opened it. Inside was a Georgia Aquarium t-shirt and a stuffed shark, the mascot of his favorite team. Joe smiled, thanked her and said hers was on the bed.

Emma walked over and brought it to the table. It was a small box and he smiled when she rattled it. Emma carefully unwrapped the little gift and was brought to tears when she realized what it was.

"It was your mother's," Joe said.

Emma held the pearl and diamond necklace on its delicate gold chain in her hand. She had to wipe her eyes to see the clasp well enough so she could try to put it on. She moved her long hair out the way and went to the mirror her father was using earlier. Emma softly touched the pearl and diamonds as if they were bubbles that might disappear at the slightest touch.

She came and gave her father a hug and a kiss on his cheek. "Thank you, dad. I love them."

Just then they heard the commotion down the hall and an announcement that Santa had arrived. Emma supposed that she should accompany her father to the main room, so out they went to join the others. There were kids and entire families having their pictures taken with Santa. He was patient with the residents who were children and kind to the adults who came, too.

Everyone gravitated to Santa. Emma supposed it was hard being in a facility over the holidays and this was a wonderful escape for them. Even Sam couldn't stop standing next to Santa and stealing the occasion hug from him. It was sweet for Santa to be so giving of his time. What Emma didn't realize was that every resident was to receive a gift, so when her father's name was called out, she quickly got her phone out to take a picture. Joe's gift was a new pair of sneakers. Santa had really done his homework, Emma thought.

Joe posed with Santa as Emma snapped a few photos and there was something very familiar about that Santa. The person who came to mind surely wasn't the one dressed in a red suit and white beard, could it? Then Santa winked at her. The shock on Emma's face made Santa laugh. When all of the gifts were handed out, Santa walked to the baby grand piano and started playing Christmas Caroles.

If there was any doubt left in Emma's mind that Santa was none other than Andy Anderson himself, it was wiped away by his singing of Rudolph the Red-Nosed Reindeer. Emma saw the director, Mr. Brown, smiling and singing along in the back of the room and Emma went over to talk to him.

"Well, hello Ms. Reese, I hope you're enjoying the Christmas party," Marc Brown said.

"Yes, sir, it's wonderful," Emma replied. "Thank you for inviting me."

"Oh we always invite the entire family. It is the holidays after all," Marc said. "And we enjoy having your father here. He gets along so well with our other residents, especially Sam. They have a real special bond."

"I was actually wondering how you managed to get Andy Anderson to play your Santa? Isn't he a little busy to come here for this?" Emma asked.

Marc's laugh was deep and genuine. "He comes every year, many times a year," Marc started, then became serious. "You don't know?"

"Know what?" Emma asked, still very confused.

"This is Andy's facility. He started it as soon as he made it into the major leagues and started the foundation, The Samuel F.

Anderson Foundation, named after his brother. Sam is his brother," Marc said.

Emma was feeling her knees buckle and quickly walked to the nearest chair. Marc Brown went to grab a bottle of water and handed it to her. Concerned that she might need medical attention, he asked if she was okay.

"Yes...I...just...I didn't know," Emma whispered.

After repeatedly confirming that she was okay and did not need the doctor on call, Marc went back to the party. Emma, on the other hand, was having heart palpitations that had nothing to do with her health. She was just given information that literally brought her to her knees and needed a minute, or several hundred, to process.

From where she sat Emma watched Santa as he played the piano and sang to every request the children wanted. Sam was right by his side. Then it hit her...if Sam is Andy's brother that meant the woman who came and visited Sam everyday was...Andy's mother. But Andy said he never saw his mother. Did Andy not know she came here every day? Surely the staff would have let him know...

Maybe Andy knew but didn't want to see her. It was a possibility. Emma would stay out of it and stay away from Andy. But watching him today, it made her smile. Marc came back into the room and announced that Santa had to leave and that dinner would be served. As the residents and their families moved into the dining room, Santa made a gesture to Emma that meant he wanted her to follow him. She did.

Andy had a room set up for his costume change and closed the door when Emma entered.

"I'm glad you came," Andy said.

"How did you know I'd be here?" Emma asked.

"Well, because your father is here," Andy replied. "I figured you'd come to celebrate with him. In fact, when I was sent his application to be a resident here, I knew we had to find a place for him. I hope he likes it."

Emma needed to sit down, again. "What do you mean?"

"Well, you told me in the truck, after the game, that you didn't like where your father was staying, so when I saw your application for a room at Sunnyside Home, I knew we had to get him out of that place. I hear stories of Rainbow House and knew he could do better here," Andy replied, gesturing around the room.

"My family is beyond help. I told you our mom left when I turned eighteen and left me with a deadbeat father. I knew I wanted to do better for me and my little brother, Sam, so when I finally got my first paycheck from the Sharks, I created a foundation and built this home for him. I wanted him to be taken care of better than I could do," Andy continued.

"I move around too much and I am hardly ever home. At least here he has everything he could ever want, besides family, but these people are his family now. And I stop in whenever I can," Andy explained.

Emma opened her mouth and was about to mention his mother coming everyday but decided against it. She wasn't exactly sure why she kept that to herself, it just didn't feel like the right time for that conversation. Besides, she had enough to process right now without adding more new information.

Andy was now back in regular clothes, his Santa suit back on its hanger and ready for next year. He could tell Emma was still in shock from information overload, so he gently took her hand and led her out the back door.

"I don't know how many of them know it's really me in the suit but just in case the little kids don't know, I like to walk around to the front and make a grand entrance," Andy explained as they walked through the grass and entered from the lobby.

Shouts of joy were heard as they recognized the star pitcher of the St. Pete Sharks enter the building. Now everyone wanted pictures of and with the MVP of the World Series. Famous in both roles, Andy was patient and generous with his time. Emma stood back and marveled.

Emma admitted she still had a hard time merging the two individuals. The celebrity pitcher with the real life individual who cared enough to help find her father a room and play Santa at a Christmas party in the home of his foundation. And Sam, now it made sense how that young man was glued to his side. Now Emma could see the resemblance that was so obvious before.

Every day Emma spent in Andy's presence she was surprised and enchanted by him. She was learning new things that made him feel real and genuine. These were things that normally would want her to go on a date with him. What was still holding her back? Then she remembered Atlanta and the advice of her friends and family, she needed to do what was best for her and her alone.

As Emma stood there and watched Andy pose for photos, he looked over and smiled right at her. She felt that smile deep in her soul. Andy was a decent and caring man, could she really choose Atlanta over him? Emma wasn't so sure anymore.

Chapter 17

Emma and Andy found a quiet bench in the back garden of Sunnyside Home to sit and talk. *His* garden and *his* Sunnyside Home. It was still a lot for Emma to wrap her brain around. Andy ran his hands through his short brown hair then breathed in deep through his nose and clenched his jaw.

"I know you must have a million questions," Andy finally said. "Go ahead."

Emma did but she didn't know where to start. After taking a deep breath herself, she asked, "Why didn't you tell me this was your facility?"

"I really don't go around and tell anyone," Andy replied matter-of-factly. "Fans know that Sam's my brother and usually put two and two together. But I don't go around and broadcast it."

"So you didn't tell me because I am a reporter and you thought I would bring a news crew here and announce it to the world?" Emma shot back.

Andy shifted in his seat, it was obvious that things were coming out all wrong. "Look, it's not like I knew much about you. We spent a few quality moments together but when I told you I'd like to go out with you, that I liked you and wanted to get to know you better, you ghosted me. I didn't see the point of divulging my secrets to someone I cared about but who didn't feel the same."

"But I do, I mean I did," Emma blurted out.

LIFE GOES ON

"Then why won't you let me take you out?" Andy asked. "I'm really a nice guy."

Emma hesitated, she never really did come up with a good answer to that question and now sitting here in front of the man himself, she was having a hard time thinking of *any* response.

"Okay, listen, let's start over," Andy said. "I'll admit, we met under very unusual circumstances and I didn't make it any easier with the 'Gary' comment, twice." They both laughed. Emma began to relax a bit.

Andy held out his hand. "Hi, I'm Andy. I play baseball and have a younger brother named Sam. He has autism and I can't take care of him so I started a foundation and a home who does." Andy glanced over at Emma who was smiling. Encouraged by this, he continued.

"My father is an alcoholic and only comes around when he needs money. My mother left when I turned eighteen and left me and my brother alone with him. When I started earning a paycheck through my baseball career, I made sure we had a better life." Andy's eyes met Emma's. It was like she was looking into his very soul.

"Hello, my name is Emma," she began with a giggle as she played along. "I am a reporter and live alone. My brother and his wife run a very success restaurant on Madeira Beach." Emma looked at Andy who was actually blushing a little at that comment. "My mother died a few years ago and a year later my father had a stroke weakening his left side. He is now in a home that not only is making him stronger but they take care of his every need..." Emma started tearing up at the end when she realized that so many good things had happened to her ever since Andy came into her life.

Not wanting to see her cry, Andy gave her a hug. It was warm and comforting and exactly the medicine she needed for her heartache. She had carried so much stress and anxiety around for years and it was slowly melting away thanks in part to the man who comforted her now. Her cavalier attitude towards him was turning to appreciation and could almost be called love.

Andy already loved Emma. He was just afraid that saying it out loud now might just scare her away for good. Just saying he wanted to date her sent her into a tail spin he wasn't sure she would ever get out of. Andy knew there was no other woman in the world like Emma and would fight for her, even if she wouldn't.

When Andy finally released her, Emma had regained some of her composure. She wiped at her eyes with a tissue from her pocket and blew her nose. Andy patiently waited. He was on her timeline now.

"My father really likes it here," Emma said.

Andy smiled. "I'm glad. Sam talks non-stop about him, so I know he likes that he's here, too."

"My hope is that he can come home, eventually," she replied. "Maybe even take that trip he's been dying to go on."

Andy asked where he wanted to go and Emma replied, Scotland, without hesitation. It was where his family was from and he had always wanted to visit. He was getting stronger every time she saw him, so maybe they could take that trip sooner than expected. Andy remembered and nodded knowing that nothing would stop Emma from eventually making it happen. Then he asked where *she* would like to go.

Emma said that for her, she would love to go anywhere in Europe. Andy said even though he has been to Europe more times than he could count, he has never really seen it. He saw airports, hotel rooms and limos, but never the city. How he longed to tour the Eiffel Tower or walk along the canals of Venice. Emma agreed, that was her dream, too.

Emma asked about his music, why he didn't play more. Andy simply said he never had the time. When life got hard, he found himself drawn to the piano. He even wrote a few notes or words and in the end realized that he had written a song.

"You wrote a song?" Emma asked, surprised by this news.

"Yes, several in fact," Andy replied with a smile.

Emma couldn't believe that he was actually writing songs. She asked to hear them, but he would never perform them here or in public anywhere only at home, which would require her to come inside his home. She considered this for a moment and then agreed.

"Really?" Andy asked, trying to be clear that he heard her correctly. "Just so we are on the same page, I am considering this a date. A date means that I will pick you up for dinner then take you to my house to play my songs and then take you home."

Emma laughed and nodded. "Yes, I understand, it is a date."

In full Andy fashion, he stood up, yelled at the top of his lungs and then sat down next to Emma again. Andy watched Emma laugh and joined in. He felt wonderful after weeks and months of thinking about this woman, she finally agreed to go out with him. He was so excited he could shout again, but based on the looks he had already received, he decided not to.

Because they were both very busy people in a very busy holiday season, they both pulled out their phones to check their calendars. Andy said he was busy for the next several days but suggested New Year's Eve. They would celebrate the New Year together. Emma smiled and said it sounded perfect. What did Emma have to lose? She would probably be leaving for Atlanta soon anyway, one date wouldn't hurt.

"Shall we rejoin the party?" Andy asked.

"Sure, my father's probably wondering where I went anyway," Emma said.

Andy stood up and held out his hand to help Emma up and she accepted. He hoped he was giving Emma an insight into his real personality. He may not have had proper nurturing growing up, but he knew how to treat people, you treated them the way you wanted them to treat you.

Inside, the festivities were still going on. Mr. Brown had taken over at the piano and cookies were being served. Andy led Emma into the dining room and asked for two plates of food. Emma didn't realize how hungry she was until the plate of turkey, mashed potatoes, stuffing and green beans were in front of her. Another plate with rolls were also brought to the table.

Andy was always given the royal treatment there, even though he insisted they shouldn't do it. They loved him and it showed. The foundation covered most of the expenses of running the home, and he covered the rest. Emma enjoyed spending time with Andy and began to consider what it would be like to date him. Maybe it wouldn't be so bad, but she had to be honest with him.

"There's something I have to tell you," Emma began.

Andy looked up, the tone of her voice let him know it was something serious. "What is it?"

"I've been offered a job in Atlanta, a news anchor position," she said.

"That's great!" Andy replied, genuinely happy for her.

"I think I might take it," Emma said.

Andy now understood the seriousness of her tone. She was moving to Atlanta. Just as they agreed to go on their first date, she said she was leaving. To Andy it didn't matter, he still wanted to see her whether that meant a long distance relationship or not. He could travel to see her, maybe even get a place there. Spring training didn't start for a little while yet, of course once it did, he would be busy until the end of the baseball season.

It wouldn't be easy but he was willing to give it a try. Emma was relieved at his reaction and glad she had told him now, just in case he wanted to back out. Andy insisted he wouldn't, he really liked her and was ecstatic that she said, 'yes' to their first date.

When Andy received a notification on his phone, he checked his watch. He had to go. Andy didn't tell Emma, but it was the alarm company saying there was a breach in his security, a potential broken window at home. Andy got a sinking feeling of what, or who, it could be.

"I'm sorry, Emma, I have to go. Something came up that I have to take care of," Andy said as he took his plate to the kitchen. "Please stay and enjoy yourself. I will see later."

Emma watched Andy as he rushed out, hoping everything was okay. She decided to rejoin the party and find her father. She touched her pearl necklace and wished her mother was here to see all of this. She found her father sitting with Sam and playing cards. Emma sat down, patted her father's shoulder and watched Sam. She marveled at what he had been through as a little boy and how caring and friendly he was. It was a true testament to his older brother how they both came away better human beings, despite what their parents had put them through.

Emma was beginning to wonder if Andy wasn't also Batman or Spiderman secretly working behind the scenes. She was learning each day that her first impressions of that man were way off base and slowly felt excited about their upcoming date. She wasn't afraid to say the word any longer...it was a date. In fact, she was ready to tell her father.

"I have a date with Andy for New Year's Eve," Emma said.

"Well, it's about time!" Joe replied.

Emma pretended to be offended as Joe and Sam started laughing, but she couldn't help but join them. It was a moment of love and happiness that wasn't just because it was Christmas, it was because of Andy Anderson, too.

Chapter 18

Emma was so nervous about her date with Andy, she had styled her hair three different ways in the last thirty minutes. Her choice of dress was easily decided since she only had one real fancy one, the red strapless one that she had worn to the gala six weeks ago. She had a black faux fur jacket that she would wear with it.

She decided to wear the pearl and diamond necklace of her mothers and found pearl earrings to wear with it. She hadn't heard from Andy in the last couple of days, but they originally arranged for him to pick her up at seven o'clock, that was exactly ten minutes from now. Just enough time to let her hair down, again.

Emma was still fussing with her hair when she realized it was a quarter after seven, perhaps he was delayed in traffic. Finally ready, she decided to pour herself a glass of wine to calm her nerves. She didn't know why she was so jittery, she spent more time with Andy than any other man in years, she was comfortable with him. But this was a date...

At eight o'clock she decided to call him and it went straight to voicemail. She sent another text and got no response. Now she was starving and worried. She didn't want to eat anything, but the open bag of chips on the counter was too tempting. She decided to text her address again, just in case he was lost and too embarrassed to ask her for it.

By nine o'clock she didn't know if she should be more mad or concerned. She didn't know who to call except the Sunnyside Home.

She didn't have any other numbers of his family or friends. The woman at the front desk said that she hadn't seen him or heard from him, either. She was sure he was okay otherwise they would have been the first to hear. That news was both comforting and frustrating at the same time.

Emma came to the conclusion that Andy was not coming because he didn't want to, he had changed his mind and couldn't tell her. Angry at herself for believing he wanted to try dating her, she ran to her room and undressed. After a hot shower and a microwave meal, she sat in front of the television and watched the ball drop in Times Square.

Why should this year be any different? This is what she did for New Year's every year. Andy can have his fancy restaurant and fancy clothes, Emma was happy in pajamas and eating frozen pasta. The more she thought about how he sucked her in, the angrier she had become. He was probably laughing right now about how gullible and easy she was to manipulate.

Emma decided that tomorrow she was going to call Atlanta and accept the position. Next she would book her plane ticket and schedule the movers. She was done trying to accommodate a man in her life. Her family and friends told her, warned her even to do what was right for her. Well, this felt right, it felt so freaking right she could scream. In fact, she would have screamed if she wasn't already crying.

THE NEXT FEW DAYS AND weeks were a whirlwind of activity. She did book her flight and scheduled her movers, in fact, they were arriving at her new apartment any minute. Her new boss, Tyler Holcomb, helped her with finding a place near the studio. It was small, only one bedroom, but a perfect location and close to everything.

She had a small balcony that overlooked the city that was big enough for a chair and a table. Pat had come by to help her set up her television and other electronic items she knew nothing about. It was nice to have someone she already knew to call on for help. As Emma put her dishes and clothes away, Pat reassembled furniture and carried heavy boxes wherever Emma wanted them.

In all that time she never once heard from Andy. Emma was ready to leave him behind. Now that she was moving forward in a new city with a new job she was not looking back. Her daily calls to her father were about every subject except Andy. Joe knew that he was a sore subject and never brought up his name even though he never fully understood why or what happened.

Her phone calls and texts to James were also everything except Andy. It was hard for James to not ask about him because his presence was still being felt in the restaurant because of the Salty Waves' growing numbers and profits. It was a record year that was continuing to get better and better with each passing month. It was hard for James to just sit back and let Emma be mad at him for missing their date.

But Andy didn't just miss their date, he never showed up or called to explain after, either. Emma refused to be the one who kept calling and texting a man who didn't want anything to do with her. No, Emma would move on.

She loved her new job as anchorwoman. The news broadcast that she was on started at six, so she had to be at the studio at five each morning. So when her alarm went off at four, she was ready for the day. Unfortunately, that meant she also had to be in bed by eight at night. No more late dinners or going out with friends for her.

When Emma got out of work around noon, she would often find lunch somewhere and take it to the park to eat. She rarely used her car and even considered selling it, but decided to make sure this was where she wanted to stay first. Sometimes she felt her decision to come to Atlanta was rash and sudden, other times she felt like she had been waiting for this moment for years.

Today was too cold and rainy to walk to the park so she opted to go home instead. She brewed some tea and found a good movie to watch when her phone rang. Pat was downstairs and had pizza and wondered if she wanted company. Emma invited him up.

Pat showed her that he had changed. She still wasn't sure she would ever be in a relationship with him, again, but he was turning out to be a good friend. One day he asked about Andy and Emma was in a talkative mood so she answered. She admitted that they had planned to date and that they did like each other, until he called it off.

"He called it off?" Pat asked.

"Yes, he wasn't serious about it," Emma said and then changed the subject. "So I hear Atlanta has their own groundhog for Groundhog's Day. Do you think we'll have an early spring?"

Pat took that as a cue to move on. He never brought up Andy again and neither did she. They talked about an upcoming concert and maybe climbing Stone Mountain some weekend. Emma wanted to stay busy. The more quiet time she had to get melancholy she might actually regret moving there. Pat was happy to accompany her anywhere.

Emma also kept in touch with Miriam and Don. They were more than happy to fill Emma in on everything happening around the newsroom. They hired someone else and she were sitting at Emma's desk, they didn't like that even though the girl was nice. Emma laughed and scolded them for not making friends with her. They said they would try.

Miriam had a new boyfriend she believed he might be worth keeping. Emma laughed, again, thinking the last one was Mr. Right. Miriam sighed and explained that he was married, more laughter. Oh, how she missed her friends! She had hoped she would find replacement friends in Atlanta, but that kind of bond was hard to replicate. She just had Pat for now.

JOE WAS PROUD OF HIS daughter, but he was also worried about her. He wondered whether she told him the truth about Andy breaking up with her right before she moved to Atlanta. After seeing them together at the Christmas party, it was a little hard for him to believe that was what really happened. Joe also respected her enough to stay out of it.

One day while he and Sam were playing cards, Joe couldn't help but comment on how Andy hadn't stopped by in a while. Sam said his brother was okay. When Joe asked what he was doing, Sam simply said he was doing good. Well, maybe that was all Andy told his brother so that he didn't worry, or maybe that was the truth. Andy could be okay and just wanted to stay away.

Maybe Andy didn't want to come around because he was avoiding Joe. He didn't want it to get awkward around here, that wouldn't be good for any of them. Joe really wanted to reach out to Andy and offer an olive branch if that's what it would take to get him to come around again. He knew Sam missed him, too, even though his mother still showed up each day, it wasn't the same.

Joe went to the concierge desk and asked to get Andy's number. They informed him that they were to never give that out to anyone, they were sorry but they couldn't. Could they at least get a message to him? They said they would try, but Mr. Anderson asked to not be disturbed. Joe thanked them and went back to his room. He didn't know what that meant.

Joe felt bad. Something happened between Andy and Emma and no one was talking it, or at least not telling the truth. There was nothing else he could do, he had tried. Hopefully time would heal their wounds. Joe, however, felt strong. One day James picked him up and took him to the Salty Waves to see it for himself.

His father was so impressed he became emotional. Joe noticed the family picture on the wall and smiled. His wife, Nora, would have loved to have seen it now. James brought him to the bar and asked what he wanted to eat. Joe requested a hamburger and a beer, but asked him to not tell the doctor.

Joanne returned with a juicy burger and a small beer. Joe laughed and thanked her. It was the best beer and burger Joe had ever tasted. The restaurant wasn't open yet, so when he finished eating he walked around and admired the decor. He noticed another picture of some familiar faces. It must have been taken on the night the Sharks invaded the restaurant and turned business around. It was of Emma and Andy.

Joe turned to his son, "Did Emma ever tell *you* what happened?" James replied, "No, just that he broke up with her."

They both agreed it didn't sound right but neither one wanted to push the subject with Emma. She was moving on and thriving in Atlanta, maybe everything turned out for the best. No one wanted to be the one to question Emma about Andy, so they left it alone.

They all sat down at a table and talked about the future. James said that when his father felt up to it, he'd love to have him move in with them. It was the family home, so it was only right that he move back in. Joe said he didn't feel ready yet but would let them know when he did. Joe was only now getting his mobility back, he didn't want to commit to something he wasn't comfortable with because he didn't want to be a burden to his children.

James was proud of his father's hard work at getting better but to learn that Sunnyside Home was run by Andy was even more astounding. They all had been touched by Andy's generosity, that was for sure, but they were also concerned that Andy might be all in the past.

One thing they could agree on is that they would always support Emma, no matter what she did or said, she was family. Health, money and fame may come and go, but your family was always there to pick you up and carry you forward because forward is the only way to go. Life goes on.

Chapter 19

Atlanta in the spring was beautiful with all of the flowers and trees blooming and the Bradford Pear blossoms falling to the ground like snow. Emma's boss had been pleased with her performance since day one. Tyler Holcomb was nice but he was not Liane Lincoln. Emma still found herself comparing them in her head. She knew it wasn't fair to him, but she couldn't help doing it.

To make matters worse, she had to report on spring training for the baseball season. Baseball was just one of those subjects that crossed over from sports to news. She had even had to comment on the lineup for the St. Petersburg Sharks and wondered if they could top their winning season from last year. So far no one was being mentioned by name and she dreaded the day she would actually have to say Andy's name on the air.

Emma had not returned home since she left after the New Year. It was a long time for her to be away from family and she was starting to get homesick. She wondered if she could take some time off around Easter or spring break and see her family and friends again. It would do her good to laugh and gossip with everyone just like the old days.

It caught Emma a little off guard when she received a phone call from Joanne that afternoon. As Emma knew, James's birthday was coming up and Joanne was planning a big surprise party for him, was there any way she could get away for a few days to join them? Emma did not need any further encouragement, it was the final push she needed to make plans.

"Yes!" Emma announced.

Emma was surprised how planning a trip home made her very excited and anxious at the same time. There were so many people she wanted to see, yet one person she really wanted to avoid. Surely Andy wouldn't just be wandering around town during spring training, right? Actually, Emma didn't really know where they trained in the spring, so anything was possible.

Most teams from up north come to Florida, if you are from Florida where did you go? She hadn't really thought about it, maybe they stayed right where they were, which meant everywhere Emma normally went. That was when the butterflies came back into her stomach. In her mind she tried to prepare herself for running into him and imagined what she would say. Even in her mind she just turned and ran away.

To make it worse, James said the team and coaches still came into the restaurant regularly. Even when they were on the phone Coach Walters was sitting at the bar. She made her brother promise that he would not say he was talking to her and he didn't. Maybe one day she could talk about it openly with everyone, but not now. It was still too soon, even after four months.

What Joanne didn't tell Emma was that she warned everyone that Emma was coming. Just in case Emma didn't let everyone know herself. She told Joe, everyone at Sunnyside Home and she even called Miriam and Don. She even warned them not to bring up Andy, even though everyone knew that topic was off limits for good. The only one who didn't know Emma was coming was James.

James, of course, had a hint that there was a party because he was in charge of ordering the food and when his wife added some extra items on his weekly shopping list, he questioned her. So the party may not be a total surprise to James but he didn't know Emma was coming, which meant he may have mentioned the party to Coach

Walters and a few other team members. So, it'll be a complete surprise to some people who show up that was for sure.

Joanne was just hoping she did the right thing by inviting her, it was his sister for goodness sake. If Emma felt uncomfortable at any time she could leave whenever she wanted. Hopefully that didn't happen, but it could. Joanne would be fully responsible.

EMMA ARRIVED IN ST. Petersburg the day before the party and checked into a hotel. She messaged her friends and they all agreed to meet at Ferg's that evening. Spring break was always busy in Florida, but Ferg's Sports Bar and Grill was extra crowded. Emma was relieved to see Miriam, Don and Cindy already there and she made her way to them.

There were cheers, hugs and laughter as everyone took turns catching up from the last four months. It seemed like a lifetime ago. She told stories about how she had the hiccups on camera one time and they had to cut to her partner until she got them under control. Emma had also never really dealt with a teleprompter much before and had to practice before they let her on the air.

They ordered more food and a bottle of champagne so they could toast to being back together again, even if only for a few days. Emma missed this and she missed her friends. Miriam said how the new girl spilled Liane's coffee all over her dress one day because she bumped into her in the hallway. Miriam felt bad when Liane yelled at her, but it was all part of the learning curve. You learn to stay out of Liane Lincoln's way. They all laughed knowing they had their own Liane stories in their past.

They all wanted to know everything about Atlanta. Emma said they would never believe how large the city was and how terrible the traffic could be. She said it was something she needed to get used to, even though she now was getting pretty good at the Marta train system. There was so much to see and do around the city that she and Pat were busy each weekend.

"Excuse me...you and Pat?" Miriam asked.

Emma forgot to tell them just how much time she and Pat had been spending together. "Pat McNeil is different," Emma replied. "And we are just friends, really my only friend in Atlanta so far."

Her friends watched Emma's demeanor change when she talked about not having any friends there yet. They knew that it was a big issue for her because Emma always got together with friends whether it was a good or bad occasion, she shared those moments with her friends. It worried them that all of those moments were with Pat, the ex-boyfriend.

Pat McNeil may be different, but he'll never be good enough for Emma. She put up with enough controlling behavior when they were together, they didn't want her to fall back into that whether she saw it coming or not. She may already be sucked back in, they had no way of knowing for sure.

"Maybe we should come visit you some time?" Don replied.

"I would love that, there are so many tourist attractions in the downtown area," Emma said.

They let Emma talk about Atlanta some more before watching her mood change again. The big city might be fun for a while, but they knew she missed St. Pete. In fact, it was becoming clearer that she was avoiding the subject of one certain person. It was a waiting game to see who was going to bring Andy's name up first.

It really was a sad situation because none of them even caught a glimpse of Andy since Emma left. It was as if they were both avoiding the entire city for fear of running into someone who might ask about the other. Maybe Andy will be at the party tomorrow and it will all be out in the open again, no more hiding around corners.

JOANNE STARTED DECORATING the restaurant early, since James already knew about it, he even helped. The food was almost ready and the cake was being decorated. The Salty Waves was nearly ready for guests. Emma was the first to arrive because she was afraid she might be forced to leave early if a certain pitcher arrived. She at least wanted time with her brother in case it became uncomfortable at the party and she had to run out the back door.

James was so surprised that she was there that he became emotional. They hadn't seen each other in months and they had never gone that long before. James made her promise to not let it happen again. Emma had brought their father and he was walking pretty steady now. They even joked that he'll be driving in no time at all. Emma laughed but it was a nervous laugh, her eyes were glued on the front door.

James and Joanne took this moment of calm to finally tell her and Joe the good news...they were expecting! Emma was so happy for them and excited to be an aunt! It was bittersweet for Joe to become a grandfather without his beloved Nora to experience it with him, but he was happy. Emma's new niece or nephew would arrive in October and she couldn't wait to spoil the new addition to the family.

As people started arriving, Emma started to feel more at ease when Andy wasn't showing up. No one really knew for sure if he would, so they couldn't put her mind totally at ease. Emma tried to keep busy by refilling glasses and offering to bring out more food. When Joanne tried to remind her that she didn't work there anymore, she laughed another nervous laugh.

Emma did her best to make small talk with all of James's friends, some she knew and others that were strangers to her. It was a large crowd and a good indication of how loved James was in the community. The community had embraced him, too. James was able to offer trivia and bingo nights, open mic and karaoke nights as well as special events and parties.

Emma stopped in her tracks when she saw Greg Reynolds, Bobby Bishop and Coach Walters walk in. She held her breath waiting for a fourth member of their party to emerge, but he never did. Emma's breathing turned shallow and she debated whether to run out the door or not but was too late, they waved at Emma to come join them. There was no getting away now.

Emma took her time walking through the crowd until she was face to face with the team. Emma asked what she could get them to drink and listed what they were offering for food. They placed their order and Emma escaped into the safety of the kitchen. It was only a temporary peace because the food was already prepared, she just needed to bring it to their table.

Coach Walters pulled over another chair and asked her to join them. She wiped her sweaty palms on her jeans and sat down. They were enjoying their food and soda when they asked how life in Atlanta was. At first she was surprised they knew, then remembered they were now friends with her brother and then immediately regretted not clarifying with James exactly what he told them about her.

Emma explained to them all about her new job and how wonderful the city was even though it was so big she was constantly getting lost. They laughed and seemed genuinely interested in her stories of Atlanta. She was more than a little surprised when they were treating her like they always treated her, not with animosity or blame. Didn't Andy say how she just left and never called him or that he never called her?

She was desperate to know what was going on but didn't know how to ask. She didn't want them going back and telling him that all she did was talk about Andy all night long. No, she would have to be sly and careful how she brought him up. She thought about her spring training story the other day and would ask them about the team.

"So how is the team looking this year, do you think you'll be able to pull off another World Series win with your MVP?" To Emma, it sounded like another pre-game interview, the one that actually put her face to face with Andy the first time.

"Oh, I don't know," Coach Walters started. "It'll be tough, we had such a great team last year, it will be hard to duplicate it."

Emma looked around the table from one man to the next for any further explanation. Since none was forthcoming, Emma asked, "Why?"

"Because of the accident," Coach Walters said matter-of-factly. When they saw the still-confused look on Emma's face, it clicked. "You don't know!"

"Know what?" Emma asked loudly. "Coach, what are you not telling me?"

Coach Walters suddenly looked very uncomfortable and looked to the other two men for help, they just shrugged their shoulders and let Coach continue. "Andy was in a car accident on New Year's Eve, he was driving with his father and veered off the road. It was bad."

Emma felt like an elephant was sitting on her chest, she couldn't catch her breath. Greg handed her his water and she drank it eagerly. Coach Walters wasn't finished.

"Now we have to use another pitcher. Andy Anderson will probably never play baseball again."

Chapter 20

Walking on the beach was quickly becoming Andy's favorite thing to do. Just like at home on Clearwater Beach, the sand here was soft and clean. He loved watching the sunset each night and the sunrise every morning. Andy could almost believe the whole world had disappeared and all of his troubles with it...almost.

He walked with his feet in the water and breathed in the salty air. It was making him homesick and he missed Emma. The sunrise this morning was particularly beautiful and it made him think of Emma's eyes, such a deep shade of green. He hated himself for not contacting her, especially after what happened, but he was wondering if now it was too late anyway.

Andy bent down to pick up a seashell that was such a vibrant pink and slipped it in his pocket to add to his growing collection. He turned around and looked back at his house and knew it was time to return. He let the waves wash over his ankles one more time before heading back. The phone in his pocket started ringing which brought him back to reality. It was his doctor.

He had an appointment later that day and Andy already knew what they were going to say, that his shoulder, arm and neck were healing perfectly, just not enough to get full mobility back. He still walked with a slight limp, too. When he added all of this together, along with his already injured elbow and shoulder from before the accident, it equalled the end of his career.

Andy had already been through many stages of grief, he was now entering the acceptance stage. He was allowing himself time to envision a life without the Sharks, without pitching, without baseball. Maybe even without Emma. He thought about staying here, at his home in Hawaii and never going back. It would be so easy to do.

He purchased this house in Kahala, a sort of Beverly Hills of the islands, when he first started playing for the Sharks. It was originally meant to be a party home during the off season. In fact, Greg might still have a home around here, too. But over the years, its purpose had evolved. Andy even thought about bringing Sam here to live. He would have staff to take care of his every need but the only drawback was that it would be too difficult for Andy to visit.

Thinking of Sam made Andy miss St. Pete, again. Now, he was using his home on Oahu as a place to recuperate. Another phone call. Andy looked and saw it was his father, he wanted to stop by later today. Andy invited him for dinner tonight and then hung up. His relationship with his father was also slowly evolving.

Andy didn't remember anything about the accident, only that the night he was getting ready to pick up Emma, on New Year's Eve, his father was at his home. Apparently he had already been celebrating and couldn't find the key to Andy's house, so he threw a rock through the window and that alerted his security team, again.

When Andy arrived at this home in Clearwater, Ron was staggering through the house looking for another bottle of liquor but Andy always kept what little he had in the house locked. Then for the next couple of hours, Ron went from rage to tears, apologizing for everything and wanting to be better. Andy had heard it all before and was done cleaning up his father's messes. Ron promised he would get help and Andy called his bluff.

They both had gotten into Andy's truck and he told his father he would take him to the hospital to check on his hand, unaware that he had cut it coming in through the broken window. But Andy wasn't taking him to just any hospital, he was taking him to rehab. Ron was sobering up enough to know they were driving in the opposite direction and grabbed the wheel.

Taking Andy by surprise, he tried to push his father back and veered to stay in his lane. Ron became more and more agitated in the truck and was now using both hands to get Andy to turn around or pull over. The final jerk to the wheel landed the truck in a ditch but the speed made it roll over with Andy getting the worst of the injuries.

Coach Walters was immediately called. Andy always had him listed as an emergency contact, since, well...there was no one else. When Coach arrived at the hospital and learned that he was driving his father, he knew there had to be some sort of argument to make Andy drive off the road. He asked that all news accounts of the accident keep his name out of it, it was what Andy would have wanted.

Andy was in intensive care for over a week and they weren't even sure he would make it. Ron was released the next day and checked himself into rehab. It only took one visit with his son to know that enough was enough, he had to get clean. Ron wept as he signed himself in and worked hard on his recovery while his son lay in the hospital hooked up to machines.

When Andy finally regained consciousness, three surgeries later, he asked for his phone. Coach Walters said they never found it, probably laying on the road and smashed to pieces by now, he would buy him a new one tomorrow. The only thing he wanted Andy to focus on now was to get better. But Andy kept asking about Emma. Coach Walters didn't have the heart to tell him right away what he learned from James, that she had packed up and moved to Atlanta. He knew he would have to eventually, but for now, he just wanted Andy to worry about himself.

Andy didn't agree! He tried to get up, he tried to contact Emma but didn't know her number. He became such a handful for the medical staff that they called Coach Walters and he brought Andy a new phone. In the end it didn't matter, as much as he tried to call or text Emma, he stopped himself right before he made the call.

He didn't want to be the reason she returned out of pity, he was no longer the man she knew, maybe never would be again. His baseball career was over. He loved her enough to let her go and find happiness in Atlanta.

That much Andy remembered from four months ago. He remembered the pain and anguish of learning the details of the accident and then the consequences of his not showing up on their date. The hospital had to cut him out of the tuxedo he was wearing that night. The aftermath of the accident was so far reaching, even Andy didn't know all of it.

When Andy told Coach Walters he wanted to do his physical therapy and recuperating in Hawaii, he was both sad and understanding. There would be less distractions and reminders of what he was leaving behind. Andy's days were filled with doctor appointments of all types and music. His home in Kahala contained a piano, he made sure of it.

Inspiration came to him from so many sources and he wrote them all down on paper and then translated that into music. He could look at the sunset, a palm tree or a seashell and feel the need to write and play. At a local bar in town, he connected with some guys who were performing and he got to talking about music. It was music that bonded them and later, the guys invited him to see their studio.

To call it a studio was being generous, it was a padded closet converted to a makeshift studio with a microphone and recording equipment. Andy had never been more impressed and asked if they would help him record some songs and they were excited to do it.

Andy spent the next few weeks getting some songs finished and recorded.

Andy kept in touch with Bobby, Greg and of course Coach Walters, and when Andy told them about his latest hobby, they wanted to hear his songs. What Andy didn't know was that those songs were being passed all around Florida and were actually getting some major attention. When Greg told everyone that this was Andy Anderson, MVP pitcher turned songwriter, they couldn't wait to play it. All of this was going on in the background, while Andy was doing physical therapy in Hawaii.

All Andy knew was that he was getting stronger and sending some songs to his friends. He was enjoying a quiet life of fresh squeezed juice in the mornings and fresh sashimi for dinner. He envisioned staying in Hawaii and selling his home in Florida, or giving it to his father, he was very unsure of where his life was headed now.

Speaking of his father, he would be coming by any minute. Andy asked the cook to prepare a couple steaks for them tonight and he poured some lemonade and waited on the lanai for him. When Ron heard that Andy was coming to Hawaii for a few months, Ron transferred to a rehab facility near him. Andy knew it was guilt, but Ron insisted it was love. They had a lot of time to work on their relationship and it would take baby steps to make up for all the years of abuse and neglect.

Ron came that evening and sat down next to his son. They hadn't done that in years and now it was a nearly daily occurrence. Andy poured his father a glass of lemonade and they watched the sunset together. Ron showed Andy his newest prized possession, his one-month sobriety coin and it wouldn't be long until he received his three-month coin as well. Andy was skeptical that Ron would keep at it, but so far he had. He had been a drunkard all his life and never saw his father sober, but now he was starting to believe that his father's sixties, might be his best years after all.

The new normal for father and son took some getting used to on both sides. Without alcohol, Ron had to learn to cope in life without the one thing he wanted most. For Andy, what was he without baseball? The one thing he had trained for his whole life was now being taken away. Ron was turning to golf and Andy had his music, maybe they could find a way to a new life.

They ate their dinner in silence. Ron had spent weeks trying to make things up with Andy before he finally had to tell him to stop. Andy no longer wanted to dwell in the past, they could only move forward, the damage was already done. Ron was now in his acceptance phase and was working on building a friendship with this son, it was the best he could hope for.

After dinner, his father left and Andy was alone with his piano. He was singing softly to one of his new compositions about love and loss. Emma was always the muse for his music and one day he hoped he could see her again, to explain…to apologize. As if he manifested it, his phone rang and the caller ID said Emma.

Immediately Andy stopped playing and remained still, as if that would make the caller go away. Too panicked to answer, it stopped. A notification let him know there was now a voicemail. Andy thought about what Emma would be calling him about and decided to just listen to her message.

"Hello, Andy? It's Emma. I'm so sorry, I just heard about the accident, Coach Walters told me…I'm home for a few days…Joanne is pregnant, I'm gonna be an aunt," Emma said through tears. "Why didn't you call me? Why didn't you tell me you were hurt!" Emma paused to steady her voice. "I could have come and helped…somehow…I should have known about it." Emma could no longer hold back the sobs, "I love you, Andy."

Andy held the phone to his ear until he heard the final click, then silence...

Chapter 21

Ever since yesterday, when Emma learned of Andy's accident and career-ending injury she had not thought about anything else. Nothing else mattered. The look on the Coach's face when he told Emma the news let her know that she was never to find out. Why? It wasn't as if they were a couple, but they were friends, good friends. Shouldn't she have been told if her good friend was near death?

Emma was angry and frantic to find out any more details about the accident and how Andy was now. She combed through every news article around that night and couldn't find anything until a small news story was buried on page three on New Year's Day. It only mentioned an overturned truck with two passengers on Gulf to Bay Blvd., both were taken to the hospital with injuries.

That's it? Where is he now? Emma thought she knew where his beach house was, but it was dark and she wasn't paying attention to street names and numbers as he directed her back to his house in November. Wow, when she thought about how long it had been since they saw each other, she had to stop and pause.

Maybe he never told her because he really did want her to go away. Maybe all this time she was right, he didn't want to see her again. Emma was sitting in her hotel room when this realization finally made her stop looking. Andy had so many opportunities and so many months to let her know about his accident and he didn't. He didn't care about her anymore.

Emma got dressed and went down the elevator. With her new perspective, she could go about her day without obsessing over Andy. She drove her rental car to Sunnyside Home and greeted Sam with a hug and he said that he missed her. Emma missed him, too. Even Sam's mother waved to her and said hello. Life had gone on without her, it was humbling.

For someone who had felt like she had carried the world on her shoulders, it was a little disheartening to learn that sometimes people just needed you to step back a minute before they could take over. Emma wasn't used to stepping back and letting others take the wheel, but she finally saw that it was okay. All the while she was in Atlanta, life had continued here without her just fine.

Joe was happy to see her today, he had worried about how she left the party last night and knew that she had received some upsetting news, they all had, but Joe knew it would hit his daughter harder than the rest of them. He was more than a little surprised when she came in smiling and humming to his room.

"You're in a good mood," Joe said.

"Why not? Life is good," Emma replied.

"Indeed," Joe answered, skeptical of her cheerful outlook.

Joe didn't push her, he knew better than to get her to open up about her feelings when she clearly didn't want to discuss it. Instead, they went out to the back garden and sat in the warm April sun. There was a chance of rain later in the day, but right now it was beautiful. Joe watched her daughter as she looked at her phone.

"Waiting for a phone call?" He asked.

"No," she answered quickly. "I just...well, I left a stupid voicemail that I wished I wouldn't have."

"Do you want to talk about it?" Joe asked.

"No."

Joe didn't need to ask what it was about or who it was that she had called, he knew it was Andy. He *was* surprised that she told him as much as she did right now, it was obviously eating at her and he prayed that Andy called Emma back. Joe tried to change the subject by offering to take out a paddle boat on the lake, when Emma kept staring at her phone, he relented and just kept quiet.

They both jumped when Emma's phone rang. It had broken the silence that had fallen between father and daughter. Joe thought it was bad news when Emma's face went white as a ghost.

"It's Andy!" She proclaimed.

"Answer it!" Joe demanded.

Emma hesitated a brief moment before hitting the green button. "Hello?"

"Emma?" Andy asked.

"Yes."

"I, uh, got your voicemail," Andy paused. He was just as nervous on the other end. "Where are you?"

"I'm in St. Pete for a few days," Emma replied.

"Okay, where in St. Pete?"

"I'm with dad, at Sunnyside," Emma answered.

"Okay, thanks." Then Andy hung up.

Emma stared at her phone for a minute, trying to piece together the conversation and what it meant. When Joe asked what Andy wanted, she didn't even know how to answer that. She said it was strange, he wanted to know where she was but...why?

"Turn around," Joe said, smiling.

Andy was walking towards them in the garden. She could tell he was nervous because he was wiping the palms of his hands on his pants. Emma's breaths were becoming so shallow she was afraid she would hyperventilate. She looked him up and down and the only clue that something was wrong was a slight limp and the sling that his left arm was in now. Other than that he could be walking to the pitcher's mound instead of to Emma.

But here he was, Andy was walking towards her. She felt her chin start quivering as he got closer and she couldn't hold back any longer, she ran to him. She hadn't noticed the tears in Andy's eyes until she collided into his embrace. He held her tight with his good arm and they held each other tight.

For Andy, he never dreamed this day would come, that he would be able to get out of hospital bed and still lead a full life, even without baseball. For Emma, she thought the man she loved never wanted her, never wanted to see her again. But here he was! They released each other and took a step back. Too emotional for words, they wiped at their tears and started giggling a nervous laugh because neither one of them knew where to start.

Joe walked up and shook Andy's hand. "Welcome home, Andy. We've missed you and prayed for your full recovery."

"Thank you, sir," Andy replied and they all went to sit down under the oak tree.

"I'm sorry," Emma blurted out. "For not following up and checking on you. I didn't know..." Andy stopped her.

"No, I'm the one who needs to apologize," Andy replied. "I should have called you. When I heard you moved to Atlanta I thought that was it, you were done with me and you had moved on. I loved you enough to let you go and live your life."

Emma's tears were returning. "No, when you never showed up for our date, I assumed you changed your mind, that you didn't care...I never thought that...that..." Emma couldn't talk any more. She put her head in her hands and let the tears fall.

Andy moved beside her and put his right arm around her. He kissed the top of her head and asked her to stop crying. If they only had a short amount of time together, then he didn't want to waist a minute on tears. Instead, he texted Emma his address and asked her to meet him when she was done visiting with her father and she agreed.

Just then Sam came running out to hug Andy followed by their mother. Andy didn't notice her at first and because this was such an unexpected visit, she couldn't avoid seeing her eldest son. When their eyes met, Andy released Sam and walked towards the woman he hadn't seen in fifteen years. The woman who walked away from her family when he was eighteen years old. The mother who abandoned her children and left them with a drunk of a father that made Andy in charge.

They stood just feet apart but the tension was felt for miles. It was Wendy Anderson who spoke first. "Hello, son."

Andy remained unmoving, his stare never wavering. Emma had no idea what was going through his mind but she watched as he clenched and unclenched his jaw. Emma attempted to move closer to them but Andy just backed away and shook his head.

"I can't deal with this right now," Andy said quietly and left.

Wendy must have been holding her breath because she let it out in one big gasp as Andy walked past her. Silent tears flowed unchecked as she turned and went back inside. Emma's heart ached for them both but she didn't know how much more Andy could take. He had already lost his career, his father almost killed him, Emma had left him and now his absent mother returned.

There was nothing Emma could do to help, she would see him later today and they had their own issues to talk over. She wasn't sure where she stood in his life right now but she wanted to be somewhere in it. Now that she knew how close she was to losing him for good, she didn't care about long distance, she loved him.

Joe persuaded her to stay for lunch and they sat in the dining room at a table near Sam and his mother. They all gave each other sideways looks, unable to talk about what had just happened. Emma wondered what Andy thought about seeing her after all of these years, of not knowing if she was even alive or dead.

But Emma knew, had known for months.

AT HOME, ANDY CALLED Coach Walters and let him know he was in town. Coach wanted to see him and suggested they meet for lunch tomorrow. Andy suggested they go to Salty Waves, there was a couple there he needed to congratulate. They set up a time and Coach welcomed him back, even though Andy wasn't sure if it was for good or not, yet.

Andy hadn't been back to his house on Clearwater Beach since that night. Today he had come straight from the airport to see Emma. He made sure his staff kept some basic food in the fridge and freezer in case friends needed to stay for a night or two. Today he was lucky it was well stocked with food. He even found a beer.

Unsure of how to process everything that happened to him today, Andy turned on the television and tried to make the time go faster. He was both anxious and eager to see Emma again and hoped that they would finally be back on the same page. Four months was a long time to be apart without any communication, he was sure they had a lot to discuss if they wanted a future together.

Andy called Greg and asked him about lunch tomorrow and he said he'd be happy to meet. Greg also had news to share and was excited to see his friend. Andy asked about spring training and tried to sound interested. He was, but it also hurt to hear about the team preparing for another season without him. Life went on.

Time seemed to move achingly slow for Andy. The moment he heard Emma's voicemail he had jumped on a plane and flew straight here. He was so happy to see her but they couldn't say what they needed to say in front of so many people. They had to be brutally honest with each other or it would never work. Andy knew that honesty wasn't always kind, so it was best to be alone. He would even offer his good shoulder if she wanted to punch him, but it was her decision now. Andy was ready to agree to anything Emma wanted.

Chapter 22

Emma followed the directions to Andy's house and was trying to remain calm the whole way. Having to focus on the street signs instead of what she was actually doing helped steady her nerves. Emma would be alone with Andy for the first time in months and it made her anxious again. She had tried listening to music and even talked to herself to stay calm but now that she was pulling into his driveway it was all coming back.

Andy was waiting at the door when Emma got out of her car. He had obviously been anxiously waiting by the door for her. He held it open as she entered his house. Her first impression was that it was a beautiful home but lacked that cozy feel that only a woman's touch could provide. It was a very luxurious bachelor pad with a large, flat screen television on one wall and a massive couch facing it. There were other chairs, tables and decorations but Emma could only focus on the man standing behind her.

As if they could hear each other's hearts beating loudly, Andy took her hand and led her to the couch. They sat with their bodies slightly angled to each other. Neither one of them knew where to begin and instead just felt the comfort of being in each other's presence. Their eyes searched each other's faces and then the faintest of smiles softened Andy's appearance.

Emma smiled back and reached out to take his hand. He looked down at their hands on his knee and smiled again.

"Thank you for coming," Andy finally said.

"Of course," Emma replied. "I've missed you."

After that, the conversation flowed easily. Emma told him all about Atlanta and her new job. She was up front about saying that she was hanging out with Pat, but only as friends, nothing more. Andy simply nodded. She then talked about how big and exciting the city was and how difficult it was to learn how to get around. Emma wanted him to know everything.

Andy absorbed it all. He watched her eyebrows raise when she got excited about a particular part in her story and the small lines in the corner of her eyes form when she smiled. These were all details he remembered, loved and missed. He was only half listening but when she stopped talking he looked at her and smiled.

"Can I kiss you?" Andy asked softly.

At first Emma blinked, wondering if she heard him correctly then nodded. Andy approached her slowly looking from her eyes and then to her lips. The kiss was soft and delicate as if she might fade away into a dream. Andy lingered before pulling away. Their faces only millimeters apart, Emma leaned in for more.

This was their first kiss and Emma wanted it to be memorable. Their lips parted and their bodies moved closer together. They were like magnets that could no longer ignore the attraction to each other. Emma moved her hands up Andy's back and ran her fingers through his hair. Andy, with one arm trapped in a sling, ran his right hand down her back and stopped at her waist.

It was Andy who pulled away first. This was not why he invited her here and he apologized. Emma wasn't sorry, she was only sorry it took them this long for their first kiss. She never wanted to stop kissing him, but she did, for now. They needed to define what they were. Emma had a life in Atlanta and Andy was unsure about his own future.

"I don't care," Emma said. "I love you Andy Anderson, not your fame or your money."

"But you have a career and I won't stand in the way of your happiness," Andy replied.

Emma was afraid to make too many promises and they agreed to take it slow. They didn't need to define this...them... right now. There were things they still needed to discuss, like Andy's mother and father who were now suddenly back in the picture.

"I'm still processing it," Andy replied as they ate frozen pizza at the kitchen island. "I think part of me is still in shock that she was there today of all days. Did you see her when you came?"

Emma hesitated, "Yes."

Andy stopped chewing and looked at her. "Wait," Andy said with a concerned look on his face. "How long has she been coming there? Have you seen her there before?"

Emma wiped her hands on her napkin, trying to think of how to answer him. "Well, I've seen her as long as dad has been at Sunnyside Home."

Andy shook his head, wondering if he heard her correctly. "What? You've known since November...and never told me?"

"Well, not just me...but I didn't even know Sam was your brother until the Christmas party, so technically, it was only a week or so...until..." Emma watched as Andy stood up and walked around the room.

"Yes, I will deal with my staff in the morning, but you...I told you my story and you let me just walk in there knowing she was there everyday...you could have told me at the Christmas party." Andy's voice became quiet and eventually trailed off.

Andy was feeling betrayed all over again by the mother who abandoned his family and now by the woman he loved. Emma had known she was in the same building as him and never told Andy or gave him a heads up. Emma felt horrible for opening up a wound that was still so raw. She also wished she had told him when she found out. How had things turned so quickly?

"Maybe I'd better go," Emma said, grabbing her jacket and purse. Andy didn't reply at first and then said, "I'll call you later."

"Yes, okay," Emma replied and left.

Emma was angry with herself the whole way back to the hotel. She had promised no more secrets and she still had them. She knew Andy would figure it out and it would be Emma's fault, at least some of it. His staff should have informed him years ago or however long it had been going on. Now Emma was the bad guy.

Andy felt bad for how tonight ended. It wasn't what he had planned, in fact, he didn't know what he had planned but this wasn't it. He had hoped the evening would have ended with a solid plan or a map on how to navigate this new relationship, if that's what this was. How could one woman make him feel so flustered every time she was around? That was Emma.

Later that evening Andy called her and apologized for the things he said. He also asked if they could try it again, this time he would have a proper dinner for her last night. Emma agreed and said that she was sorry, too, no more secrets. If this was going to work, they had to be completely honest and up front with each other from the beginning. Emma agreed and said she would be there.

THE NEXT DAY ANDY WALKED into the Salty Waves and saw James. The two shook hands and then embraced, it had been too long since they had seen each other. Joanne joined him.

"Congratulations," Andy said. "Coach told me the happy news! When is the baby due?"

"October," Joanne replied.

Andy promised to be there and wished them well. He spotted Gary and Coach Walters at a table and joined them. More handshakes and hugs. Coach was getting emotional because he remembered that night of the accident and how badly Andy was injured, in fact, it was an image he couldn't get out of his mind. He had tried filling in the gaps in Andy's memory, but no one should have to relive all of that horrible night.

Andy thanked them for coming, these were two of his best friends in the world. Greg and Coach Walters both looked at each other with a sly grin on their faces as they argued over who would go first with their news.

"Well, somebody better before my food gets cold," Andy joked.

"Okay fine," Coach began. "I'll start. Andy, the team still needs you. The Sharks want to offer you a position."

Andy looked at Coach like he grew a second head. "Coach, that's impossible."

"Not as a pitcher, Andy, as a coach. We are in need a first base coach who knows what they're doing. We had one retire and another moved up to Pennsylvania." They were both watching Andy's reaction.

"You're serious..." Andy replied.

"Yes," Coach Walters confirmed. "Are you interested?"

Andy hesitated and then answered, "Yes, I am."

Satisfied with Andy's answer, they started eating their food. Coach knew Andy couldn't resist being a part of the team again, even if it wasn't as a pitcher. He was a valued member of the Sharks and they would be lucky to have him back.

"Okay, now my turn," Greg said. Andy nodded. "I kind of did something without telling you." Andy gave Greg and angry look. "No, nothing bad...it's about your music. You know those songs you kept sending me from Hawaii, well I sent them to my friends at a music label and well, they loved them. They want you to come record them at their studio at your earliest convenience."

Greg sat back with a smug look on his face as if his news was better than Coach's news. Actually, Andy didn't know who won that debate he just knew he was probably the luckiest injured player in the world right now.

"Wow, are you serious?" Andy asked Greg.

"Yes, man, one hundred percent." Greg replied.

"Okay then, let's set it up!" Andy said.

Cheers rang from the table as James and Joanne looked on. Whatever was going on at Andy's table it was clearly good news. James was happy for him, he deserved all the happiness he could get.

Coach Walters said they could use him whenever he was ready, but he needed to be signed off from a doctor because it would be long days of practice until opening day. Coach wanted confirmation that he was up to the job. Andy said he would get it all taken care of. They asked about his father and Andy assured him he was sober, but would be staying, for the time being, in Hawaii. He tried to assure Coach Walters that he had changed, but even Andy had a hard time defending the man who ended his career.

Coach Walters asked about Emma. They wondered if she was back in the picture? Well, it depended what picture they were looking at because they hadn't decided anything yet. Hopefully tonight they could figure out where they stood in each other's lives. They had an argument last night and they still needed to get past that, otherwise, they were good. Andy thought about the kiss. Yes, they were good.

Coach hoped they could all get together but Andy said that Emma might not have time this trip. He would try to get her to come back to St. Petersburg soon. He mentioned that they were having dinner together tonight but they weren't invited. Everyone laughed and they enjoyed the rest of their lunch. Andy didn't know where he would be without these men in his life and after today, knew they would forever be in his future.

Coach paid the bill and they said goodbye to their hosts. James waved and told Andy to come again soon. He would since it looked like he would be staying in St. Pete for the foreseeable future.

On the way home, Andy thought about how his day had already started off with a job offer and he just couldn't believe it. He hoped Emma would be happy for him, too. It would mean he could continue to be a part of the game he loved even if it was only as a coach. He would be the best first base coach ever.

Feeling optimistic for the first time in months, Andy decided to stop at the florist and pick up a dozen roses. He was going to make up for last night if it was the last thing he did. Andy turned up the music and sang at the top of his lungs. Life went on and he was ready for it.

Chapter 23

The next morning, Andy went to Sunnyside Home. On any other day Andy would just have strolled in and greeted all of the residents and checked in with Marc Brown to see how his day is going. However, today was different. Today Andy knew his mother was inside and that the staff had known for a very long time without telling him.

Andy went inside, ready to lay down some new ground rules for his staff. Andy smiled as he passed the front desk but went straight to Marc. Andy was in Mr. Brown's office for thirty minutes before he came out and went to the dining room for a soda. Mr. Brown called other senior staff members into his office to relay the warnings that Andy had given him.

Andy went in search of Sam and saw him busy in the back garden. As Andy approached, he didn't realize their mother was sitting with her back to him. Sam was painting and Andy went to him and gave him a hug and a high five then sat and joined them at the table. Wendy watched as Andy fidgeted in his seat without meeting her gaze.

"Hello, Andy," Wendy said.

"Hello," he replied dryly.

"I'm sorry I never told you that I come to visit Sam most days. I've seen you come and go but I've always been too afraid to say anything to you," Wendy said.

Andy remained quiet, waiting for an excuse that made sense, that made up for the last fifteen years of silence and disappearances.

"I don't know what I can say to you that will make you forgive me, but I want to explain that I know I was wrong for walking out, but your father threatened me if I didn't. I didn't even know where I was going and thought you would be better at home than on the streets with me."

Wendy stopped and waited for a response. Andy never moved, his gaze focused on Sam and his paintbrush.

"I never stopped loving you and I'm so proud of the man you have become. You've taken good care of Sam, too," Wendy said.

Andy looked at his mother. "I did it because I had to, our mother left us." Andy stood up and walked out of the garden and out of the facility. He got in his truck and drove.

He didn't want to listen to his mother any more. It took all of his restraint not to yell and argue with her right then and there, but he would never do that in front of Sam. Sam loved her and that was fine, she could have Sam but not him. Andy couldn't forgive her.

EMMA STOPPED IN TO visit her father later that afternoon, unaware of the turmoil that Andy caused with his visit to Mr. Brown and Wendy. Andy was ready to take back control of his own life and everyone wondered how many people would be sent overboard in his wake. Emma hoped it wouldn't be her again tonight when they had dinner later.

Joe expressed his gratitude for her visit this week. It was short but very welcome. Emma promised to come more often, especially since things were better between her and Andy. They weren't perfect, but they were working on it. They each still had their trust issues that needed to be worked on, but maybe with time, it could become something more.

Her father could tell there was already more. Emma's whole face lit up when she talked about Andy. They might be taking a bumpy, roundabout way of getting together, but it will happen eventually. He was sure of it even if Emma wasn't.

Emma decided to take her father to see James. It would be her last chance before she left town tomorrow and she wanted some quiet time with them to properly celebrate their baby news. It was a nice drive to the beach with her father. The afternoons were warming up as a hint that summer was right around the corner.

Salty Waves was busy. Emma was glad things had finally turned around and that they could open up at eleven for the lunch crowd. It was a full-time job now for James and Joanne and Emma wondered how they would handle a baby this fall. She wished she could be there to help babysit, but her plans were very much tied to Atlanta...and Andy.

It was such a welcome distraction for Emma to be around her family and Joe loved asking how his new grandchild was doing. Joanne just patted her belly and said he or she was doing fine. She was lovingly scolded for being on her feet but Joanne just laughed and said there was plenty of time to rest later. It was nice for Emma to sit around the table and be a complete family again.

Emma missed that so much. She loved her job and was getting used to her life in Atlanta, but it wasn't this, it wasn't home. Her father was so close to being able to live on his own again, it was great to witness. She knew it was going to be hard to say good bye when she left this time. James asked her to be the Godmother of their child and she was thrilled to accept. It was an honor she would do her best to live up to.

Emma looked out at the beach and decided to put her toes in the water. She excused herself and walked out in the sand. The breeze blew her hair as she carried her shoes. It was nice to feel the sand under her feet again. She walked out to the waves and let the salt water wash over her feet. She rolled up her pants so that the water could hit her ankles.

She stood like that for several minutes, just watching the horizon. Emma used to always envision a pirate ship sailing out in the distance, just waiting for the right time to come ashore to search for treasure. It was a story they were always told as kids and it kept the pirate spirit alive. Pirates were romanticized enough that every kid wanted to be one.

It was at moments like this when Emma just took a moment to reflect on where she was going and where she had been that made her appreciate where she was. She had finally gotten to a position in her career that she was proud of, but she also loved being the hard-hitting investigative journalist. That was still inside of her, too. She wished her mother was here to discuss it all with her.

Emma turned when she heard footsteps behind her. James had come out to check on his little sister and see if there was anything she needed.

"No," Emma said. "I was just wondering if I could see the pirates today."

James laughed. "Haven't spotted any so far, but there's still time."

James put his arm around her and hugged her. He had always let her pick up the slack when he was too busy to pull his own weight. Maybe he relied on Emma too much, he had thought that once the restaurant became successful he would have more time to take over, but he just became busier.

"I promise to do more and be better," James announced.

Emma looked at him. "You are already the best."

James asked what her plans were for the rest of the day and she said she was meeting Andy for dinner. James simply smiled and asked her to pass on his well wishes before they both headed back inside the restaurant. Joanne had slices of pie ready for everyone and they all sat down to enjoy their dessert.

James thanked everyone, again, for such a wonderful birthday party the other night. He was truly grateful for everyone who came but most importantly, the ones around the table. He didn't know where he would be without any of them but it certainly wouldn't be here and in a position to be serving the usual lunch crowd at the Salty Waves. Joanne touched his arm and smiled.

It was sweet to see James and Joanne still so in love. Emma was happy for them, but her own inner chaos was something she had to deal with tonight. For now, she watched her brother and his wife enjoy the last few months of being a family of two, knowing that everything would be changing in the fall. Emma hoped that they all had changes for the good coming soon.

James and his wife had to get back to work, so Emma took her father home. Joe loved his time out in the real world, as he called it. It made him feel normal again. He had been living in a facility that took care of him for years and he longed to have his old life back again. It made him enjoy and appreciate his time out even more.

Emma made sure he was settled in his room before she finally left him. He was tired and would take a quick nap before his dinner. Emma said good bye to Sam, who was quietly reading on the couch, his mother was nowhere to be seen. She hoped that Andy hadn't scared her off because Sam loved her visits.

Emma went back to the hotel to get ready for tonight. She thought about how dinner had gone the night before and was hoping that Andy had calmed down since then. He had texted a couple times today just to check on her and ask if she was still coming and she said she was planning on it. She still had time to change her mind, but she didn't want to leave things the way they were.

Whether they parted as friends or more than friends depended on how things went tonight. Emma didn't think there was anything else she needed to tell him, no hidden secrets or buried treasure, she was just eager to see him. Emma was willing to work through whatever problems they might have just for the chance to start a real relationship with him, she felt ready.

Emma chose her purple, long-sleeved wrap dress and black heals to wear to dinner. She left her hair down and wore her mother's necklace and sprayed on some perfume. If this was the last time she saw Andy for a while, she wanted to leave an impression. Satisfied with her reflection, she went down to her car.

Emma remembered the way to his house this time and she was feeling more excited the closer she got to his mansion. She was hoping for the grand tour tonight, having only seen his living room and kitchen before she left yesterday. She had liked what she saw, she just wanted to see more. How much more she wanted to see was still undecided.

Part of her wished they could go out to eat and be seen together, then she remembered how last night had turned out and decided that maybe it was good they weren't in public. She did want to be seen with him, though, to go on a proper date but that would have to come in time. She had criticized him having women on his arm and walking all over the globe, but now she was imagining what it would be like to *be* one of those women. Andy was tall and handsome, who wouldn't want to be seen with him?

Emma pulled into Andy's long driveway and sat in the quiet car to collect her thoughts. After taking a deep breath, she got out and walked towards his door. There, standing in a white shirt and trousers was Andy, holding a dozen roses.

"Wow," Emma said. "Are those for me?"

Andy nodded. "Come inside, Emma. We have so much to talk about!"

Chapter 24

Emma stepped into Andy's house and was immediately greeted with the bouquet of roses. She smelled them and smiled then she let Andy place them in a vase he had ready on the kitchen island. The next thing she noticed was the delicious aroma of dinner. It made her mouth water.

"Can I take your jacket?" Andy asked.

Emma nodded her head and let Andy help her remove it. He placed it on a chair and came back to give her a kiss. It was quick and welcoming and then Andy took her hand and led her to the dining room. The table was set for two, complete with candles burning and a bottle of wine chilling. There was soft classical music playing in the background and Emma felt like she was in a five star restaurant.

"Did you cook?" She asked.

Andy smiled. "Well, not exactly. My cook prepared it, but I said that I would serve it."

Andy brought in a large platter that contained roast, potatoes, carrots and onions. Then he carried in a serving dish of rolls and French bread. It was so wonderful and delicious. At first they ate in silence, letting themselves get comfortable with each other again. As they ate, they were finally able to relax a little. Andy said he had so much news to share.

He told her all about his lunch with Greg and Coach Walters. Andy could continue to be a St. Petersburg Shark, only now he would be a coach. He knew his injury would end his pitching career, but it didn't have to derail him completely. Emma was happy for him. Baseball was his life and it was in his blood. She wasn't sure he knew how to be anyone else without baseball.

She asked if this meant he would be staying here for good or would he be returning to Hawaii. At first, Andy planned to return, but now...his life was here. Hawaii was a great retreat, but it wasn't home. This was home.

Then Andy asked her about Atlanta. Would she be staying there? For Emma, Atlanta was home now. She loved her job and wanted to give it a real try. She had only been there a few months and she thought she had a real chance at living her dream. Emma wasn't ready to give up on that right now.

Andy understood. This was the only thing standing in their way, a distance of about five hundred miles. It wasn't the end of the world, lots of couples made it work, but were they a couple? They still hadn't defined what they were. They were living in two different cities going in two different directions, could they ever be one?

"Let me ask you one thing," Andy said, taking her hand. "Do you want this, us?"

Emma smiled. "Yes, I really do. I thought about it a lot and considered what it would be like to leave here tomorrow and say good bye to you as friends and I started to panic, like that would be the end of us and I didn't want that."

"Neither do I, the saying good bye part," Andy joked. "I want us to try and make it work. I want us to be together."

"I love you," Emma said.

"And I love you," Andy replied.

Andy leaned over and kissed her. "Oh, there's more," he announced. "Greg also told me that he shared the songs I had written to some label friends of his, without my knowing, and they liked them. They liked them enough that they want me to record them!"

"What!" Emma exclaimed.

They both stood up and Andy hugged her lifting her feet right off the floor. Then they kissed again, dinner forgotten.

"When am I going to get a chance to hear these songs?" Emma asked.

Andy took her hand and led her to his piano in the living room. He sat down, lifted the cover off the keys and looked over at Emma. She was standing in front of him, watching. Andy looked down at his hands and started playing the melody. Emma was immediately drawn in to the soft notes and then he started singing. His voice was just as soft as the touch of the keys.

> "*Warm embrace*
> *I miss your touch,*
> *Remember your face*
> *Where did she go,*
> *I can break but I am not broken*
> *I can bleed but I let you in,*
> *If you're lost*
> *Call to me*
> *Call to me*
> *I'll come to you.*"

Andy stopped playing and looked up at Emma who had tears in her eyes. It was about her, she knew it. Andy had given her a glimpse inside and it made her sad. His voice was so hauntingly beautiful. It expressed the hurt and hope that only music could show her. Andy was waiting for Emma to respond.

She couldn't speak. Instead she sat down beside him on the bench and kissed him. With arms wrapped around each other in a desperate embrace they let the kiss speak for them. Emma was still so emotional. She stood up and wiped at her eyes.

"I'm so, so sorry," Emma said. "I should have tried to find you."

Andy stood up and rubbed her arms. "It's okay. You were mad and hurt, I didn't expect you to know what happened. I didn't even know what happened until two weeks later."

Emma kept sobbing and Andy held her close. "It's okay. We are okay." After letting Emma dry her tears and calm down, Andy finally asked, "Did you like it?"

Emma laughed through her tears. "I loved it."

"Good," Andy replied.

Andy went back to the table and cleared their dishes. There was still dessert and Andy was determined to keep this date on track. When everything was properly put away into the kitchen, Andy carried out a cheesecake topped with cherries for dessert. It was almost too pretty to eat.

Andy cut a piece for Emma and one for him and instead of taking the first bite, he fed it to Emma. She did the same to Andy. Between each bite, they kissed until they finished their dessert. Emma looked into Andy's eyes and felt so safe and welcome.

"I, uh, haven't gotten the grand tour, yet," Emma said.

Andy smiled and took her hand. He led her through the living room and into his office. This was where he displayed his awards and baseball memorabilia. Impressed, she asked to see more. Andy led her upstairs and Emma followed. He showed her bedrooms and bathrooms and then at the end of the hall he showed her his bedroom.

This room contained absolutely no baseball memorabilia at all, that was reserved for his office. This room was his sanctuary, his escape from the fame and fortune of the baseball world. The large, king-sized bed was the main focus of the room. There was little else besides bedside tables and a dresser. There wasn't even a television.

Emma stood in front of Andy and started to unbutton his shirt. He put his hands on hers to stop her as if asking if this was what she wanted, she continued. Andy waited until she was done and unbuttoned her dress. With shallow breathing, Emma loosened his belt and pants and they were standing inches apart and baring themselves to each other.

Andy pulled her hair back and kissed her neck while Emma's hands ran down his back. His hands moved from her hair to her sides and down to her waist. They kissed until it was no longer enough. Andy laid her on his bed and their hands and mouths explored each other's bodies. It was as if foreplay had lasted months and they were now ready to move forward.

Emma climbed inside the sheets and Andy joined her. They made love into the early hours of the morning, never getting enough of each other. Andy couldn't believe she was really here, in his bed. He had thought about her since the first time she stepped on the field with a microphone in her hand. Back then it was nothing more than lust, this was love.

For Emma, she couldn't stand this egotistical baseball player the first time they met. She had the impression that he was full of himself and saw women as a trophy to be won and paraded around. How wrong she was! She learned that fact right after he drove her home and then helped her brother and her father. Andy was the most sensitive and caring man she had ever known.

Andy's music proved that his talent was never ending. He was showing her things she had never dreamed of before, that a man could be so soft and warm yet passionate and intoxicating. She didn't see how she could ever get enough of him. She also didn't want to think about tomorrow, only tonight.

Andy had never felt so complete in his life before tonight. He had been with plenty of other women but tonight he had bared himself and his soul to this woman and she loved and accepted him. Even his flaws and inadequacies were accepted as part of him. He was not broken or unlovable, he was enough in Emma's eyes.

They fell asleep in each other's arms and remained in bed until Emma felt thirsty. When she stirred, Andy awoke, too. Andy put on sweatpants and Emma put on his white button down shirt he had worn earlier and they walked down to the kitchen. Andy handed her a bottle of water and took one for himself as well.

"Play me another song," Emma said quietly.

Andy obliged. He would do anything for her. They walked to the piano and this time Emma sat next to him, her hand on his thigh. Another soft melody came from the keys and Andy's voice was so emotional.

> "*Standing strong, but empty*
> *Smiling easy, but lost*
> *Call to me, Set me free*
> *Alone, life goes on.*
> *My heart is beating, but broken*
> *My eyes are searching, but blind*
> *Save me, Release me*
> *Alone, life goes on.*"

Life does go on, Andy could attest to that. Since he was a child he felt like he was swimming upstream and being hit by everything life could throw at him, but he didn't break. It molded him into someone he wished his parents were, a strong survivor.

Emma kissed his cheek and laid her head on his shoulder. These were more lyrics about his pain and struggle. She wished she could help him, but it was something he had to work through himself. Maybe music was his therapy. Emma was glad that more people would eventually hear his music and feel his emotion. It was powerful.

Andy put his arm around her and held her. She was helping him more that she would ever know. All his life women had wanted to be with him because of what he could give them, whether it was status or things, but not Emma. Andy had to fight for her and prove he was worthy to be with her. He knew he wasn't but he was glad that she thought so. He was totally and completely hers.

Andy played the piano a little while longer, he couldn't help it. The piano had become his constant companion when he wasn't with Emma. The melody was soothing to her and she didn't interrupt his playing. With her head still leaning on his shoulder, she felt the muscles in his arm move as he played each note. She was melting into him.

When he finally stopped playing, she brought her head up and looked at him. He was smiling and then he kissed her.

"Let's have more dessert," Andy said.

Emma stood up and headed towards the kitchen only to have Andy grab her hand and shake his head.

"Not that way," he said. "Upstairs."

Emma smiled and followed him back up to his room. Neither one of them wanted to think about tomorrow and how they would have to say good bye, they still had tonight and they weren't going to waste a minute together.

Chapter 25

Emma was learning that summers were hot in Atlanta, almost as hot as in St. Petersburg. She had really fit in with her Channel 4 morning crew. They had been able to find a cute hang out place near the studio and got together at least once a week. Emma had really started to feel like she could stay here, if only the thought of Andy didn't keep pulling her home.

Ever since her trip home in April, they had talked often but never had another chance to visit each other. In fact, the longer they stayed apart, the less frequent even their calls were. Emma was worried that their relationship would not be able to withstand the distance after all. She knew that he had been very busy with the Sharks but he used to make time for her, too.

Emma listened for every mention of the Sharks during the daily sports report and smiled when they won. It was all she could do to still feel close to the man she loved. She was torn between enjoying her career and missing Andy. Staying busy was the only thing that helped her. Emma went for walks on the Beltline and joined a book club at the local bookstore. It helped some.

It was her co-worker, Brian, who also wanted to help her stay distracted by asking her out. She always refused but it was clear that he wasn't used to it. Sometimes in an elevator or at her desk his hand would wander where it shouldn't and Emma would have to set him straight. Instead, she called on Pat to do things with her.

Pat was glad to have his best friend back. He would often meet her on her walks and invite her to dinner. She had mentioned to Andy that Pat was still in the picture. He didn't like it but he also knew there was nothing he could do about it. Andy knew that Emma and Pat were friends and he would never be *that* boyfriend who would insist she only have female friends. Emma didn't want to hide anything but she also tried not to bring it up too often.

Atlanta was full of festivals, flea markets and outdoor concerts all summer. It seemed like there was something fun to do every weekend. She always invited Andy to come visit, but his response was always the same, he was too busy. Emma was afraid this would always be the case, no matter what time of the year it was. They would both be busy with something. The problem was, it was never involving the other person.

Emma was beginning to wonder if a long distance relationship would really work after all. It felt like they were drifting further and further apart. The connection they once had when they were together was fading with each passing month. As one month rolled into the next, all of a sudden two months turned into three months since they saw each other last. This was not the kind of relationship Emma wanted or deserved. Were they even still happy? Is this what Andy wanted, too?

It was hard to know because they didn't even talk that often anymore. They were texting or leaving voicemails for each other and Emma even wondered when the last time they talked on the phone was. Emma was getting lonely. One night when she and Pat were at an outdoor concert she told Pat she was missing Andy and feeling very alone.

It was such a warm evening and they were laying on a blanket listening to the music and talking about their week. Pat rolled over to look at her and leaned on one elbow. He was sorry she was so lonely and wanted to know how he could help. She just shrugged and said that she didn't know if anyone could. Then Pat kissed her.

At first Emma wanted to push him away. She didn't think she was saying or doing anything to encourage him or make him think that was what she wanted. But Emma let him kiss her. It did help and it made her feel desired in a way that she missed. After the kiss, Emma sat up and said it was a mistake.

Pat remained quiet, which led Emma to believe that he didn't think it was. Emma stayed only a little while longer until the guilt was too much. She packed up her things and said she had to go. The whole way back to her apartment she felt terrible. Tears were blurring her vision and she went to bed crying into her pillow that night.

Emma cursed Andy for staying away. But wasn't it *her* decision to stay away? She refused to leave Atlanta which was ruining everything. If she would just go back home to St. Pete, this would all be better, right? But she couldn't, not yet. She had dreamt of this anchor job for so long that she wasn't willing to give it up. Emma supposed she had made her choice.

ANDY LOVED BEING ON the field again. The smell of the turf, the sound of the crowd and the crack when the bat hit the ball was as close to heaven as he could imagine. He had come back to life being here on the field. His shoulder was stiff and limited but he didn't let that stop him. He could massage most of the pain away, but the ache in his heart was throbbing and relentless.

Hanging out with the team passed the time but it wasn't how he really wanted to be spending it. He thought of Emma's last night in St. Pete, how they had spent it in his bed. Andy had been trying to contact Emma and talk during the day but their schedules never matched up. It was frustrating because they had promised to make a long distance relationship work but he wondered if they were really trying?

Emma was blaming Andy for not being available and Andy was blaming Emma for pulling away. It seemed like she was becoming more distant and even wondered if she had met someone new...or an ex. Andy was too busy to find someone else. Between morning workouts, afternoon practices and evening games, he barely had time to play his music.

His music was also taking on a life of its own. He was still amazed how a record label was begging him to come in and record another song. They loved the song 'Broken' and were waiting for him to record 'Life Goes On'. Andy was even working on another one. It was more than he could ever imagine and it was all because of Emma.

Andy thought about flying up to visit her but as soon as he made plans, he would have to cancel because something came up with the team, his music or the foundation. He was only one man and he was starting to think it was getting to be too much. He never wanted to lose the joy in any of those things because as soon as they felt like work, he would have to stop.

Right now, baseball was his priority, that was what was paying the bills and keeping the other two in business. Without the Sharks there would be no foundation or the freedom to pursue the music at all. He had to remain loyal to them and to Coach Walters. Andy was grateful that they were giving him a chance at coaching. It was hard at first because his instinct was to walk to the mound.

He could still feel the dirt under his feet and the ball in his hand. The way he watched the catcher and nodded his agreement to a pitch. His stillness as he glanced over his shoulder to hold a runner at first or third. It was in his blood. He could still look out at the stands and wave to the fans, they still wanted his autograph. He was still their MVP.

LIFE GOES ON

When the Sharks were playing the Savannah Storm for three nights in a row, Andy wanted to call Emma. It still meant they were over two hundred miles away, but it was closer than they had ever been geographically in months. They hadn't been talking to each other as often as they had been, so Andy wasn't sure what her reaction would be when he asked her to come see him in Savannah.

He knew it was a risk to be so vulnerable but wasn't this what they were in a relationship for? If they couldn't be open and honest with each other, what was the point of any of this? When they arrived in Savannah, Andy called Emma. At first he wasn't sure what to say. Did he come right out and ask her to come or should he be the one to try and get away?

Andy decided to just tell her. If she asked him to come, he would be on the first flight out, he was sure of it. When Emma answered on the first ring he was startled.

"Hello?" Emma said.

"Hi," Andy replied.

A few seconds of silence before Emma asked, "Is everything okay? How are you?"

"Yes, I'm good, we're in Savannah for three games," Andy replied then added, "I want to see you, Emma."

Emma didn't tell him that she already knew the Sharks were going to Savannah. She could fly there in one hour or she could hop in her car and be there in three hours. Either way, she was waiting for the invitation to come. Emma had the weekend off, so she could have two days and one night with him and she could be packed in ten minutes.

"I'll catch a flight this afternoon," Emma replied.

All afternoon, as Andy helped the players warm up, he kept scanning the stands. He had told her to just come. He left word at security that a reporter was coming and made sure they had Emma

Reese on their list. When Andy finally saw her walking in the stands behind the dugout, he nearly got hit in the head with a ball.

"Hey, sorry...continue to practice with one of the other coaches..." Andy told the player as he threw down his mitt and ran to Emma. Coach Walters was giving her a hug and escorting her down onto the field. To Andy she had never looked more beautiful. She was wearing white denim jeans and her Sharks jersey with her hair up in a ponytail.

Andy's hug lifted her feet off the ground. He even swung her around as she let out a holler to put her down. The other team members who knew her came over to say hello, too, until Andy took her hand and went to a quiet corner of the field and kissed her. They had waited months to be able to hold each other like this. It had been agonizing to be apart, but all of that hurt and frustration was forgotten in that moment. They were together again, even if it was for only one night.

When the game started, Emma was given a chair right behind the dugout. She had the perfect view of the action and of Andy. He was the first base coach and it took all of his concentration not to take his focus off the game and look at Emma. He still couldn't believe she was there! Luckily, the Sharks were getting plenty of hits, so Andy stayed busy at first base.

He was good at reading the pitcher and in telling the runner when he was faking a throw. It was the small nuances of being a pitcher in his former life that helped him now coach. Andy was a natural. If he couldn't pitch again, at least he could be a part of the action on the field. He had already gotten plenty of guys to steal second base in this game.

The Sharks were winning. It was now the bottom of the ninth and the Storm had the home field advantage of batting last. The score was three to two. The Storm could tie it up now or even pull out a win. The Shark's pitcher on the mound was doing his best, but Andy

LIFE GOES ON

could tell he was tired. The speed wasn't there anymore and he was taking too long between pitches. He would shake off too many that the catcher was showing him and it was now down to the player at bat.

There was no one on base and there were two outs. The batter was a strong hitter but he already had a three balls and two strikes count against him. Andy hoped his pitcher had one more strike in him to end this inning and the game. As he leaned down and focused on the catcher, he shook off the signal he received. Andy didn't like that.

Finally, the wind up. The pitcher raised his knee and extended his arm and the ball was released. All eyes were on the catcher's glove as he caught it and held steady. The umpire leaned down and with his arm outstretched and yelled, "Strike!". It was over. The Sharks pulled out a win in their first of three games. It was always a glorious victory when it came during an away game.

The Sharks fans who were in the stands cheered, the rest were silent and headed for their cars. Andy looked for Emma but she was already on the field and making her way to him. Again, they hugged and her feet were lifted off the ground. They kissed and then joined the celebration with the rest of the team.

As the players cleared the stadium and headed back to their hotels, Andy took Emma to the hotel restaurant and ordered some drinks. They both got iced tea and cheesecake.

"Don't you want something more celebratory, champagne perhaps?" Emma asked with a smile.

"I don't drink anymore," Andy said after taking a bite of the cheesecake.

Emma considered this for a moment. This was new information and wondered why he decided now. "Why?"

"I just don't want to," Andy replied. "There was nothing good about drinking. I didn't like how I acted when I drank, it made me more…I don't know…angry maybe."

Emma didn't comment further. She wondered if it also had something to do with his father but didn't say anything more about it. They ate their cheesecake and Andy paid the bill.

"Do you need to get a room or are you okay with staying in mine?" Andy asked. It was an awkward question and he felt strange asking his girlfriend if she wanted her own room, but he wasn't sure what she wanted anymore.

"No, I want to stay with you," Emma replied.

Andy took her hand and they went up the elevator to his room.

Chapter 26

Their night together was just as they remembered. They kissed, cuddled and talked before the physical closeness was too much for them. Andy and Emma surrendered to the passion they had been hiding and denying for months. This was still new to them and they had to get used to each other all over again.

They managed to get some sleep during the night and when the sun coming in the window woke them up, it was with a realization that Emma had to get back to Atlanta. She could stay a little while longer, maybe see some of their warm up, but she had to get back to the studio. They were quiet through breakfast and on the ride to the stadium. Emma still wondered if a night together every few months was enough to keep them together and their relationship alive.

She felt like she was holding him back, keeping him from a real and physical relationship with someone back home. When they were together, they were great...but was it enough? Andy made her feel special and included but how long could he keep it up. She didn't want to be the one to question their longevity, she would wait until he needed more from her than she was willing to give.

As much as she missed him and St. Pete, she still wasn't willing to give up Atlanta. She had worked too hard to get there and she couldn't give it up now, not even for Andy. He understood, they had discussed it last night in the wee hours of the morning. Andy was willing to let her live her dream, he would wait and they would figure it out.

Emma watched Andy on the field doing what he loved, playing baseball. She didn't want to dwell on the reasons why he wasn't on the pitchers mound, it was still too painful. Emma never brought it up, never even mentioned his father although Andy did in passing, saying he was doing good in Hawaii. She nodded and wished him well, what else could she do?

Andy watched Emma check her watch and knew she had to leave for the airport soon. They had only been able to spend a few hours together, but that precious time meant so much to both of them. Who knew when they would get the opportunity again? It could be months. Emma came down on the field to tell Andy her ride was here, she had to go.

Andy thought this was the hardest goodbye he had ever experienced, he didn't want to let her go. They hugged, kissed and then she was gone. Andy tried to get back to practice but his head just wasn't in it. He went into the dugout and closed his eyes, he needed to regroup and focus. They still had two more games in Savannah before heading home. He couldn't let anything prevent them from reaching their goal, not even Emma.

After a few moments to collect himself, Andy returned to the field and continued with warm ups. It wasn't until the game started that Andy got the text that she had made it home safely. He was grateful for that and replied to her text thanking her for coming out to see him. They texted back and forth for a few minutes before they each had to get back to work.

If he didn't have the texts as evidence, he might have convinced himself that it was all a dream. The Sharks ended up losing the second game but won their third. It was a bitter sweet ending to their time in Savannah. Andy had good memories, no matter whether they won or lost. Emma called to congratulate him and promised that they would see each other soon. Andy wanted to believe it was true.

EMMA HAD BEEN GLUED to the television each night that the Sharks played the Storm. Every once in a while she would catch a glimpse of Andy on screen. She agonized along with him when they lost, but cheered when they won their final game in Savannah. She longed to be with him and had to admit that the time apart was harder to bear with each passing week.

Emma had invited Pat over for the second game but after he tried to kiss her again, she asked him to leave and didn't invite him back. She was angry with herself for putting herself in such a vulnerable situation with him. She would have a talk with Pat so that he understood her boundaries better. Pat could not cross that line or she would cut ties with him completely.

The following week was busy for Emma and she was thankful for the chaos. It kept her mind occupied with other things besides Andy. There was a protest on the streets of Atlanta and crews were covering it day and night. Emma had to provide breaking news reports and needed to be ready at the studio in a moments notice. By the end of the week, it was taking a toll on her. Some nights she didn't even go home, she just slept on a couch in the lounge.

Emma did love the excitement of it, though. This was why she loved journalism. Real stories of things that mattered to the people. There would always be crimes in small groups or neighborhoods, those were everywhere but they didn't usually involve a whole community of people. Immediate families were devastated and Emma always sympathized every time they had to report on another death or injury. This protest was ever changing, fluid and evolving. It was as if it was alive and growing.

Emma was just on air reporting that more streets were being blocked off so that the police could set up a perimeter for the community's safety. She was walking back to the lounge to get more coffee, and maybe lay down for a few minutes, before the evening news when a group of female interns came in watching something on their phone. They were laughing and giggling about a cute singer who was suddenly very popular according to them.

"I can't stop listening to it," one girl said.

"I can't stop watching him!" Another replied.

"Play it again, play it again," a third girl insisted.

Emma was laying on the couch with her eyes closed when a familiar melody floated across the room. She knew those piano notes and chords. Then when Andy's voice started singing, Emma sat up.

"*Standing strong, but empty. Smiling easy, but lost. Call to me, Set me free. Alone, Life goes on...*" Andy's voice sang through the girl's phone.

"I wonder who he wrote it for," the first girl said.

"Whoever she is, she's stupid for not staying with him," the second girl added.

"I read that he used to be a famous baseball player," the third one replied.

All three girls left and Emma sat straight up in the silent room. She didn't notice the tears that flowed until they dripped on her hand. She wiped at her eyes and felt terrible. Yes, she was the one who left him, she was the reason he wrote sad songs about being empty and alone. Emma grabbed more tissues and let the tears fall.

The song had been released and Andy Anderson was, again, a household name. Fans were flocking to the baseball stadium to see the songwriter who wrote such heartfelt songs. Women wanted his autograph, his picture and to give him their phone numbers. It was just like the days when he was famous for being an MVP pitcher, but this was different. This was his heart on his sleeve and it was a little frightening to Andy.

Andy's record label had warned him that the song would be played everywhere, then the next song. Eventually Andy would record an album and they assured him it would be a success if the reaction from the first song was any indication. Outlets around

Florida, the United States and the world were clamoring to get Andy Anderson to come and perform on their stages. Soon Andy would have to make a decision about where he wanted his life to go.

Baseball required his complete attention for more than half a year. Could music wait? Would baseball? Andy wasn't ready for that kind of definitive answer. For now he was walking a tight rope and hoped that the whirlwind of attention didn't knock him down.

Emma had to admit that when she heard his song on the radio for the first time she was proud of him. Even though the whole road that led him to that point was built on tragedy and heartbreak, he was successful and loved by millions for it. And Emma loved him, too. She had almost wished the love would fade or disappear altogether so that she wouldn't have to make a decision.

It was clear now what her decision must be, for her own life and sanity. She couldn't live like this anymore with one foot in Atlanta and the other in St. Petersburg, it wasn't fair to either of them. She prayed about it and considered all of the consequences of her decision and it was clear that there was only one. Only one thing she could do that would make both of their lives better and allow them to move on.

Emma looked for her phone and went to her contacts. She scrolled until she found the person she needed to talk to first. It would finally put an end to all of the guessing and confusion that surrounded her relationship with Andy. She had been putting it off long enough and now was the time. Emma took a deep breath before dialing the number and waiting for it to be answered. She was nervous but knew this was the right thing to do.

"Hello?"

"Hello, Liane," Emma said, "we need to talk."

Chapter 27

Only Liane Lincoln knew Emma was arriving today. Emma drove straight to the Channel 2 newsroom and had to get a visitor's pass from the front desk. How odd to be walking back here after nearly a year! It was mid-September and the hot, Florida air was still humid. She was glad she had just worn a short dress with a light sweater today.

As Emma made her way up the elevator to the newsroom, she started to feel her anxiety return. It had come and gone over the last few days as this meeting approached, but now that it was here, it was almost overwhelming. As the elevator doors opened, she stepped hesitantly out onto the third floor and down the hallway. It was Miriam who spotted her first and squealed with delight at the sight of her old friend. Don looked up and they both hurriedly made their way to her.

After hugs and greetings they asked why she was there. She was surprised that Liane hadn't mentioned it to anyone. Emma never told her to keep it a secret, so it was odd that she had. She informed them that she had a meeting and would chat and catch up when she came out.

"Wait...a meeting with Liane?" Miriam asked. "Are you coming back?" Miriam was jumping up and down with the potential return of her best friend.

Emma simply smiled. "I will see you when I get out."

She looked back at Miriam and Don who where both beaming with giddiness as Emma approached Liane's office. Through the glass, Liane waved her in and gestured to the chair.

"So, what is this I hear about a possible return?" Liane asked.

"Well, I have been following the recent staff changes here at Channel 2 and I noticed that one of your morning news anchors has announced her retirement at the end of the month. I want that job," Emma said.

"What about Atlanta?" Liane asked, leaning back in her leather chair.

"I am willing to leave if I can have this position," Emma replied.

Both women sat back in their chairs with arms crossed. What Emma didn't know was that Liane had already submitted her name for consideration for the position. It was hers if she wanted it. Emma had simply beat her to the punch. Liane tried her best to look uninterested and asked a few more questions about the logistics of such a move and wondered how quickly she could be available.

Emma assured her that she would handle all of the necessary arrangements. She was only wanting to know if it was possible to apply for that opening. Liane shifted in her seat and shuffled papers on her desk. Emma wondered if it was already too late, had she waited too long to ask about it. She didn't want her former boss to know how badly she wanted it but she had to know. Finally, Liane handed Emma a document that she asked her to read over.

As Emma read, she realized it was a contract. She looked up at Liane in disbelief.

"Is this...is it...?" Emma started.

"That is a contract," Liane said with a smile. "A legal document that you read and if you agree to the terms, you sign at the bottom."

Emma smiled. She knew what a contract was, she needed clarification that it was for her. "So this means I have the job?"

"If you want it," Liane teased.

Emma signed the paper and handed it back to her boss. Her boss. Emma was an official staff member and news anchor of Channel 2 news in St. Petersburg, Florida. She calmly stood up and shook Liane's hand. A wave of relief washed over her as she turned to leave the room.

"Thank you," Emma said and walked back out into the hallway.

Miriam and Don motioned for her to be quiet but to join them near the studio. They whispered to her that the timing was so odd for her to be here today. Emma wasn't sure what they meant or why they were whispering until she saw the 'on air' sign lit up, they had an in-studio guest that was being interviewed. Miriam glanced at Emma with an anxious look and then Emma realized what was happening.

There was a reporter on one chair and Andy Anderson on another and he was being interviewed in their studio. A piano was off to the side with a spotlight on it. Emma couldn't take her eyes off the guest.

"Well, we would like to thank you, Andy Anderson, for coming in today and speaking with us," the reporter asked.

"Thank you for having me," Andy replied.

"There is a lot of excitement around this new single because it has just skyrocketed to the top of the charts. And, in the midst of your successful music career, you are back with the Sharks. How are you able to manage both careers?" The reporter asked.

Andy wiped his hands on his pants, Emma could tell he was nervous. "Well, it isn't easy right now. I never really expected my songs to be loved by so many people. I really only wrote them for myself and maybe one other person, but I'm glad people are embracing them."

"Of course your songs are loved, almost as much as you are loved as the MVP of the World Series. It's amazing to us that St. Pete is now home to our own singing baseball player. What do your teammates think of all this extra fame?" She asked.

Emma could tell that Andy was getting embarrassed by this line of questioning, but he had always been good at interviews. "I get teased about it a little, but they know it's something that I love, so they support me very much."

"How did you feel when you were nominated for two Grammys? I think one was for Best New Artist and the other for Best New Single."

"I was honored. I owe all my success to someone very special and none of this means anything without her," Andy said.

"Well, maybe she's watching you right now as you get ready to perform you new single, 'Stronger Together.' Everyone, Mr. Andy Anderson."

Andy stood up and waved at the camera. He walked over to the piano, sat down and took a deep breath. Emma didn't realize she had been holding her breath until the reporter mentioned a Grammy. How did she not know he was nominated for Grammys? Why didn't Andy tell her?

The lights around the studio dimmed and all eyes were on Andy as he sat in the spotlight with the piano. Emma watched as Andy started to play and listened as the words he sang were directed at her.

"There were moments in my life when I was scared
Of being unworthy of you,
I would close my eyes and dream of a day
You could see me as complete.
But not today
But I'm on my way
We are stronger together.
I am still searching for a reason to be loved
Then you came along and believed in me,
I'm on my knees praying for truth
You gave me the strength to run to you
Today is the day

> *I'm on my way*
> *We are stronger together."*

Andy stood up to a few applause in the studio. He thanked everyone for their time and the interview and performance was over. Emma wiped at the tears that had fallen during Andy's performance. She had never heard that song before and it was achingly beautiful. As Andy left the studio and entered the hallway, he stopped in his tracks at the sight of Emma.

"Emma!" Andy exclaimed. "What are you doing here? How did you know I'd be here?"

"I didn't," Emma replied. "Why didn't you tell me?"

Andy and Emma looked at each other with love and hurt in their eyes. Andy took her hand and led her into an empty office to talk. But first, Andy held her. Still trying to control her tears, Emma felt secure in Andy's arms. They had so much to talk about but this was not the place.

Andy held Emma's face in his hands and angled it up to meet his gaze. "Everything will be okay. Let's meet tonight to talk, I don't want to discuss this here."

Emma nodded her head and he kissed her. She returned his embrace and then they each stepped back. The shock and joy melting into calm and happiness. Emma suggested they meet at Salty Waves tonight because she had a lot to say and she may as well have everyone together. Andy felt a little nervous at the mention of an announcement but he agreed.

After Andy left, Miriam and Don waited for Emma to fill them in on her little secret. "So...why are you here?" Miriam asked.

Emma smiled as she announced, "I am going to be the new Channel 2 morning news anchor."

More squeals and jumping from all of them as they welcomed their long lost friend back to St. Pete. It was so unexpected but desperately needed. Miriam never did find anyone else to hang out with the way she did with Emma.

"We need to celebrate! Let's go to Ferg's tonight," Miriam said.

"Sorry, I can't tonight," Emma said. "I'm meeting my family for dinner."

Miriam looked over and Don and added, "And Andy?"

Emma blushed slightly. "Yes, and Andy."

They were too happy for her to be mad. "Okay, fine, another time."

Emma agreed and left. She had so much to prepare for moving back home which included finding a place to live. All of her preparations could wait a little while longer. For now, she wanted to see her father. After being away for about four months, she was sure he had made more progress and was probably mad that she didn't come home more often. It was a promise she had broken.

Emma walked into Sunnyside Home and gave Sam a hug. He was so excited to see her. Emma missed these small moments to, of walking in here and seeing familiar faces or hearing the laughter of the children playing a game in the corner. It was like coming home. Emma walked to her father's room and leaned on the doorframe. When Joe looked up, he half expected to see his physical therapist but when he realized it was Emma, he stood up and hugged her.

She apologized right away for not coming more often. The good news was that she never had to break that promise again because she was moving back. Joe was so excited he hugged her again then asked her to tell him the whole story. Emma did, even the part about arriving at the studio and running into Andy.

"That wasn't luck or chance," Joe replied. "It was fate."

Emma shrugged her shoulders. She wasn't sure about that. Secretly, she suspected Liane had a hand in which day and time the meeting was scheduled, but she liked the sound of 'fate' better.

Maybe she was wrong, maybe it was the universe telling them that they were supposed to see each other at that moment.

All Emma knew was that she and her father were to meet Andy at the Salty Waves in an hour and she and her father had so much to talk about. She also wanted to hear all about his progress. He was using his left side so much more than before and it made Emma smile. The Sunnyside Home had done so much for Joe and it was all thanks to Andy and his foundation.

It really all came back to Andy, didn't it? In the end, Atlanta didn't work out. She gave it a good try but the pull to come home was just too great. She was missing out on the lives of her loved ones and that wasn't worth all the money in the bank. Not to mention she had a nephew that was going to be born soon and she wouldn't miss it for the world.

Chapter 28

James showed everyone to a reserved table in the back of the restaurant. Salty Waves was busy for late September. There had been talk of a possible hurricane on track to enter the Gulf of Mexico but today was business as usual. Emma and Joe joined Andy and Joanne at the table and hugs and greetings were shared. It felt good to Emma to be back with family and Joanne looked like she could be giving birth at any minute!

"How much longer, Joanne?" Andy asked, having not seen her in months either.

Joanne rubbed her large belly. "Two weeks, but I'm ready now."

Everyone laughed but all eyes were on Emma. It was clear that everyone really wanted to ask Emma why she was here, but it was just so refreshing to be back in the Salty Waves that she wasn't ready to talk about it yet.

"Do you think I could get a soda?" Emma asked James.

"Of course, what would everyone like?" James asked the group.

With drink orders taken, the focus was back on Emma who took a deep breath and started to explain her sudden appearance. Emma started by saying how much she loved Atlanta and tried hard to make it work. She had explored the city, tried to make new friends and embraced her new job but...something was always missing.

When she quickly mentioned Pat, she glanced at Andy to see his reaction. It was nearly imperceptible, but Emma noticed the few extra blinks at his name. Emma had been honest with him about everything except the kiss, but her family wasn't aware they had been hanging out. Emma continued to explain that even with all that Atlanta had to offer, her heart was calling her back home to St. Petersburg.

It had been easier to stop communicating as often then to let the homesickness grow. If she didn't remember the people she left behind then she couldn't miss them. What she didn't count on was the strength of the tether that kept her bound to St. Pete. In the end, it felt more like she was running away from something or someone then running to anything. Until she allowed herself to reevaluate the reasons why she was in Atlanta in the first place, she would never be able to fully accept it.

As Emma looked at her family around the table, and Andy, she was reminded why she needed to return home. These people were more important to her than anything else in the world.

"So what will you do?" James asked Emma.

"Well, I accepted a new position at Channel 2 News," she replied. "I will be their new morning anchor very soon."

They all congratulated her but it was Andy who looked like he just won another MVP award.

"Really?" Andy asked. "Are you serious? You're home for good?" He couldn't believe it. It was something he had dreamed about but never thought it would happen. Andy would never have asked her to move back home, that was a decision she had to make on her own but he was filled with joy that she had finally decided.

Emma looked at him and nodded her confirmation. Andy took her in his arms and held her. His life may have given him an equal amount of things to be bitter about and proud of, but Emma was his center of gravity in it all. With Emma by his side, Andy felt he could weather any storm life threw at him...and she was back by his side.

"This is fantastic news, Emma," Joanne said. "Now I have a babysitter."

More laughter filled with love enveloped the table and Emma certainly felt it today. Part of her was frustrated with how long it took her to realize she needed to come home, she had missed so many important events in her loved one's lives, which reminded her about Andy's big news.

"Hey, what's this I hear about a Grammy?" Emma asked Andy.

Andy blushed and ran a hand through his hair. He was still very uncomfortable with the whole topic and now he had everyone at the table watching him so intently.

"Yes, well, apparently it's really happening," Andy replied. "I have been nominated and now I have to go to the Grammys. I was just hoping someone might want to come with me."

Emma looked at him with something that resembled fear. "Me? You want me to accompany you on a red carpet at the Grammys?" She could feel her heart racing already.

"You have time to think about it, they aren't until February, but I would very much like it if you did," Andy replied.

Emma remained silent as the idea of walking a red carpet on the arm of Andy Anderson suddenly came into focus, she would be just like one of the girls she made fun of in those magazines. But she knew this would be different, they were in love and he wanted her to be there with him. How could she refuse? Andy was asking her to be by his side on one of the most important nights of his life.

"That's great news," Joe said. "I need to hear these songs."

"I will be sure to get you a copy," Andy responded. "I'll get you all copies."

James brought food out from the kitchen even though no one ordered anything. He said it was his way of celebrating this occasion. So many wonderful things were happening to his family that he couldn't help but offer food, his love language. James considered Andy part of their family and it was Joanne who cleared her throat to speak next.

"Andy," she started. "James and I want to ask you for a favor."

"Anything," Andy replied without hesitation.

"Will you be our son's Godfather?" Joanne asked Andy.

Andy's sudden intake of breath made everyone aware that he was not expecting that as the favor. "Are you sure?"

James and Joanne laughed. "Andy, we wouldn't be asking you if we weren't sure. Besides, Emma already agreed to be his Godmother."

Andy looked at Emma and she nodded. Andy was feeling emotional. He had grown up without this type of family bond and he had never really known what he had missed all those years, but he was learning. He had come to terms with Sam probably not getting married and having a family and part of him had even given up on himself. It was Emma who was showing him a whole new life he never dreamed of before. Andy was part of a family again.

"Yes, I would be honored," Andy replied.

Joanne looked relieved when he finally answered. After watching the wave of emotions play out on his face, she wasn't completely sure he would agree. Now Joanne could lean back in her chair knowing that everything was ready for their son, they were as prepared as they could be for their baby. She could relax a little more for the next couple of weeks.

"Great," Joanne said. "Thank you."

Attention was then turned back on Emma. "Where will you be living?" Joe asked his daughter.

Emma had thought about it but she didn't want to decide now, at first she thought she might like to live in her old neighborhood in Pinellas Park, but now that everyone was in St. Pete, she might like to look closer to the beach. "I'm not sure, yet," she replied.

Andy wanted to offer her to move in with him, but that was a conversation for when they were alone, not in front of her entire family. He was afraid to make her feel like she was being rushed into a relationship, but the fact was he had so many unused bedrooms that it seemed silly for her to waste money on rent. But Andy also knew that Emma was very independent and would do whatever she wanted to do. Andy could live with that.

"Well, there's an extra bedroom at Sunnyside Home, right Andy?" Joe said.

"Yes," he replied.

"There you go," Joe responded. "You have a few different options. I just want you to feel welcome and at home."

"Thanks, dad," Emma replied. "And thanks, everyone. I do. I feel so welcome and I'm grateful for all of your love and support. You helped me feel like this decision to come back to St. Pete wasn't seen as a failure, but just another step in my journey and I'm so grateful for that."

They all assured her that they had been proud of her journey to Atlanta as well as her journey that brought her back to them. They would never think of her as failing at anything, she was the toughest fighter they knew. Without her perseverance, Joe would still be in the old and dirty facility in a wheelchair and James would have shut the doors to the Salty Waves months ago. Emma always put her family first and they were proud to see her put herself first for a change.

James brought over a key lime pie he made earlier and they all had a piece while still digesting all of the news from their dinner. There were still things to work out and questions to be answered but it didn't matter. They would figure things out together because that's what families did. Andy was eager to have some time alone with Emma, so after pie and coffee, he suggested they take a walk on the beach.

Andy took her hand and they walked down to the water. The gulf was still warm and they took off their shoes and let the water wash over their feet. Emma inhaled deeply and looked out over the horizon. The wind carried her hair in all directions.

"Still no pirates," she said.

Andy tried to decipher what she meant but couldn't. "What?" Andy finally asked.

"Pirates," Emma said matter-of-factly. "You know, stories our parents tell us about pirates coming to invade for buried treasure and if we didn't behave they would take us away."

Andy simply shook his head. "Nope."

"You never heard them?" Emma was surprised.

"Emma, you have to remember that my childhood was very different then yours," Andy began. "I grew up listening to fighting and cursing, then wondering when someone was going to go grocery shopping that week. We never sat around and encouraged each other or shared fun stories...." His voice trailed off. There were so many things Andy missed out on but he had never dwelled on them before, not until it was shown to him how it could have been.

Still watching the horizon, Emma gave Andy a side hug and leaned into him. She hated to hear about his childhood and how much horror he had lived through and survived. It always impressed her how, even after all he had been through, he managed to turn into such a giving and empathetic man. He had such strong faith in people despite what he knew they were capable of.

"I love you," Emma said softly but loud enough to be heard over the waves.

"I love you, too." Andy replied. "And I want you to know that I always have a bedroom available for you, no pressure, just a bedroom. It can be temporary or permanent, it is completely up to you."

This time Emma turned to face him with both arms around his waist and laid her head on his chest. She had so much to be thankful for and Andy was always at the center of it. "Thank you for the offer. I will think about it."

That was all Andy needed to hear. He offered her an option and it was now up to her to accept it or not. He would not take it as an acceptance or rejection of him personally, he was smart enough to know that she needed to feel independent. Emma had to figure out her own future and how she would live it. Until then, Andy would be her biggest cheerleader.

"So, where are you staying tonight?" Andy asked her.

"Um, tonight? I'm not exactly sure," Emma replied.

"How about I show you one of those bedrooms I was offering," Andy teased.

Emma looked up at him. "Why Mr. Anderson, are you trying to bribe me?"

"Yes, ma'am, is it working?" Andy asked with a smile.

"We can discuss it after the bedroom tour," Emma replied.

Chapter 29

Andy was standing in his kitchen making scrambled eggs while wearing his boxer shorts when Emma entered the kitchen. She kissed him and then sat down to wait until he was finished cooking. There was an entire spread of toast, fruit, bacon and juice already laid out on the dining room table. Andy had been up for a few hours and had decided to make breakfast.

He had to leave for a few days because the Sharks were playing some away games in the playoffs. They had to travel to Nashville but he would be back home in a few days. Emma was welcome to stay at his house until she got settled in her own place, if that was what she still wanted to do. She thanked him and said she had already booked some appointments to look at places for the next couple of days, so it worked out fine for both of them.

Maybe she would even be in her new rental when he returned. Part of him didn't want her to ever leave, but he knew this was what she wanted and he would support her. She would also use that time to visit her friends and catch up on lost time. She had asked Liane for some time off before she started her new position and she allowed it. There was no hurry or time frame for her to get settled. As long as she was ready to work when she needed to be.

After breakfast Andy had to pack and get ready to leave for Nashville. Baseball season was winding down but Andy wasn't confident that they would make it to the World Series this year. There was always a possibility, but not a strong one. Andy knew it wasn't only because he wasn't on the mound this season, but he knew it was definitely a factor. Maybe next year they would make it.

Andy wasn't sure what his future looked like with the St. Petersburg Sharks. He played a vital role, but he was also aware that other people could fill in as a coach, too. He was replaceable. Andy wasn't sure he wanted or needed to be a Shark anymore. He hadn't mentioned this to anyone yet because he still wasn't sure about it himself. The Grammy nominations really surprised him and it could be a way for him to transition into something not so physical anymore. Andy wasn't getting any younger and now he had options.

He had a lot to think about during the next few days. He knew he wanted more time with Emma now that she was back and he didn't want to let her get away again. He was eager to have another dinner together and maybe even go to an actual restaurant but it would have to wait. He couldn't wait to make more plans with Emma, but he also didn't want to scare her off.

IN NASHVILLE, ANDY did not have much free time to call or video chat with Emma. She was either busy with her day or Andy was warming up on the field. His arm felt good but would always have limitations. It was the only physical remnant of the crash, the rest was all mental. His father would call to let him know his progress and when he received another token. Andy was proud of his hard work but also a little resentful that it took so long. If he had only done this ten, twenty or thirty years ago...

His mother, on the other hand, had been working on herself since she left. Wendy had gotten a job, her own place and found a therapist that listened to her. Andy would never understand what would make a mother leave her family and never look back, but she was part of Sam's life and that was probably a good thing. Andy was still trying to understand why his parents were the way they were, even if he were to forgive them he would probably never understand it. Everyone had their own demons to live with, some never got past them.

Andy's job right now was to get through this baseball season. The Sharks won one game out of three, which took them out of the running for the World Series. The team felt deflated after such a great season last year, but that was the fickleness of the game. Andy understood it and it was also partly the reason he was willing to finally step away from it for good.

After his career-ending injury as a pitcher gave him another shot as a coach, it just wasn't the same. Andy knew it would be a struggle to feel satisfied with the shift, but he was realizing now that it just was not enough anymore. For some people, he was living the dream, but he took the job thinking this was all he could be, a base line coach. His world was opening up now in ways he never expected and he was excited to follow this new path.

His record label was wanting him to devote more time to recording and he was having to shift and juggle them around his baseball schedule. Maybe it was time to jump in and see how it all played out full time. Emma had tried it and he was proud of her courage, why couldn't he? He would have to sit down and have a serious conversation with Coach Walters soon about his future as part of the team.

WHILE ANDY WAS AWAY in Nashville for a few days, Emma took that time to find a place of her own. She appreciated Andy's help and hospitality, but she didn't want to be dependent on him for her housing or for anything. She wanted her own sanctuary back where she could relax and invite people in or keep people out. Emma wanted control back in her life. Her and Andy were just getting back into a relationship and it didn't feel right to be under the same roof, yet. Maybe in time that would be something they could consider, but not now.

Her realtor took her to several rentals on the beach. They looked all the way up the Treasure Coast from St. Pete Beach to Clearwater and it had become overwhelming. She wanted to be convenient to everyone and ultimately decided on a cute beach bungalow on Indian Rocks Beach. She was halfway between Andy and James which made her feel connected again.

She was able to move in right away and had her things delivered the following day. She invited Miriam over to help her unpack and also to catch up. Emma also just needed some girl time. Miriam thought she was crazy for not moving in with Andy in his huge mansion on the beach, but ultimately she understood why she didn't. She would rather have her small, cozy place on the beach then be dependent on anyone, too.

Miriam told her all about her latest boyfriend. Emma hadn't kept up with how many there had been since she left last time, so she just nodded and agreed when Miriam said he was the perfect guy. Emma had confidence that Miriam would in fact find the perfect guy, but she wasn't sure if this one was it or not. Miriam also gave her the scoop on what had been happening in the newsroom since she left and Emma laughed at all the drama.

They were so excited to be working together again, but their schedules might be slightly different now that Emma would be a morning news anchor. Either way, they would see each other everyday again. Emma talked about Atlanta and even told her everything about Pat, including the fact that he kissed her.

"Are you going to tell Andy?" Miriam asked.

"I don't think so, what good would come out of it," Emma said. "It didn't mean anything and it's in the past." Emma had been confident in her decision, but Miriam was making her question it.

Miriam wasn't so sure that Pat would keep it in the past and she was worried that if Emma didn't tell Andy, he might find out some other way. That would be much worse. They each decided to stay out of each other's love life unless specifically asked to give advice so they just unboxed items and put them away. Miriam was concerned for her friend, but she wouldn't say anything, it was her decision.

When the women took a break in the afternoon, they were impressed with the progress they had made. The kitchen, bedroom and living room were pretty much done and items put away. She could get her bathroom organized and pantry ready later. Emma decided to order pizza so they could sit out on the back porch and admire the view. They had worked hard and now it was time to relax.

Emma had beach access and a pretty decent view of the water. For her price range, it was as good as she could get. For Emma, it was perfect. She could envision herself having her morning coffee on the back porch, dinner at the kitchen table and having Andy spend the night in her cozy little bedroom overlooking the water. She was glad she stayed firm in wanting her own place. She wanted Andy to feel welcome, but she also wanted the freedom of being alone when she needed to be.

Miriam stayed a couple more hours before she finally had to leave. They had done a fantastic job at getting her place in order and Emma thanked her for coming over. Emma had enjoyed the help and also Miriam's friendship. There were only small items to be organized, but the larger things were done. They agreed to meet up for dinner in a few days and Emma thanked her again before she drove away. Andy should be getting in later tonight and they agreed to meet up tomorrow.

Seeing him again soon was a luxury she never wanted to take for granted. She had gone months knowing she couldn't be with him or touch him, but now he was within reach, even if he went away for a few days, he would be back. Thinking of him now, she longed to hold him and feel his arms around her. She played his songs and it made him feel closer to her. His words were so raw and emotional, it was like he was telling her his deepest fears and biggest dreams.

Emma hoped she fit into those dreams somehow. She wanted to build a future with him and now that she was settling back home, it was a good time to have a long conversation about it. Emma moved around her bungalow from room to room admiring their handiwork. She felt comfortable here and sat on the couch with a blanket and turned on the television. She found an old movie on television and went to make some popcorn.

It felt like her other apartment, but knowing that she was close to family and friends made her smile with contentment. She could picture herself running over to babysit for James and Joanne or if they needed extra help, she could be at the Salty Waves in no time. And if she needed Andy to come fix something, he could be there quickly, too. She felt safe.

Emma was longing to hear Andy's voice but sent him a text instead, just in case he couldn't talk. He knew they were coming back soon but maybe he was surrounded by teammates. She asked him how things went and how he was feeling. She already knew they lost a couple of the games, even watched some of them, but she wanted him to know she was thinking about him.

It was a little while until Andy texted back saying that he was fine, had to run a couple errands on his way home, but he was home now. They confirmed meeting up tomorrow and Emma smiled. Emma also texted Joanne to check on her and make sure she hadn't run off to the hospital without telling her. Joanne laughed and said that she was still at home, no baby yet. She also confirmed that Emma would be one of the first to know when the time came.

Satisfied that all of her loved ones were okay, Emma still longed to hear Andy's voice. She decided to call him since he had said he was home now. She imagined him coming home to an empty house, especially since she was there when he left and now moved out when he got home, she felt bad. It wasn't that late, so he should still be up. Emma pulled out her phone and dialed Andy. It rang a few times before it was answered.

"Hello?"

Emma immediately hung up because even though she dialed Andy's number, she could tell that it was a woman who answered.

Chapter 30

Andy woke up still exhausted from yesterday. He had a long day of travel and then as soon as he got into town he received an unexpected message. Andy had been too tired to argue or refuse, so he did what was being asked of him and would deal with it in the morning. Well, it was the morning and Andy couldn't even find his phone.

He put on a t-shirt and sweatpants that he found on the nearby chair and walked downstairs. As soon as he saw her sitting on the couch, it was all coming back to him from the night before.

"Good morning, Andy," she said.

"Good morning," Andy replied politely.

As Andy made his way to the kitchen, he kept looking back at her. He was still a little confused how his mother ended up on his couch last night and was not looking forward to having any sort of in-depth conversation about it, either. He needed coffee first.

"Are you hungry?" Andy asked.

"I'll have some coffee, if that's okay," Wendy replied.

Wendy walked slowly into the kitchen and sat at one of the chairs around the island. She watched as her eldest son poured them both a cup of coffee and then waited. Andy noticed a small book that she always carried and even now she was reluctant to put it down when he handed her the cup. Wendy took a sip and then looked up at Andy.

"Thank you for...picking me up last night," Wendy said. She knew he did it out of obligation, but she also felt like he deserved an explanation.

"You're welcome," Andy replied.

"I've been staying with a friend lately and, well...he passed away," Wendy's voice grew soft and quiet. "He was so kind to me, he took me in when I had no where else to go."

Andy straightened up and inhaled deeply. He was in no mood to hear how hard she had it when she abandoned her children to a monster. Were we really going to debate who had it worse? Andy didn't want to listen any more.

"Listen, I'm sorry your friend died, I am, but if you need a place to stay, I will get you a room at Sunnyside Home. It's not a big deal. I'm sure Sam would love it if you even shared his room. Just give me a day to work it all out and we can get your things sent over," Andy said.

Wendy moved her fingers over the little book next to her when Andy mentioned her things. "I have everything of value right here."

"What is that?" Andy finally asked.

"Oh, it's a collection of things really. The book is a poetry book your father gave me when we first met. He knew I loved poetry and, well, he was good to me back then. I keep it as a reminder of the good times."

Wendy leafed through the pages and Andy saw there were other papers, school pictures and cards tucked in almost every page. She pulled out some random items and then held them up to show Andy.

"This was a mother's day card you made for me when you were three. You drew a heart and colored it in." Wendy took out another paper from the pages. "This one is a birthday card Sam made me when he was four." Wendy wiped at her eyes as she continued. "This card is a birthday card from you. You were eight and said how you would always love me..."

Wendy put back all of her cards and letters and held the book tight to her chest. "I keep them to remember that I still have children that I love and maybe will love me back, too...someday."

Andy was surprised that he had gotten emotional. He had never considered her side of things because his side hurt too much. His eyes had watered a bit, too. He cleared his throat and said, "Mom, I may never understand why you did what you did, but I want you to know that I forgive you. I've learned a lot since then, about people. We all do things that hurt each other and sometimes we don't even know why we do it." Andy looked at his mother. "I've held onto hurt and grudges for so long that I think it's holding *me* back and I don't want that any longer."

Wendy came over to Andy and hugged him. "Thank you," she said through her tears. "Trust me, I've lived with what I've done all these years. I've followed your career and was so proud of you. I tried to reach out but I didn't think you wanted to hear from me."

"To be honest, I probably didn't," Andy replied. "But now that you and dad are back in my life, maybe it's time to start moving forward."

"Your father?" Wendy asked, confused.

"Yes, you didn't know?" Andy replied. "He showed up last year here as drunk as a skunk and just now got sober."

"Wow," was all Wendy could say. She never even considered Ron being back in Andy's life. Maybe people could change after all. "Oh, you had a phone call last night after you went upstairs. I answered it but there was no one there."

"Wait, you answered my phone?" Andy asked.

"Yes, I hope it wasn't a problem," Wendy replied. "I personally don't have one, I'm used to the old home phone where whoever was closest to it answered it."

Andy went to his phone and looked at the last call...Emma. Shit.

"Is everything okay?" Wendy asked.

Even though Andy was shaking his head, he replied, "Yes." He would have to call Emma back and explain who had answered his phone, later. Right now he just wanted to get his mother settled and out of his house. As much as their little bonding moment was helpful, it was still too much to deal with right now. He didn't want to spend any more time alone with his mother.

Andy went upstairs to get dressed. He would leave his mother at his house while he went too Sunnyside Home to get a room ready for her. Andy gave her instructions to stay there and make herself comfortable and he would be back later. As Andy drove away, he was starting to wonder if he was living in the twilight zone. Why was his father and mother both coming back into his life now? They acknowledged most of what they had done but they were now completely different people.

At Sunnyside Home, Andy walked into Marc Brown's office determined to get a room for his mother. Even though it was very last minute, they were able to fit her into a room, Sam would be thrilled. His meeting with Marc didn't take as long as he thought, and Andy probably could have been handled it over the phone but he needed to get out of his house. Too many childhood memories had been dredged up from the long forgotten depths and he needed to clear his head. Andy walked out into the back garden and that was when he spotted Emma.

Andy ran a hand through his hair and took a deep breath before heading in her direction. She was sitting with Joe, but he hoped he could get her alone for a minute.

"Good morning, Joe, Emma," Andy said.

"Good morning," they both said in unison.

"Emma, may I talk to you a moment, in private." Andy said to her and Joe.

Joe nodded as Emma stood up and walked over to Andy. They went over to another side of the garden that had orange and grapefruit trees. They sat down on chairs and Andy watched as Emma sat back with her arms crossed. She obviously thought the worst of him and that concerned him.

"Emma, I know you called last night," Andy started. "Why didn't you call back?"

"Are you really asking me that?" Emma asked. "I guess I figured you were too *busy*."

Andy shook his head. "Emma, did you really think I would sleep with another woman? That I would jeopardize what we have for a one night stand?"

Emma just sat there, staring at him.

Andy took a deep breath and then exhaled. "That was my mother who answered my phone last night."

Now it was Andy's turn to sit back and cross his arms. He watched as Emma's face showed signs of anger, confusion and then surprise at Andy's news.

"Wait, what?" Emma finally said.

Andy smiled. "Listen, it was as much a surprise to me, too. After I got home last night, my mother called me from here and said she didn't have a place to stay. Our guest rooms here were full and she didn't know what to do. I came and picked her up and she slept at my place last night."

"But why did she answer your phone?" Emma asked, still trying to piece it all together.

"I don't know. She saw it ringing and answered it, old school style," Andy replied. "What hurts is that you automatically assumed I had cheated on you."

He was right. Emma *had* thought that and now she was ashamed of herself. She knew in her heart that he would never cheat on her, but it was also so unexpected to hear a woman at his house.

"I'm so sorry, Andy," Emma replied.

Andy took her hands and said, "I got her a room here, her own room. She will be moved in later today and then we can spend time together."

"That sounds fantastic," Emma replied.

"So, dinner tonight?" Andy asked.

"Yes, I'll meet you at your place."

"No! I'll meet you at yours, I want to see the new bungalow you have been talking about the last couple of days," Andy replied.

Before Andy left, they hugged and kissed. They had both felt hurt by the other in some way and knew that they had to do better on their relationship. Just when they thought things were moving in the right direction, it appeared that a simple misunderstanding had the power to derail the entire thing. They were still building this relationship on a sand foundation and it could give way at any time.

Emma hadn't mentioned any of this to her father, so for Joe, it just looked like a man saying good morning to his girlfriend. To Emma, it was a reminder to trust Andy. She had jumped to conclusions and was wrong. The worst thing was that Andy knew it and it hurt him, the last thing in the world she ever wanted to do and she felt horrible about it.

Emma took her father inside for lunch. She stayed to eat with him so they could visit a little while longer. Sam came over to give her a hug and she wondered how it would be when his mother was living here, too. They would all be seeing a lot more of Wendy Anderson around here. For Andy's sake, she hoped that it would be a good thing and not a daily reminder of the ghosts of his past.

Joe always enjoyed Emma's visits but he knew she had other things that she needed to do. After lunch, when Emma left, he decided to ask Mr. Brown if he could help out with chores around the facility. At first, he was hesitant, he didn't want Joe to overdo it and get hurt so after consulting with his physician, they agreed to let him help a little in the dining room or kitchen when needed. It was all in an effort to get Joe back on his own someday.

Joe knew these were baby steps to get him where he needed to be but it was a start. It would improve the coordination and concentration that he needed to finally drive and live on his own. Joe smiled at the thought of cutting his own yard or driving to work. The simple things that he used to take for granted suddenly seemed so alluring. He would never take any of it for granted again. There might always be obstacles in his way but life goes on.

Chapter 31

Emma finished organizing her cabinets, pantry and closets all afternoon in anticipation of Andy coming to see her new place. She suddenly felt nervous about his coming over and wanted his first impression to be perfect. She even lit a candle on the coffee table. The October air was finally getting cooler and she went outside to sit on the back porch. She had heard news reports of a tropical storm coming into the gulf soon that may get stronger. They had been lucky the last few years by avoiding any big hurricanes, but she would have to keep her eye on this developing storm.

She smiled when she realized she was looking at the horizon for pirate ships. It was sad to her that Andy never grew up with those stories or a loving and caring home. She wondered what this mother and father coming back into his life made him feel deep inside. It was odd how, after all of these years, they were both here after Andy not knowing if they were alive or dead.

Emma thought back to the first time she met Andy Anderson, interviewing him at Tropicana Field. His eyes captivated her but she would never let him see it although he probably did. His smile and wink, she still laughed at how they used to make her so angry until she learned that the public Andy was very different then the private and vulnerable Andy she now knew.

They would finally have their first real date tonight at a proper restaurant. This would be special for both of them and it meant being seen in public together. She had to admit she was a little nervous and apprehensive about being seen with Andy, but she was ready. Emma thought about what she could wear tonight when she heard a text come through on her phone.

"Hey, I'm running late. Not sure I'm gonna make dinner," Andy texted.

Emma decided to call him back. Andy explained that he was helping his mother move into her new room at Sunnyside Home and it was taking a lot longer than they had planned. Turned out she did actually have a lot more things and he had to get a bigger truck to fit it all. It was probably gonna take a few more hours and he wouldn't have time to go home and change for a proper date.

Emma really wanted to see him, to make up for the other night and suggested that he just come to her place when he was finished. He could shower there while she made dinner, she didn't care. He knew she was looking forward to a night out and felt bad for ruining it but agreed to come over. They would just have to reschedule their big night out for another time, it wasn't the end of the world.

She thought about just ordering a pizza but decided against it. This would be the first time she cooked for him and went to her pantry to see what she could make on short notice. She decided to make a pasta dish with a salad and Italian bread and got to work. She chopped lettuce and veggies for her salad and then put water on to boil for the pasta. Emma added meat and garlic to her sauce and left it to simmer. The house smelled so good when she heard a knock at her front door.

Emma opened the door for Andy and he kissed her as soon as he crossed the threshold. He had such a long day and hated to come so late but he didn't want to disappoint her. Emma insisted she didn't mind and showed him where the shower and towels were. Andy had a gym bag on his shoulder, explaining that he always kept a change of clothes in his truck for emergencies.

While Andy showered, Emma put the finishing touches on dinner and set the table. She moved the candle to the center of the table and put on some Beethoven in the background. She was just adding the sauce to the pasta when Andy came into the living room and looked around. His hair was still damp and he was wearing a clean white t-shirt and pants that he had brought with him.

"Maybe you should leave a change of clothes here," Emma suggested with a smile.

"That might be a good idea," Andy said as he embraced her and kissed her forehead.

Andy's gaze scanned the room as he saw glimpses into her life. There were photos, knick knacks and the same glass trophy on her shelf that matched his. Andy walked around the room and picked up certain items and admired them. She had souvenirs that friends and family brought back from vacations, a ceramic dolphin from her childhood and a crystal vase that used to belong to her mother.

Andy studied a framed photo that looked to be her and her family when they were younger. "Who's this?" Andy asked.

"That's mom, dad, me and James when we went to Tarpon Springs one summer. James was fascinated by the sponge divers and always wanted to go back."

Andy studied the smiling faces in the photograph. He had never seen Emma's mother before. Even Joe was nearly unrecognizable in his younger years.

"You look like her," Andy replied, admiring the photograph.

Emma came over to look at the photo she had seen a million times only now she was seeing it through Andy's eyes. Maybe there was more resemblance then Emma thought. James looked just like their father, why wouldn't Emma look just like her mother? Andy looked from the picture and then to Emma and smiled.

"Come on, let's eat before it gets cold," Emma said, smiling.

Andy put the photo back where he found it and followed her into the small dining area. You couldn't really call it a dining room since it was just an extension of the kitchen, but it was nice and cozy.

"I like your new place," Andy announced.

Emma smiled. "Thanks, me too."

As much as Andy wanted her to move in with him, he had to admit that he was proud of her for not giving in. Emma was self sufficient and he would never want to change that about her, he just wanted to be a part of her life. If that meant only dating, then he would be satisfied with that, for now. He enjoyed the glimpses into her life and yearned for the day he would be a more prominent part of it.

Dinner was delicious and Andy kept complimenting Emma with each bite. He could tell that the cooking gene ran in her family because it was the best pasta he had ever eaten. Andy offered to clear the table and wash dishes but Emma said she wasn't finished yet, there was dessert. Andy smiled when she brought a plate of homemade brownies to the table. Crumbs fell to the table as they each took a bite of one.

Andy loved watching her laugh, it was the best sound in the world and he didn't hear it nearly enough. He wiped at the corner of her mouth and then leaned in to kiss her. With brownies forgotten, they kissed and undressed all the way to her bedroom. He didn't get to see this room earlier and probably wouldn't get to tonight either. Tonight they only had eyes for each other.

Their love making tonight was swift and passionate. It was the physical release of all their built up tension and stress from the last week that just couldn't wait past dessert. Andy was making up for his time away and Emma wanted to erase her fear of his infidelity. They were becoming in sync again and they needed to be each other's partner rather than just a passing thought.

Tonight they reset their compass to trust each other and follow their instincts. They were letting doubt and outside influences cloud their relationship and they promised each other to not let it happen again. Their promise was sealed with a connection that no one could break.

It was somewhere in the middle of the night when Emma got up, put on a robe and went to sit on the back porch. The wind was picking up but the air was cool. She loved having Andy at her place and hoped he felt welcome here, too. They had overcome so many obstacles to finally be together in one place and hopefully even on the same page.

The mix-up with his mother was really silly when she thought about it. Of course Andy wasn't the kind of guy to just bring a girl home. Then she remembered Pat...and their kiss. It wasn't the same thing at all, or was it. She never wanted to tell Andy because it was nothing. There was no reason to bring it up. She had moved past it, or did she. Why did it come so easily to her mind if she had?

When the sun rose and Andy finally awoke, they ate breakfast and he left. Still so much for him to do concerning his mother, he needed to go home and change. He left only after promising her a proper dinner out tonight, no excuses this time!

IT WAS WHILE EMMA WAS getting dressed for dinner that she heard the weather alarm alerting their area of the hurricane's approach. Emma went into the living room and turned on the television. She hadn't really been paying attention to the weather, with everything else going on in her life, but she had noticed the wind picking up. In fact, she had brought in her outdoor furniture earlier today because it was getting stronger.

According to the weatherman, the impact would be later tonight, making landfall around Sarasota, not far from her. It would be coming in as a category two hurricane with the possibility of becoming a category three. When Andy arrived a few moments later, they wondered if they should stay home, that maybe restaurants were closing early or not opening up at all.

Andy got on his phone and was making some phone calls while Emma went to look out her back window. Waves were getting bigger but it wasn't raining. They would be on the western side of the hurricane which was better than the alternative. The hurricane would continue traveling east and move right over the state and into the Atlantic Ocean. If they were lucky, they would just get a little rain or wind, nothing worse than that. Hurricanes were so unpredictable, she prayed everyone remained safe.

Andy called the restaurant where they had reservations and they confirmed they were open now but would be closing in a couple of hours. They could either come now or reschedule. Just as Andy was asking Emma what she wanted to do, there was another knock at the door. Emma thought it might be her brother checking in on her, but it wasn't. In fact, it was someone she never expected to see ever again.

With Andy on hold with the restaurant waiting on Emma's answer, he went in search for her to see what she wanted to do. When Andy saw who was waiting at the front door, he hung up the phone and went to stand behind Emma.

"Pat, what are you doing here?" Emma asked, shocked.

"Emma, I had to see you!" Pat said as he pushed his way in the door. "Ever since you left Atlanta I have been thinking about you! I was wondering how you were doing and if you were okay."

"I'm fine," Emma replied.

"Yes, she's fine," Andy repeated, putting himself between Pat and Emma.

"You never returned my phone calls or answered my texts..." Pat said and then sat on the couch. "I was worried that something might have happened."

"Like what?" Emma wondered.

"That maybe *he* got mad," Pat replied.

Emma felt her cheeks get hot. No! He wasn't going to say what she thought he was going to say! Emma looked from Pat to Andy and then back to Pat but it was too late.

"Why would I get mad? What happened?" Andy asked but was looking straight at Emma.

Pat smiled. "Oh, you never told him about the night we kissed, did you?"

If Emma wasn't watching Andy, she would have missed the flash of sadness in his eyes right before he looked from Emma and then to Pat. After that moment, everything else happened so fast. Andy ran over to Pat and punched him in the jaw. Pat McNeil wasn't as tall or as muscular as Andy, but he could definitely hold his own in a fight.

After Andy punched Pat, he fought back by punching Andy in the ribs and then the face. Andy was able to protect himself and throw some punches before Pat cornered him and put all his weight into a punch that connected with Andy's arm, the one that was still recovering from the accident. Andy doubled over and Pat punched him in the face again. Tables were being overturned and furniture was being pushed across the room.

Andy, in pain but also furious about why Pat came there in the first place, landed a solid punch to Pat's side that dropped him to the floor. Emma had been yelling for the two to stop fighting, but no one heard her. They were too caught up in fighting each other that now she wondered if they both needed a doctor.

Pat was wincing in pain on the floor but looked like he would be okay, it was Andy who thought Pat actually did damage to his arm by breaking or dislocating a pin or plate. Andy sat on the chair cradling his injured arm.

Emma was in tears as she yelled at Pat to leave and never come back. She never wanted to see him again, ever! With a smirk on his face, Pat left. Emma tried to help Andy up and led him to her car as they made their way to the hospital.

Chapter 32

At the hospital they asked Andy what happened. He said he had gotten into a fight and the doctor looked at Emma for a more detailed explanation. They were both dressed up, expecting a nice evening out, so they weren't sure what the doctor was imagining. The televisions all over the hospital were broadcasting the latest about the hurricane. It would be making landfall soon and everyone was advised to stay indoors.

"I really need to check on Sunnyside Home," Andy said.

"Well, you aren't going anywhere until we x-ray that arm, Mr. Anderson. You could have really done some permanent damage," the doctor replied.

Emma and Andy could only exchange quick looks at each other. It was all her fault he was there in the first place. Pat showing up was only part of the problem, if Emma had told Andy about the kiss in the first place she could have given it some context, that it didn't mean anything. Now she knew Andy's mind was imagining the worst case scenario and she needed to talk to him about it, to say that nothing had happened.

As the doctor wheeled Andy away, all she could do was wait in the sterile waiting room for him to return. So white and cold, she longed to be by Andy's side. A text came through from Pat but Emma deleted it without even reading it and then blocked his number. She didn't want anything to do with him again, he may have already ruined the best relationship with the warmest man she had ever met and it wasn't even all of Pat's fault.

It took an hour for Andy to be brought back out from the x-ray. The doctor said to give them some time to look at it and he would get back to them with the results. That left Andy and Emma alone.

"I'm sorry for not telling you. I wanted to but then again, I didn't. It was nothing, it meant nothing," Emma pleaded.

"What exactly happened?" Andy asked softly.

"It was a night that we went to an outdoor concert. It was nice, we were sitting on the ground and he leaned over and kissed me. I've felt guilty about it ever since but that was all it was," Emma replied.

"That's it, do you promise?" Andy asked.

"Yes, Andy, I love *you*!" Emma declared through tears that were streaming down her face. She desperately needed Andy to believe her, that Pat meant nothing to her. It was all just a stupid mistake.

Andy reached up and wiped at them with his good hand. "Okay, I believe you," Andy said. "I love you, too."

That was it, she would never bring up Pat's name again and she hoped Andy meant it when he said he believed her. This was turning into a terrible night and she just wanted to go home. The doctor came back and said his arm looked good, there was no damage and he was lucky. It may be swollen and sore for the next few days and would prescribe some medication to help with that, but he was good to go.

Andy's phone started ringing and he searched his pockets for it. It was Sunnyside Home.

"Hello, Andy?" Marc Brown started. "Um, I have to tell you something. With the hurricane coming, we've been making sure everyone was secure in their rooms but we, uh...can't find your mother."

Emma's phone rang while Andy was talking to Mr. Brown, so she stepped out into the hallway, it was James.

"Hello, Emma?" James started. "Joanne is in labor and we are heading to the hospital now. Can you meet us there?"

"Hi, yes, I'm actually already here," Emma replied. "I'll wait for you!"

"Wait, why are you at the hospital?" James asked.

"Long story, I'll see you soon," Emma said and hung up.

Emma walked back into Andy's room just as he was standing up and removing wires. "I have to go," Andy said. "They can't find mom at Sunnyside Home, I have to go help look for her."

"Okay, well, Joanne is having the baby and they're on their way here, so I'm staying," Emma replied.

Andy took Emma's hands and reassured her that they were good. He wasn't mad but he also had to go and hoped she understood. She did, of course, and would keep in touch through the night. The storm was coming and they knew that anything could happen.

Andy held her and kissed her hard, not knowing when they would manage another moment alone.

"Raincheck on that date?" Andy yelled as he ran down the hall.

"Definitely!" Emma yelled back and then waited for James and Joanne to arrive.

AT SUNNYSIDE HOME, Andy ran in the front doors followed by a gust of wind from the hurricane. Marc was there to greet him and filled Andy in on where all they had checked. Andy asked if they checked outside.

"You don't think she'd go out in *this* do you?" Marc asked.

"Marc, to be honest, I don't know her all that well and frankly, I don't know what she would do," Andy replied and headed for the back garden and into the storm.

LIFE GOES ON

Andy and Mr. Brown split up and searched every bush, tree and out building while the storm grew stronger. It was raining now and the wind made it hard to walk straight.

"Wendy!" They both shouted as they made their way through the expansive grounds. It was dark, cold and windy but neither man would give up until every inch was searched. Marc had a flashlight but Andy just had his phone. Using the last of his battery, Andy turned the flashlight on and tried to see in front of him.

Alternating between calling "Wendy" and "Mom," Andy thought he saw movement ahead of him but it turned out to be just a stray cat. Almost ready to give up, Andy walked to the end of the property to the small shed that housed their lawn mower. There, crouched behind the small shed was Wendy. Andy took her hand and she stepped forward.

He took off his suit jacket and wrapped it around his mother. Andy led her back to the main building to get warm and dry. Mr. Brown was both relieved and embarrassed that Wendy was found so far away and in the storm. A nurse came and took Wendy to her room to help her change into warm, dry clothing.

Andy sat down on the couch and Marc joined him.

"It's been one hell of a night," Marc said to Andy.

Andy started laughing. Maybe it was part relief and part hysteria, but Andy couldn't stop laughing. When he thought about how this day started, in bed with Emma, and how it ended up, he couldn't make this up if he tried. Marc was now noticing the bruises on his face and asked about them.

"Well, it's been one hell of a night," Andy said and Marc laughed, too.

The nurse brought Wendy out when she was put in some dry clothes because she wanted to thank Andy. "Thank you, I'm so sorry for all the fuss and trouble," she said.

"It's okay, it all turned out fine and that's what really matters," Andy replied. "But why were you all the way out there?"

"I couldn't find my book," Wendy said. Andy watched as she clutched it to her chest. "I knew I left it when I came in to use the restroom but then I got distracted. When I went back out, the wind and rain had moved it and by the time I found it I had become so disoriented..."

Andy gave his mom a hug and shook Marc's hand. "If you don't mind, my night isn't over yet," Andy said. "I have to get back to the hospital." Then Andy paused. "Do you mind if I borrow Joe for a few hours? He is becoming a grandpa tonight."

Marc Brown's face lit up, "Oh how wonderful! Maybe something blessed will come out of this terrible night, yet!" He shook Andy's hand again and he and Joe drove to the hospital.

Andy had been gone only a few hours, but Emma had kept him updated on the baby. Joanne was almost ready to push and she was blaming the hurricane on how fast the baby was coming. Andy had to smile thinking what a hurricane of chaos they were creating themselves. It was difficult to see on the road, but they weren't far away.

Andy parked and helped Joe get inside. It didn't take long to find Emma, she was waiting in the hallway and ran to her father first, then Andy. They let Joe go in the room while Emma waited with Andy. They sat next to each other and held hands, Emma was thankful that Andy made it back safely. He told her all about his mother and that she was okay now.

"Thanks to you," Emma said.

"I never want anything or anyone to come between us again," Andy proclaimed.

"Me, either," Emma agreed.

"Are you free for dinner tomorrow night?" Andy asked.

Emma laughed. "Let's wait and see how tonight goes. We have a baby and a hurricane to consider now."

"Okay, but when this is all over, let's go back to your place," Andy said.

"I might have some cleaning up to do," Emma replied. "A couple of knuckleheads broke out into a fight in my living room. Plus, you don't have a change of clothes."

Andy smiled. "I will help you clean up and yes I do, I have a bag packed in my truck right now."

Emma kissed him and they sat in each other's arms in the waiting room for word of her nephew being born. Word didn't come for several more hours and in that time Andy searched for coffee and food. He found coffee but no food. When Joe finally came out to tell them the baby arrived, they asked to go in.

James was holding him and Joanne looked happy but tired. Emma hugged Joanne and James and kissed her new nephew on the forehead. James offered Emma to hold the baby and she held out her arms for the small bundle.

"Meet your Godmother," James said. "Emma, meet Justin."

Emma rocked the new baby and stared at his sleeping face. Justin looked so peaceful all swaddled up without a care in the world. One by one, everyone around the room yawned and felt like it was finally time to go home.

"It's been one hell of a night," James said.

Andy smiled and Emma agreed. Emma took her father home and on the way Andy fell asleep. When she pulled into her own driveway, she had to wake him up. Disoriented at first, Andy got out and helped Emma to her door. Andy didn't need much persuading to stay the night because he fell asleep as soon as he sat on her couch.

Emma cleaned up the mess, took a shower and laid a blanket on Andy before crawling into bed. Andy looked too peaceful to disturb after such an ordeal. She said a quick prayer of thanks that all of her loved ones were safe tonight because it was one hell of night.

Chapter 33

It took a few days for everyone to adjust to their new normal. For James and Joanne, being first-time parents was frightening and exhausting. Every cry that Justin made caused anxiety and stress in the new Reese household of three. There were many times that James called his father or that Joanne called her mother to get help and advise. In the end, Justin was healthy and thriving and that was all that mattered.

Emma couldn't stay away. She loved being an Aunt and holding her little nephew while Joanne could fold laundry or take a shower. And now that the storm had passed, Emma even took him for a walk down the street. The air had warmed back up and the sun was shining. Thankfully, their area was not badly damaged by the hurricane and they prayed that those who were could be helped soon. It made Emma smile to think that this little boy had been born during such a chaotic night, she hoped that he would bring calm and stability to their family.

James worked at the restaurant as much as he could and even Emma went to help a little, too. It was just like old times, only busier. James hired some more staff so that Joanne could have all the time she needed at home with her mother who came to help around the house. Little Justin James would be the most loved baby in all of Florida.

While Emma spent her free time with Joanne and little Justin, Andy was spending his at Sunnyside Home. After the scare with his mother, Andy made sure Wendy had everything she needed and he even got her a cell phone. A cell phone was new technology for her and it took him several days to explain the different functions and services it could provide. It was important to Andy and Mr. Brown that she could get ahold of them and vice versa whenever they needed to.

Wendy liked having her own phone and would routinely call people throughout the day. Andy had to remind her that usually people text first and if they wanted to talk on the phone then they could call, so Andy worked with her on how to text. Wendy secretly loved all the attention Andy gave her. She would never fully be able to explain why she left him and where she had gone, but it was good to know they were building back a future together.

Wendy had been able to show Andy more of her book. It was worn and yellowed with time but housed some of her most dearest possessions. She had already shown him some of the cards, but she also had photos. Some were school pictures of the boys and others were family portraits or holiday pictures around the Christmas tree. Andy looked at the smiling faces in the pictures and honestly didn't remember any of them. For him, all of the fear and anxiety in the house overshadowed any love that might have been there.

Andy just looked at the photos and cards and handed them back. He let his mother hold on to the dream of a nice family life. Everyone had their perspective and she never once asked Andy his. That was okay, though, Andy was ready to move on...had already moved on.

He didn't think his father was ever coming back. Every time he talked to him, he told Andy how wonderful Hawaii was and that his golf game had gotten very good. He was playing whenever he could and enjoyed his job. He had even gotten another token. Andy was happy for him and allowed him to stay at his home as long as he wanted. Maybe Andy would even go back for a visit soon.

Andy received a phone call and excused himself from Wendy and went outside. It was his agent telling him that he had booked a venue for Andy and it was big! It was just the right size for a Grammy nominated artist, the Hard Rock Hotel and Casino in Tampa. They had a wonderful venue where some of the biggest names in music had performed and they wanted Andy Anderson. He couldn't believe it!

"When?" Andy asked.

"December," his agent replied. "They are working on the promotional materials now!"

Andy hung up and sat down to let it all sink in. He had done small shows here and there, but this would be the biggest place he will have played so far. He and his album were ready, it was just so new. He had played baseball in front of packed stadiums but it wasn't just him on the field. This would be like playing baseball all by himself in front of a sold out stadium. He couldn't wait to tell Emma.

Andy texted Emma, always assuming that she was in the vicinity of a sleeping baby, and said he had big news. Emma immediately called back explaining that she was actually in the car on her way home. He didn't want to tell her over the phone and suggested they have dinner. Emma laughed considering the last few times they planned a nice dinner out and that it hadn't actually happened yet.

Andy tried to point out that it wasn't his fault, he still intended to have a proper first date with her and tonight would be the night. Emma agreed but explained that she needed to rest first, babysitting and waiting tables was exhausting. Andy admitted that he also needed some time to prepare this afternoon, so he would pick her up at seven.

Before Andy left Sunnyside Home, he made the usual rounds to visit everyone he could. He stopped in to see Joe, but was told he was in the kitchen. That was where he saw him chopping vegetables and measuring ingredients for the cakes. Andy was impressed with how well he did in the kitchen and gave him a high five before looking for Sam.

Sam loved to stay active and was always on the hunt for someone to do a puzzle or a game with. Today Sam was at the pool table with another young man who lived at the facility, Reggie. Reggie hadn't been there very long but they were both in their twenties and became fast friends. Andy simply went over and hugged his brother and let him continue his game.

One of the places Andy had to stop at today was his record producer to find out more about the concert in December. They would have to work out a schedule of rehearsals and performances. Andy was excited that his music was being taken seriously and that fans loved it. He had to make sure that all of his friends and family could come.

Andy found out he would have an hour on stage and could perform from his album or even new music. He had been working on lots of new songs, so he might try out a couple at the Hard Rock Hotel. He couldn't wait to tell Emma all about it and he hoped that she would be just as excited for him. She knew her new job would be starting around then, too, so he might have to pull a few strings to make it all work out.

When Andy finally got home after running all over town to finish his errands before their date, he had a few minutes to relax before picking Emma up. The reservations where made and he checked his pocket to make sure he had the envelope, yes it was there. Andy set his alarm before closing his eyes, he was not going to miss this date with Emma.

AT THE RESTAURANT, Andy didn't even have to give his name, the hostess recognized him and showed them to their table. Emma watched as heads turned when Andy walked past them. It was like the night she met him for dinner in the hotel, Andy was a celebrity and Emma had to get used to it. It was easy for her to forget when she was watching him get beat up by an ex or holding her newborn nephew in his arms, but he was.

Some looks were in Emma's direction, mostly trying to figure out if she was famous, too, but it was always Andy who stole the show. Emma didn't mind, she secretly enjoyed it knowing that he only had eyes for her. That took her a very long time to accept and believe, but after everything they had been through, she finally did believe it. Emma held her head high and held onto Andy's hand as they made their way to the table.

Andy held out her chair as she sat down, careful that he didn't step on her sequined black dress she wore tonight. Andy wore a tuxedo and unbuttoned his jacket as he sat down and looked at Emma.

"You look gorgeous tonight," Andy said.

"Thank you, so do you," she replied.

They felt like teenagers on their first date using a brand new credit card. They smiled at each other, unable to believe they finally made it out on a proper date after months of trying. This time parents, fights and hurricanes couldn't keep them from ordering a bottle of champagne and toasting to a great night.

"Do you remember out first date was supposed to be New Year's Eve?" Emma asked.

"Of course I remember, every time I try to use my left arm," Andy joked, even though the memory of that night still haunted him. He hadn't realize until much later how close he had been to dying that night.

"That was nearly a year ago now," Emma said. "And after all that has happened, we are still here, together."

"I'll toast to that," Andy said as the waiter poured their glasses.

It was bittersweet to think of all their time wasted on misunderstandings and hurt feelings. They were adults and they knew better, now they could move forward knowing that it could all be taken away in an instant. Emma never wanted to lose Andy and would try to always make him a priority.

Andy told her all about his upcoming concert in Tampa. Emma felt tears come to her eyes knowing how much it really meant to him to share his music with the world. He was being modest and demure right now, but she knew that he was excited on the inside, perhaps even more than becoming MVP of the World Series because he did this all by himself. She was so very proud of him.

Emma reached out for his hand and smiled. Andy explained that the concert was before Christmas, so it would all be over when they celebrated the holidays and he could play Santa again at Sunnyside Home.

"Well, that's a relief," Emma said with a smile. She knew how important it was for him to do that every year for his brother and all of the residents.

"I actually have a Mrs. Claus costume and an elf costume if you'd like to join me..." Andy said.

"I'd love to!" Emma replied and they laughed.

Their conversation was only interrupted by the waiter taking their orders and then bringing out their dinners. Emma ordered the salmon with rice and vegetables and Andy ordered a ribeye steak with a baked potato and carrots. As they ate, Emma talked all about Justin and how fast he was growing. Andy explained how he bought his mother a cell phone so he would always know where she was and she could get ahold of him if she needed to.

Andy felt like they had all finally settled into a rhythm, a new normal for them all. He was not going to be returning to the Sharks, his baseball career was finally over. Emma heard a tinge of sadness in his words but there was also something else there...acceptance.

They were all learning to accept their limitations and embrace new opportunities. Like Andy had said once, he had already made his millions, now it was time to live.

It was time to focus on their future. Andy took a deep breath as he pulled a small velvet box from his jacket pocket.

Chapter 34

Andy nodded to the waiter as his cue to get the second bottle of champagne ready to open if things went the way he planned. With the black velvet box in one hand, Andy stood up and then got down on one knee beside Emma. Immediately brought to tears, Emma brought her hands to her face and watched Andy kneel beside her.

"Emma, from the moment you came to the stadium and tried to interview me the first time, I knew you were special. You saw past the facade and the public persona and saw *me*. No one had bothered to do that before, only you. God knows my life hasn't been a smooth ride, but you stayed with me and by my side the entire bumpy road. You loved me, even with all of my flaws and scars and I never want to lose you. I love you, Emma. Will you marry me?"

Emma didn't know if she could speak, her chin was quivering and tears were blurring her eyes but she managed to say, "Yes!" Andy opened the box to reveal a large diamond ring and slid it on her finger. Emma hugged him and the waiter came over to pop the cork on another bottle of champagne.

"She said yes!" Andy yelled inside the restaurant. Emma, embarrassed, covered her face as the restaurant cheered the newly engaged couple. They toasted each other and Andy kissed his fiancé. The waiter brought out their dessert, a cherry cheesecake in the shape of a heart, made at Andy's request.

Emma didn't know what could possibly be next but she loved all of his surprises. She couldn't wait to tell her family and said she would make arrangement for them to all get together for lunch tomorrow so she could tell them together.

"Perfect," Andy said with a smile. His surprises weren't finished, but they could wait. Right now he enjoyed the look on her face as they ate their cheesecake. Emma kept looking at the ring when she thought he wasn't looking. Andy simply laughed.

"I still can't believe it," Emma kept saying. She didn't expect it, not now after so much chaos and confusion in their relationship. But seeing the ring on her finger confirmed that Andy's feelings for her were real and would withstand anything.

They savored the champagne and cheesecake but asked for the rest to be wrapped up for later. As Andy stood up to pull out Emma's chair, the restaurant applauded the happy couple as they made their way to the exit. Andy and Emma waved at everyone as they finally made it out into he cool night air. She had entered the restaurant a single woman and left engaged to Andy. Tonight was magical.

When Emma commented that Andy had missed her turn, he said, "You're coming home with me tonight."

THE NEXT DAY EVERYONE had gathered at the Salty Waves for lunch. Emma made it sound as if Andy wanted to see how everyone was doing and the baby in order to hide her real news. Emma hid her ring as best as she could until they sat down to eat. Justin was sleeping which gave them all time to talk and share their good news.

Emma cleared her throat and said, "Andy asked me to marry him last night and I accepted!" Then she showed them her ring.

Cheers and congratulations were shared around the table. Justin fussed a little at the sudden outburst, but went right back to sleep. Everyone wanted to see the ring and shake Andy's hand.

"Welcome to the family," Joe said to him.

"Thank you, sir," Andy replied.

"Wow! Finally," James said with a smile.

Emma and Andy hugged and thanked everyone for their support. They had all been so kind to Andy this past year and it made it so easy for her to accept his proposal knowing that her family loved him, too. They all admitted that they knew a proposal was coming, they were just waiting to hear that it did.

Andy told them all about his concert in December and wanted them to know they were all invited and pulled an envelope out of his jacket pocket. He laid down enough tickets for them all to see him at the Hard Rock Hotel in Tampa. There were VIP passes and everything they would need to make it happen. He even offered to get them rooms if they didn't want to drive home.

They were all so happy for him and hoped he would win a Grammy or two in February. Emma held the ticket which made it feel more real. She loved that there was a ticket with his name on it because he had worked so hard for it. This was something Andy had done all by himself and they were all so proud of him.

"And there's more," Andy said. "I haven't even discussed this with Emma yet, but I'd love to have the wedding in Scotland...with all of you there, if that's okay."

Every face looking at Andy was full of shock and surprise. No one was saying anything and he was starting to wonder if it was a bad idea. He produced some brochures and vouchers from the envelope he held that showed venues and accommodations in Scotland that he had been to. They would be beautiful locations for a wedding and hoped they liked the idea.

"What?" Emma asked. "You want to get married in Scotland?"

"Well, you said once that you'd love to take your father there one day and I thought this would be the perfect time," Andy replied, still not sure if she liked the idea.

"I can't believe you remembered," Emma said quietly.

"Of course I did," Andy replied.

"I love the idea," Emma said and looked around the table. Everyone was in agreement and started looking through the brochures. "You did all of this for me?" Emma asked looking up at him.

"For us, yes," Andy replied.

Emma didn't know if she could handle any more surprises. She needed time to digest what had happened over the last day or two and wanted to be alone with Andy. After lunch they said their goodbyes and excused themselves and drove up the coast.

Andy didn't know where she wanted to go, Emma just told him to drive. When he saw the sign for Tarpon Springs, he turned. Tarpon Springs was a lively Greek fishing village and Emma immediately remembered it from her childhood. They ordered some food to eat on the beach and found a secluded place to sit.

They ate their greek salads and gyros while watching the waves roll in and out on the sand. Neither one needed to talk, they had said enough already. Now they each needed to process what was happening. They were getting married...in Scotland. Emma was caught off guard with Andy's generous announcement but she loved the idea as soon as she heard it.

Emma couldn't believe that he remember her comment from a year ago. Did she say it at the city's gala award's night? Even *she* didn't remember. But Andy did. Andy remembered everything about her. They had joked about where they would live and Andy said they would live at her place. Emma had burst out in laughter thinking about the impossibility of such an idea.

They stayed on the beach in Tarpon Springs for the rest of the afternoon. Emma would look from her ring to the waves and then to Andy. Was it a dream? She could feel him next to her and knew that it wasn't. If she could only stay this way forever, life would be perfect. Emma didn't know how it could get any better.

Andy suggested they head home. It was getting dark and chilly and they weren't prepared for either. When they got back in Andy's truck, Emma thought of how important Andy had become in her life and it scared her a little bit. She had been so independent all her life and now she had to make room for Andy.

Maybe that was part of marriage, the compromise of giving your life to someone else and incorporating them into yours. Was she just letting him in or letting him take over? Emma asked Andy to take her home instead of his place.

"Is something wrong?" Andy asked, concerned he had said or done something to upset her.

"No, I think I just need some time alone to process things," Emma replied. "I'll be fine in the morning. We can go tell your mother and brother then."

Andy wasn't exactly sure what was going on, but he agreed to take her home and leave her alone tonight. If she was having cold feet about marrying him, she would let him know. He knew they had been through a lot and he didn't want to push her. Andy dropped her off at her door step and kissed her goodnight.

Andy drove away, unsure of what just happened. They were so excited about everything just a few hours ago, but now she looked scared. He tried to convince himself that everything would be okay in the morning. When he got home, he called to check up on her and she insisted she was fine, just tired.

Emma had taken a long, hot shower, eaten a microwave dinner and would either walk on the beach or watch a movie before bed. Andy wished her good night and would call her in the morning. Andy was tired too and carried the left over cheesecake to the kitchen and went to take a shower. Exhausted, he fell asleep as soon as he got into bed.

Emma called Miriam to tell her the good news. Miriam screamed so loud Emma had to hold the phone away from her ear. She was so happy for Emma and would start planning the bachelorette party tomorrow. Emma laughed and said that it sounded perfect.

Miriam went on to tell her all about the new guy she met at the coffee shop. She thinks he is the one and wanted Emma to meet him. Again, Emma laughed at Miriam's ability to find so many eligible men in the city, it was just a shame that she couldn't make any of them last longer than a month or two. Now that Emma was so happy, she wanted her friend happy, too.

After Emma hung up, she went to sit on the back porch, her favorite place in her house. It was dark but she could hear the waves as they rolled onto the shore. Still no pirate ships, she thought. She wished she could tell her mother all about Andy and how wonderful he was to her. She was sure her mother would love him, too. Sometimes Emma talked out loud to her and it brought Emma comfort to think she heard her.

When it got too cold for her, Emma came back inside and stumbled. She was about to find the television remote when Emma started to feel very dizzy and had some shortness of breath. Emma almost made it to the couch before she collapsed.

Chapter 35

Andy woke up feeling very rested and realized it was past nine o'clock. Had he really slept nearly ten hours? He tried to call Emma but she didn't answer her phone. Apparently she was sleeping in, too. Andy went downstairs to make coffee and find something for breakfast. He noticed some missed calls and decided to call his manager back first.

Plans were underway for the concert and five hotel rooms were booked for him and Emma's family. Andy thanked him and said he would be over later to go over the set list and review a practice schedule. He mentioned that he had a wedding to plan, too, and there were cheers on the other end of the phone.

After a few sips of coffee, Andy texted his mother back and smiled as he did so. He was glad they could communicate so easily now without him having to go there each time he wanted to check on her. She had acclimated well to living at Sunnyside Home and he was glad. Wendy confirmed that she was well and Andy said he would be over later to check on things.

Andy tried texting Emma again, but no reply. He then texted his mother back who had written that she heard the news and Andy replied, 'thank you'. She didn't think to call his mother about his engagement, but maybe he should have. Andy decided that he would stop by later with Emma and see her.

There were other texts and calls but Andy just put his phone down and made some toast. He thought about going to pick up

Emma which would give them time to discuss travel plans on the way to Sunnyside Home. James would need to get little JJ a passport and if they planned the trip for spring, he would be six months old by then.

Andy refilled his coffee and went upstairs to change when his phone rang, it was James. Andy considered letting it just go to voicemail, but answered it.

"Hey James," Andy said.

"Hello," James said. Andy could tell he didn't sound like himself.

"What's up?" Andy asked.

"Um... it's about Emma," James started. "I've been trying to reach you. You didn't hear anything?"

Andy waited for James to explain then asked, "Is she canceling on me?" Andy thought he was making a joke, but James wasn't laughing, in fact, it sounded like he was blowing his nose.

"A jogger on the beach saw her back door open and...oh, Andy...he called the police when they found her..." James was crying, there was no mistaking it.

"Where is she?" Andy demanded.

"She's at the hospital, but..." James was trying to steady his voice. "She's dead."

Andy let the phone drop from his ear and started sobbing uncontrollably. "No...no...no!" Andy yelled. This wasn't happening, it was a mistake. Andy grabbed his keys and ran out the door. He jumped in his truck and drove straight to Emma's house. Andy pounded on the front door and then went to the back, it was still unlocked.

Andy stood in the doorway but couldn't go in any further. He didn't know what to do so he called James back. He confirmed that the ambulance took her to the hospital but she was in the morgue. The doctor said she had probably suffered a stroke last night and wasn't found until this morning. He remembered Emma saying she might walk outside after they hung up but she was all alone.

Oh, Emma! Why? It was too much for him. Andy told James he was coming over. When Andy got to the Salty Waves he noticed that James had put a sign on the door saying that they were closed due to a death in the family. Andy broke down, again. As soon as Joanne saw him walk in the door she came to hug him. They were trying to console each other but no one wanted to believe it.

Joseph had already made plans for cremation and there would be a service on Friday. Andy had to sit down, it was all happening too fast. How could he be putting a ring on her finger and then planning a funeral all in the same week? James came and patted Andy on the back as they each let their tears fall. Their beloved Emma had died.

Andy didn't want to accept that his Emma was gone. He went out onto the beach and stood looking out into the horizon. He thought of Emma's story of looking for the pirate ship and knew that she was with her mother on one of those ships right now. He wanted to join her.

"Go find your treasure," Andy said out loud.

He felt as though he had been crying all morning and then he thought about her family. He wouldn't let his grief overshadow that of her family. Andy went back inside and asked James what he needed him to do. James said most had already been done, but someone would need to pack up her house and contact the landlord. Andy said he would arrange everything. He didn't even know where to go right now, everything reminded him of Emma and it was just too sad. Andy had to get out of there but told James to let him know if there was anything else he could do to help.

He sat in his truck for a few minutes collecting his thoughts. Normally he would be picking Emma up so they could tell everyone their great news, now they were making funeral arrangements. He made some calls and decided to continue with his day. Andy still had people depending on him and he couldn't let them down, too. He had to keep going, Emma would want that.

Andy met with his record producer and after explaining what had just happened, they asked if he wanted to cancel the show. He had to admit that he considered it, but Emma was just so proud of him and he couldn't let her down. He knew she would want him to do the show and as hard as it might me, he would do it for her. Everything he did now would be for her. The show would go on as scheduled.

THE SERVICE FOR EMMA was beautiful and the Church was crowded. Everyone who knew and loved Emma was there for her. Liane Lincoln, Miriam, Don and Cindy Day even Pat showed up to pay their respects. Everyone shed tears for a woman with so much potential, her life was only beginning. It also seemed like half of St. Petersburg along with the entire St. Pete Sharks baseball team filled the pews. Mr. Brown arranged for anyone from Sunnyside Home who wanted to attend could and then he ended up needing a larger van.

There were so many folks who wanted to say a few words, it was heartwarming. When Joe and James spoke, it was heartbreaking. The cries from little Justin in Joanne's arms were a reminder that Emma didn't get very much time to be a Godmother. Andy would have to step up and be the Godparent for both of them.

Next, it was Andy's turn to say something about the woman he loved and had asked to be his wife. Most people attending the service that day didn't know they were engaged. He could hear the sobs and tears from folks who heard about their love, their life and their plans for the future. It was a future that looked bleak to him right now but he believed that Emma would help him through it. Emma was always his cheerleader.

Afterwards, strangers were coming up to the family and offering their condolences. Joe couldn't take it any longer and went to sit in the car. One by one they all joined him and then eventually they just left. What were they all supposed to do now? Emma was the glue that held them all together. Now that she was gone, what would happen to them.

The urn that held Emma's ashes now sat on Joe's table in his room. He had already buried his wife, now he had to bury his daughter, it wasn't natural. Mr. Brown was afraid that Joe would have a setback in his therapy and encouraged Sam to keep him busy. It would be so easy for Joe to fall into another depression and Mr. Brown had to try to prevent that from happening.

Everyone handled their grief differently. For Andy, he threw himself into his music completely. He was practicing and getting ready for the concert in Tampa next week. He had a few new songs ready and he felt good about this show. There was a lot of pressure on him because this show could lead to more and his record label was already counting on that. They needed Andy to perform at his best even when he was at his worst.

James and Joanne focused on their baby and the restaurant. The regulars would know not to mention Emma but then you had those who said they hadn't seen her in a while and asked about her. Those where the moments when they had to step outside for a minute. James was always happy to see Coach Walters come in. It almost felt like old times when he and Greg Reynolds and Bobby Bishop would have lunch at the bar. Andy didn't come around as much and even his former teammates said they don't hear from him as often as they used to.

No one knew how to help Andy, though. He was keeping himself so busy with his music that he seemed to be cutting everyone else out. They worried that he hadn't really dealt with Emma's death.

LIFE GOES ON

Joe had given Andy back the diamond engagement ring and it now sat in one of his dresser drawers.

One day James thought of something to do for Andy, but it would be a long shot. He called Sunnyside Home and asked for Mr. Brown, the director. James asked Mr. Brown if he had the phone number for Andy's father. After explaining that they were concerned about Andy, Marc Brown said he would try and contact him and fill him in on what his son had been going through. James hoped it wouldn't backfire, but with the concert coming up, he just might like the support.

Marc Brown called Ron in Hawaii and explained the situation. Ron admitted that he hadn't really talked to his son much the last few months, only checking in by text or voicemail once in a while. Ron would see what he could do and was grateful for the information. Well, Marc had passed along his concerns, now it was up to Ron to decide if it was worth his effort to help his son when he needed his father the most.

THE NIGHT OF THE CONCERT, James, Joanne and Joe rode over to Tampa. Joanne's mother agreed to babysit Justin overnight and even though it gave the new parents a little anxiety, they knew their baby was in good hands. Mr. Brown drove a van with Sam, Wendy and a few others from Sunnyside Home to watch Andy perform.

Sam knew they were seeing a show, but he didn't believe them when they kept telling him Andy was singing. Sam only knew Andy to sing Christmas carols, like he would be next week for their annual Christmas party, but nothing beyond that. Wendy couldn't wait to see her eldest son on stage, she was so proud of him.

When they got to the venue and security scanned their tickets, they were escorted to the VIP section which was right next to the stage. As more friends and family filled in the VIP box, it soon became clear who was blatantly missing. They all knew Emma should be there cheering on Andy as well. Emma was always Andy's biggest fan and now she was gone. The empty seat was just too empty.

Security came to find James and said there was someone else here who wasn't on the list but insisted he was family. James asked who it was and when the man said Ronald Anderson, James was in shock. Mr. Brown spoke up and confirmed that he was, indeed, Andy's father and he could join them in the VIP box.

Marc Brown looked over at James and smiled as if to say, 'it worked.' Ron Anderson was brought to their section and it was the first time he saw Wendy in over fifteen years. There was no time for getting reacquainted because the show was about to start. The emcee announced Andy and he came out and stood in front of the microphone. At first he just stood there and his friends were afraid he couldn't do it but then he started speaking.

"Hello everyone and thank you for coming," Andy started. "I'm Andy Anderson and after an injury forced me to leave baseball, I turned to music to comfort me. Music has helped me through some of the toughest times in my life."

Andy turned to the section that contained all of his friends and family and nearly fell over when he saw his father. Just like his last game when his father said he was in the stands, here he was again, cheering him on. Andy had to quickly compose himself in order to continue.

"Um, my family and friends are here to support me tonight, except one. I got engaged a couple of months ago..." Cheers from the crowd interrupted Andy's speech. "But she passed away a couple of days later..." Silence. "This is for her."

Andy sat down at the grand piano and took a deep breath as the spotlight focused only on him. He started with his song, "Broken" with it's haunting lyrics...

*"I miss your touch... Where did she go
I can break but I am not broken I can bleed but I let you in,
If you're lost
Call to me, call to me
I'll come to you."*

Andy let the final note on the piano fill the quiet room before applause broke out. Andy stood up and thanked everyone again. He liked to talk about each song and give a little story about it. Now he explained that he was going to play a new song before finishing up with a favorite that many may have heard on the radio, again, more cheers.

This one is called, 'Gone.' Andy sat back down at the piano and only started when there was silence. Andy's voice was sweet and strong during the chorus:

*"Walking on the beach Hand in hand, Laughing at a joke
Toes in the sand,
You're here with me, Stay with me Gone."*

Andy had played a total of ten songs with heart felt introductions to each, but his final piece was, "Life Goes On." When the familiar opening notes of the song sliced through the quiet hall, fans clapped and started recording on their phones.

*"Standing strong but empty, Smiling easy but lost,
Call to me, Set me free Alone, Life goes on..."*

James looked at his family and friends in the VIP box and there wasn't a dry eye around him. He couldn't explain it, but he could have sworn he heard Emma's voice...

Chapter 36

Sam was so excited when Santa walked into Sunnyside Home with his bag of presents. Andy never asked Sam if he suspected it was him and decided to never say a word. The children ran up to him and asked if theirs was next, but all Santa could do was pull one gift out at a time. The kids were so excited when their names were called, it was such a pleasure and joy to watch.

Joe sat on a chair and looked around the room. What a different crowd it was this year. Now Wendy lived here with Sam and they were inseparable. But today, Wendy was sitting with Ron. Joe had spoken with Ron briefly but he and Wendy had spent much of the afternoon together just talking and getting reacquainted and it seemed to be pretty civil. At first he thought Ron might be angry to see her but he actually seemed interested to hear her story. It was an interesting turn of events and Joe wondered if Ron would stay in St. Petersburg after all.

Andy kept his distance, too. After Santa finished handing out gifts, Andy changed and reappeared and played Christmas carols. It wasn't the same upbeat mood as years past but he had managed some holiday spirit. After a few songs, Andy took a break and went over to get a soda, Joe joined him.

"Hey Andy, good job today," Joe said. "Thanks," Andy replied.

"So what are your plans now?" Joe asked.

"Well, I guess someone really liked my show because they want to book a tour," Andy said without much enthusiasm.

"That's great!" Joe exclaimed.

"Yes, it really is," Andy agreed. "But before that happens, I think we should consider booking that Scotland trip."

Joe couldn't hide the look of confusion on his face. "What? I didn't think you'd want to still go, it was supposed to be..."

"Joe, it was supposed to be a trip for your family and Emma. That's what she originally wanted. I was the one who tried to change it. I think we should still go, maybe even scatter..." Andy couldn't talk anymore. He took a sip of his soda and looked out over the room.

Joe was confused and concerned. He assumed the trip was called off since it was meant to be their wedding trip. He didn't know what to say. They had never discussed the trip since the day he brought the brochures over.

"We can discuss it later," Joe finally said.

"I think it would make Emma happy," Andy said, trying to smile.

Joe stood next to Andy and surveyed the room. So much change had occurred this year and yet some things stayed the same. He considered Andy's answer, that it would make Emma happy. Well, he knew she didn't want to be sitting in an urn in his room. Maybe they should reconsider the trip to Scotland. Joe would call James later and see what he thought.

Andy said goodbye to Joe and his family and left the party early. He needed to be alone with his thoughts. He remembered the night he proposed to Emma, he had the Scotland brochures in his pocket that night but waited to show them until they were surrounded by her family. Andy loved her family and still wanted to do the one thing Emma mentioned was her dream for her father.

Andy entered his quiet, empty home that night. There weren't many things he saved of Emma's when he had her place packed up but he did keep a few special items. He kept a few of her shirts that smelled of her and a few knick knacks, like the ceramic dolphin that she loved and displayed. But the one prized possession that he looked at everyday was now on his bookshelf. It was her glass trophy from the city's Hometown Heroes award's night.

Andy now had bookends. It was a joke Emma said when she really didn't like him much. He had tried to charm her but it never worked on her. It was his vulnerable side that eventually won her over, that and his piano skills. Andy thought about how Emma had changed him, not intentionally but just with him wanting to be better, for her.

"Emma, I promise I will do it all for you. I will do the tour, win the Grammys and go to Scotland...for you," Andy said in the empty room. "Because...life goes on."

Acknowledgements

To my husband, Yoshi, for giving me the time and space to write. To my daughter, Alisa, for reading my first draft and loving it.

To my son, Leo, for his constant encouragement.

To my sister for always being there for me.

To my friends for always being willing to read my first drafts and saying that they were perfect, even when I knew they weren't. Your encouragement has brought me to where I am now.

To Maggie Stiefvater for creating a writing seminar that provided life changing inspiration.

To my parents, who are no longer with us, for their constant love and support.

About the Author

Amy Iketani lives in Stockbridge, Georgia, with her husband and pet cat. Originally from Erie, Pennsylvania, Amy met her husband while working for Club Med and has lived in Florida, Japan and Hawaii. Amy enjoys crocheting, reading, spending time with her two grown children, Alisa and Leo, and traveling with her husband, Yoshi, of thirty-three years.

Follow Amy on Instagram @amyiketaniwrites

Don't miss out!

Visit the website below and you can sign up to receive emails whenever Amy Iketani publishes a new book. There's no charge and no obligation.

https://books2read.com/r/B-A-ALFAB-RPFIF

BOOKS 2 READ

Connecting independent readers to independent writers.

Did you love *Life Goes On*? Then you should read *Second Chances*[1] by Amy Iketani!

After a traumatic event that leaves Noah Wagner injured and his fiancé dead, Noah takes time off to recover. When he decides to drive to Malia's hometown in Virginia to see her family, he suddenly loses his nerve. Wanting to give himself time in Virginia, he responds to a help wanted sign at the Patterson Ranch. The three week task of repairing a fence turns into five and in that time Noah finds himself falling for Kate, the eldest daughter.

Kate's boyfriend, Mason Fisher, becomes jealous and obsessed with running off this mysterious man who he sees as a threat to his relationship. What Mason does next changes everyone's lives for good. Noah returns home to Pittsburgh to forget all about Kate, but

---

1. https://books2read.com/u/baLzev

2. https://books2read.com/u/baLzev

nothing is ever the same again. Does Noah come back to confront the man who drove him away? Will Kate be strong enough to stand up to Mason and tell him how she really feels?

Second Chances is about overcoming adversity and finding the courage to keep moving forward. This book will take you on an emotional journey as Noah questions everything he thought he knew. Follow him as he must navigate his way from guilt to forgiveness and finally love.

Read more at instagram.com/amyiketaniwrites.

Also by Amy Iketani

Coming Home
The Last Wish
I Never Knew
Second Chances
Life Goes On

Watch for more at instagram.com/amyiketaniwrites.

About the Author

Amy Iketani lives in Stockbridge, Georgia, with her husband and pet cat. Originally from Erie, Pennsylvania, Amy met her husband while working for Club Med and has lived in Florida, Japan and Hawaii. Amy enjoys crocheting, reading, and spending time with her two grown children, Alisa and Leo, and traveling with her husband, Yoshi, of thirty two years.

Follow Amy on Instagram @amyiketaniwrites
Read more at instagram.com/amyiketaniwrites.

Milton Keynes UK
Ingram Content Group UK Ltd.
UKHW031347011224
451755UK00001B/63